A GRIPPING PSYCHOLOGICAL
ROMANCE DRAMA

IT HAPPENED IN THE LOFT

BRIAN HARTMAN

Copyright © 2023 by Brian Hartman

All rights reserved.

No portion of this book may be reproduced in any form without written permission from the publisher or author, except as permitted by U.S. copyright law.

"Life is getting up one more time than you've been knocked down."

-John Wayne

To the therapists, counselors, psychiatrists, doctors, and nurses who treat the ever-growing mental health epidemic.

Chapter 1

I hate doctors. Well, I guess not every doctor, but a lot of them. Especially the ones who walk around like they're the kings of the world, looking down on the rest of us like fools.

Obviously, I can't hate every doctor because I am one. Though I guess it's possible to hate myself, and I do from time to time. Sometimes just when that third Oreo passes my lips, chasing the second, after I said I was only going to eat one.

Then there are the times I hate myself for an entire day. Like now, when I'm covering a shift for my colleague on the day after a three-day weekend. For a myriad of reasons, patients flock to the emergency department on the first business day after a long holiday weekend. And here I am, working the Tuesday after Labor Day. I didn't realize what day it was when I read the email asking for a trade. And like the kind-hearted fool that I am, I made the switch. On a Tuesday after a long holiday weekend.

I sighed as I draped my stethoscope across my neck, clipped my badge to the pocket on the front of my scrub top, and walked toward the employee entrance to St. Luke Hospital.

Labor Day is a time meant for friends and families to get together and share a meal, while they tell each other how great their summer was. Every other partner in my group is married and has children. Most of them even have parents or at least a sibling in their lives. I have neither, and it's all my fault.

Hating oneself for a day would be a relief. I've hated myself every day for the last seventeen years.

Chapter 2

"Good morning, Dr. Lee." The words came from my right as I entered the department.

"Hi, Rosanne. How's it going today?" I didn't think it was much of a joke, but Rosanne must have thought so by how hard she laughed before replying.

"I'd turn around and go home if I were you. You do *not* want to go in there." She walked away, as if she just imparted some ancient wisdom and was heading back to her throne.

I smiled and gave a halfhearted reply while continuing to walk through the department. I hated those types of comments. What choice did I have? Abandon the shift? Quit my job? Who would take care of the patients? I'd lose my license for sure. Or was it she didn't think I could handle the pace? Or maybe the complexity of the patients? Was that it? Does she not think I'm up to the job?

"Alex, I'm glad you're here. EMS just called and they're a few minutes out with an unresponsive kid."

I set my bag down in front of an open workstation and replied to my partner. "How old? What's the story?"

"He's almost two. That's all I know."

Great. A sick kid. My anxiety level rises with the amount of life expectancy remaining for my patient. A crashing octogenarian? It happens. Crashing two-year-old? Not good. "Okay Holly, thanks. Are you ready to get out of here?"

"No, it's going to take me a while to get caught up on these charts. Give me a shout if you need help."

Holly is the leader of our group and the medical director of the emergency department. It's her job to handle the scheduling of physicians, represent our group to the medical staff, and field complaints from patients and their families. That last part is the worst and the reason I've never put my name up for consideration for director. No thanks. I have enough stress in my life just dealing with my own patients. I don't need to involve myself in the complaints of others. She also lives in my condo community, along with a few other docs at the hospital.

Our ER is fairly small by comparison. We have fifteen total beds, with two of them equipped as full resuscitation bays. These rooms are stocked with supplies for any invasive procedure we may need to do immediately, such as placing someone on a ventilator or placing a large IV into a central vein. One of the two rooms was specially outfitted with pediatric equipment. Room eight. A terrible number for a pediatric resuscitation room. They chose a font for our room numbers that was wide and swoopy. Like the note you'd get passed in junior high from the cute girl sitting up front by the teacher. The eight looked like an infinity symbol. Never ending. Like events that happen in this room will never be forgotten.

It's true though. I can still remember each child I've resuscitated in here. Each summer day ruined by a frantic search for a missing child, only to find them at the bottom of the pool because "someone else was watching." When the dirt bike ride went from a great time to a heartbreaking tragedy. When the minor food allergy became a severe anaphylactic reaction.

And now, in a minute, the doors are going to open and the paramedics are going to wheel in an unresponsive toddler, probably with frantic parents wanting me to diagnose and fix whatever's wrong. And if I can't, it will be my fault. Again.

"They're here!" yelled Kendra, one of the staff nurses on shift today. She opened the doors to the ambulance bay and EMS quickly wheeled in a stretcher that was mostly empty, except for the small toddler laying on his back in the middle, motionless.

He did not look good. Uh oh. "What happened?" I asked.

"Doc, this is Eli. He was playing at his grandmother's house and everything seemed fine. She thinks he fell off her bed and struck his head on the ground. Grandma heard a thud and ran in, finding him stunned on the floor, but then he started crying. He calmed down quickly and then acted normal. About an hour later, he lay down for a nap on the couch, but when she checked on him an hour later, he had vomited. She couldn't wake him up."

That's not good. A fall with head injury followed by declining neurologic status. I'd been down this road before. It never leads anywhere good.

I helped them transfer the child to the bed and did a quick assessment. Outwardly he looked fine, except for the lack of spontaneous movement and the vomit on his pajamas. His eyes were slowly scanning around without focusing on anything in particular.

I ran my hand along the entirety of his skull, feeling for swelling or a deformity that could suggest a fracture. Nothing. My sarcastic side took over briefly. I can't help it. They're only fleeting thoughts and they help me stay calm in the moment. It's not a good thing that someone 'swelled out' because it meant it didn't 'swell in'. That's garbage. Lack of external swelling usually suggests less force was involved and less likely to cause an internal injury if it can't even lead to a bruise.

The kid's vital signs showed a fast heart rate and a borderline oxygen saturation.

"I called CT and they are ready for us," said Kendra, clearly prompting me through her friendly update.

"Yeah, let's get him to the scanner. We need to make sure this isn't an epidural bleed, but I don't see much sign of trauma on him. Are the parents or grandparents here yet?"

"Doc, do you want to intubate him before he goes to CT?" The question stopped me cold. No, I didn't want to intubate him. He's two. That terrifies me. A toddler's airway anatomy is different from an adult's. Everything is smaller and more anterior, making it more difficult to get the tube into proper position. Intubating a kid is the last thing I want to do at any time of any shift.

But it was the right question. He was unresponsive, vomited, and had borderline oxygen saturations. "No, it will delay CT. If he has a bleed, we need to know that quickly so we can arrange transfer to the pediatric trauma hospital. Plus, it'll take some time to get things ready to tube him. Let's be ready to do it when he gets back from CT in case he's not awake yet."

"The IV's in, 22-gauge left AC. I'm drawing blood now." I looked to see who said that. Rosanne. God bless her. Getting an IV on a pediatric patient is hard enough, but an acutely ill one adds even more anxiety to the mix. I'll take her snarky comments all day long if she gets my pediatric IVs first stick like that.

A loud clunk filled the room, and the bed shook as Kendra unlocked the wheels to prepare for transport. She sat the portable monitor on the mattress and began wheeling the patient out of the room.

Chapter 3

"Doc, the parents called and they are on their way. They were at a restaurant nearby and should be here in five minutes." Carla's update was brief, but to the point.

What a way to ruin a date night. But at least they got to have one. I haven't been on a date in years. I watched the cot as it was wheeled quickly down the hallway headed for the donut of truth. Emergency medicine gets a bad rap for over ordering imaging studies, but no one will forgive us for missing critical diagnoses. They can't demand limited testing and zero misses. That's just not possible. It seems our new motto is "if you don't know, make them glow." I should get mouse pads printed up with that saying.

"Rosanne, can you get me a blood sugar on that kid before you send his blood to the lab?"

"Sure Doc, hang on a sec." She took the plastic device that she had used to fill the blood collection tubes and inverted it, revealing a small column of blood in the connector piece. She touched the opening to a small rectangular card, transferring a drop of blood to it. She then inserted the card into the glucose meter and waited for a reading.

I'm an ER doctor and have no patience. I want every result back yesterday. The machine beeped after a few seconds and displayed a warning message on the screen. 'LOW'. He had to have seized because his blood sugar was low. This isn't trauma, this is a metabolic emergency!

"Rosanne, get me a 50ml syringe and a blunt-tipped needle." I yanked open a supply cabinet that held our IV solutions and scanned the labels until I found the shelf containing D10, a ten percent solution of dextrose in water. She handed me the large syringe with a blunt needle attached, and I quickly filled it from the bag of fluid.

I ran down the hallway toward CT, carrying the simplest of medication, but one that was about to save a life. My badge was attached to a retractable lanyard and clipped onto the front pocket of my scrubs. It spun in large circles as I ran toward the radiology department like I was some sort of adult stage performer.

The CT suite was just around the next corner. I rounded it without slowing down and braced myself against the wall with my forearm, shoving myself back into the center of the hallway. A "CT SCANNER IN USE, KEEP OUT" sign was illuminated above the door to the room.

"Sorry," I said as I pushed the door open and entered the room.

The well-meaning tech shouted at me around the radiation-proof wall. "Hey, Doc, we're scanning. You can't be in there!"

I ignored her and closed the distance to my patient. He was deep inside the machine, but the table was not currently moving. They must have gotten the scout images already and were preparing to run the full scan. I reached inside to release the velcro strap holding him in place, allowing his arms to fall to the side. I located the IV in his left arm and hooked the syringe up to it, pushing the glucose into his arm.

"What are you doing? What are you giving him?" asked Kendra. She had stepped around the wall and was standing next to me. Not in a challenging pose, but as a colleague, wanting to learn and assist.

"His glucose was below what our machine could read. I think he got hypoglycemic and had a seizure. I'm giving him fifty milliliters of D10." By now my thumb was touching my fingers, having depressed the plunger all the way and emptying the syringe into his arm. It was only five milligrams of glucose, but it was straight into his vein. I hoped his heart and lungs would suck that blood back to his left ventricle and then blast the sugary food into his brain. It shouldn't take long.

I removed the syringe and secured the velcro strap again before following Kendra into the CT control room.

"We're going to have to redo the scout images because he may have moved. That's extra radiation, doc." The tech wasn't pleased that I had disrupted the scan.

"I don't think you need to. He didn't move much at all, and I think the scan is going to be negative. He's altered because of a seizure due to low blood sugar."

"Our protocols say I have to redo it." She sighed and repeated the scout images before adjusting the settings and preparing for the actual scan.

"Hey, he moved his right leg!" Kendra's excited voice was a perfect way to break the tension in the room.

We looked at the patient, who now was wiggling on the bed and crying. The tech sighed audibly and stared at me. "I can't scan him like that. The images will be blurry and useless."

I nodded to her. "I understand. Let's get him back to the room and we'll assess the need for CT later."

Kendra helped me lift him off the scanner and back into his bed. He was sitting up and looking around with a fearful expression. "Buddy, you're okay. We're at a hospital. You're doing fine. Your parents are on the way."

I listened to her reassure him and pretended she was talking to me. It was going fine until she mentioned my parents were on the way. I highly doubt they'd be stopping by for a visit. Why would today be different from any other day?

Chapter 4

Seventeen Years Ago

The bell rang loudly through the intercom system, prompting my history teacher to somehow talk even louder and faster. "Remember, test on Monday over the last three chapters we've covered!"

I merged into the throng of students in the hallway, headed toward my locker to grab my lunch, but was stopped by an arm across my chest.

"Hey, slow down there Rapid Lee." A series of laughs followed the taunt and I turned to see my brother's friends from the football team blocking my way through the hallway. Luke's friend Ronny was the one bothering me this time.

"Just headed to lunch. Where's Luke at?" I asked.

"No idea. Probably trying to hit on his teacher," said Ronny with a laugh. "He's always working on someone. Confident Lee. Hey, back up," he said, pushing me backward a step.

"Sorry," I said, regaining my footing. It wasn't my fault. Someone had slapped me on the butt and I took a step forward out of surprise. I turned to my left and couldn't tell for sure who it was, but a petite girl with brown hair was walking away. What was that all about?

"Alex, what's up?" I recognized my brother's voice over my right shoulder.

"I was heading to lunch, but your friends stopped me. I need to get going." We bumped fists before I continued down the hallway toward my locker. The sounds of the passing period faded from my consciousness as I tried to figure out why I got a slap on the butt. And who was that girl with shoulder-length brown hair walking away? It must have been Stacy Griffin! She lived a few minutes down the street from us and sat near me on the bus. Once I even pretended to miss my stop so I could walk a bit with her after she got off. I'd been hitting on her for months and didn't think I was making any progress, but this could be a step in the right direction.

I rubbed my hand across my butt, trying to remember the feel of the slap, and felt my pocket crinkle as my fingers moved across it. I reached inside and my fingers touched a piece of paper inside the pocket. How'd that get there?

Now the background noise vanished as my entire focus was on the piece of paper in my rear pocket. I pulled out a folded piece of lined paper that looked to have been ripped out of a notebook. Inside was the cutest penmanship I'd ever seen. The pink ink and heart under the exclamation point completed the image.

Your barn loft, 7 p.m., bring the beer.

No way! Stacy finally acknowledged my presence and wanted to meet in the barn! With my dad's drinking, getting a few beers wasn't going to be a problem. I doubled my pace and after getting my lunch, joined my friends in the cafeteria.

"Dudes, you'll never guess what just happened to me!"

They looked at each other with smiles, but Levi was the first one to talk. "Let me guess. You were just accepted into Girl Scouts?" This drew a round of laughter and nods from the others and started a chain of guesses.

"No, I bet it was explosive diarrhea."

"Puberty? Finally? Congrats, man."

"You guys suck," I said. "I thought you were supposed to be my friends." But I didn't mean it. I loved these guys. They'd do anything for me, and of course I'd do the same. "You're all wrong. Stacy Griffin just passed me a note and wants to meet in my barn at seven tonight."

"Woah! That's awesome Alex, congratulations. You'll have to let us know all the details." Levi had stopped mocking me and instead slowly shook his head as he spoke. "Why does stuff like that never happen to me?"

I tossed a napkin at him and dropped a truth bomb. "Well, you have yogurt on your face, for starters. Do you want all the reasons or just a few?"

"Shut up. I'm just jealous. She's pretty hot."

"Yeah, and I have a thing for soccer players."

"Duh, who doesn't? Maybe we'll stop by and root you on."

My excitement vanished, replaced with a sense of dread. "No, you can't. Don't ruin this for me."

"Just joking, man. But if you screw this up, we won't let you live it down. We'll be blowing up your phone Saturday morning if you haven't checked in."

The rest of the day was a blur. Every time I shook my head to clear my thoughts, it only took a few seconds for an image of Stacy leaning back on a bale of hay, her lips pressed against the bottle of beer, smiling as she took a drink. Most of the times she winked at me as the bottle came away from her mouth.

When the last bell rang, I almost ran through the hall toward the bus. I was one of the first on it and took a seat near where Stacy usually sat. But as the minutes ticked by and the other kids climbed on, she hadn't shown up yet. The bus was getting full, and it was becoming awkward to hold the seat next to me open. I lost the battle when a friend plopped down next to me. I pulled my bag onto my lap to get it out from under his hip.

"Hey Alex, any big plans this weekend?"

I didn't even look at him, my eyes were focused forward on the stairs, hoping to see her get on. There! Finally. I recognized the top of her head before I even saw her face.

Brown straight hair, held in place by a fabric hair band across the top of her head. I smiled and tried to make eye contact with her, but she took a seat next to another girl up front. I smacked the seat in front of me, drawing a stare from the kid sitting in it.

"Sorry," I said. "There was a bug."

"You okay, Alex? I can move."

I looked at my friend and sighed. "No, it's fine. Just excited to get home and everyone is taking forever to get on the bus."

My stop is before Stacy's and I had rehearsed dozens of things to say when I passed her in the aisle. I had come up with the perfect line.

I stopped next to her and looked down, making eye contact with her and her friend, but froze. What was the line? Crap. "I'll see you later," and winked at her, drawing a smile from her and her friend. She must have told her friend about the note. A slap on my backpack got me moving again as I was holding up the line to get off the bus.

I stood still and watched the bus pull away. Idiot. How can I have forgotten the line? I'll have to apologize to her later. It will be a great icebreaker.

Dinner was great, and I impressed my mother with how quickly I ate it. We moved on to chores afterward. Dad went to light the burn pile and carried an insulated mug with him. Probably full of whiskey. Mom watched him walk outside and sighed before starting on the dishes.

"I'll clean the barn," I said, but no one acknowledged it. Mom was talking to herself at the sink, Dad was outside, and Luke was still eating.

The burn pile today was fairly large and not stacked together very well. It was going to take forever to burn, and it was already six o'clock. In one hour, my date would sneak into the barn and I needed my dad inside.

"Want some help burning the pile today, Dad?"

"Sure Alex, be my guest," he said from his Adirondack chair. He tossed me the stick lighter and then took a long drink from his cup. "I'll supervise."

I found some paper and lit it quickly, then started stacking things on top to grow the fire. Soon the blaze was expanding rapidly, and I continued to toss fuel onto it.

"Hey, that's getting pretty hot." My dad was holding his cup in front of his face and had turned away from the fire. He stood and pulled his chair back a few feet and sat back down but didn't remain there. "You made that too big. I'm headed in. I'll send Luke out to clean it up in a bit."

"Okay Dad, I'll be out here cleaning the barn. I'll be in later."

He waved and then headed back inside the house. The burn pile was half the size it was when we started. Not bad for ten minutes. It should be down to smoldering ashes in another fifteen. Then Luke would rake out the metal and other things that didn't burn and either head inside or go out with his friends. And I'll be sipping beer in the loft with Stacy.

Chapter 5

Kendra and I escorted our patient back to room eight, where two new people were pacing back and forth.

"Ollie!" The woman rushed forward and touched her son's face. He looked up at her, a blank stare looking into her reddened, tear-soaked eyes. "Are you okay? What happened? Granny said you fell and hit your head." She rubbed her hands across his skull, mimicking my exam from a few minutes ago.

"Ma'am, I'm Dr. Alex Lee," I said. I gestured to Kendra, who smiled and waved. "And this is Kendra, Ollie's nurse. He's doing much better now. His blood sugar was very low and I think he had a seizure. We were just down in the CT scanner but he woke up after I gave him glucose, so I think we can save him the radiation of the CT."

"Why was his sugar low? Is he diabetic?" asked the father.

"I'm not sure. Has he been eating and drinking normally lately? Any recent illness?"

His mother stroked his hair as she spoke. "No, he's been fine. He ate a hot dog and french fries for lunch before we dropped him off at my mom's. She even gave him a sippy cup of apple juice to calm him down after he hit his head."

Huh. That's strange. Why was his blood sugar so low if he wasn't sick and has been eating normally? Something else was going on. Crap.

"I'm not sure. I'm going to run some more tests and see what we can figure out. You are welcome to sit in bed with him if you'd like." I lowered the side rail and his mother slid into bed with him. He snuggled up quickly and laid his head on her chest. The father pulled a chair over and dutifully placed a hand on each of them.

Good for him. If I ever had a wife and kid, that's exactly how I would sit all the time. Well, maybe not in the bathroom, but as often as I could. I don't see that happening any time soon, though. Usually marriage is preceded by dating, and that's something I haven't done in seventeen years.

I walked back toward my desk to chart on Ollie and ran into Dr. Brady in the hallway. "What are you doing here?"

"I heard you had a sick kid and was in the area, so I figured I'd see if you needed a hand. I am a pediatrician, you know."

Yeah, I know. He'd been standing over my shoulder, second guessing my work for years now. He's the type of doctor I hate. Emergency medicine encompasses the emergent presentation of literally every condition in every specialty of medicine. We know a lot about a lot, but don't have the same knowledge base as a specialist in their own specialty. Unfortunately, that leads to some doctors always assuming we're inferior to them. Like Dr. Brady.

"No, we're good. He was hypoglycemic and had a seizure, but I gave him glucose and now he's better. I'll call you if I need you."

"Interesting case. Is he diabetic? On insulin?"

I exhaled deeply, trying to make his presence feel as unwanted as it was. "No, he's not diabetic, and he's not on insulin or any other meds, for that matter."

Dr. Brady shook his head and laughed. "Are you sure about that? Come on ER, you're better than that. It's a good thing I'm here to protect your patients. I was hoping after that case five years ago you would have learned something, but I guess not." He turned and headed for the exit of the ER before giving me a chance to reply.

What did that mean? Is he this patient's doctor? Does he know something he's not telling me? Him and his smugness. This is a patient's life we're talking about, not some childish pissing match. What happened to the good old days when medicine was collegial?

I shook my head to clear my thoughts and focused on the present again. I quickly scanned Ollie's chart but found no history of prescriptions other than a single round of amoxicillin six months ago for an ear infection. Dr. Brady was not listed as his pediatrician. But maybe the jerk had a point. Something wasn't adding up. I turned around and went back to room eight and asked more questions.

"Does Ollie take any medications?"

His parents looked at each other and shook their heads. "No, nothing."

"Are either of you diabetic? Is it possible he got into one of your prescriptions?"

The mother's eyes widened, and she sat up quickly in bed. "No, but my mother is. She pulled her phone out of her pocket and made a call.

"Mom, what is it you take for diabetes? Aren't you on a few pills?" She listened for a minute and then looked up at me. "She takes glimepiride, 2mg a day. Also metformin, 500mg twice a day."

Boom. There it is. He had to have taken her medications. Glimepiride will drop glucose dangerously low in non-diabetics, especially pediatric ones! "Where does she keep the pills? Is it possible he could have gotten into them?"

"Mom, could you hear the doctor?" The mother tilted her head away from the phone. "She's going to look. Said she keeps them in a pill container by her bed."

Yep. Accidental ingestion. Why didn't I think of that immediately? "I'll be right back. I need to get a glucose drip started for him." I tracked down Kendra and updated her on the history. "Sounds like he got into his grandmother's pills. Go ahead and start a D10 drip. I'm going to get him transferred for admission downtown to the peds hospital. He should be fine, but it's going to take a day for that to get out of his system."

I went back into the room and the mother confirmed our suspicion. Her mother kept the pills in a plastic case with a spot for morning and night meds for each day of the week. The pills for tomorrow were missing. Fortunately, it was only two pills. The glimepiride and a thyroid supplement. Thank goodness for relatively healthy grandmothers. And I hated to admit it, but I was also thankful for Dr. Brady. I'll have to let him know the next time I see him. But this is a small hospital and we don't see sick kids very often, so it may be a while. Which is perfectly fine with me.

I pulled my notebook out of my front pocket and made an entry on the next free line. "Pediatric ingestions and antidotes." Looks like I have some homework to take care of tonight. Since residency, I have chosen a topic or two from each case and read up on it after I got home. It's a way of keeping up the huge fund of knowledge required to practice emergency medicine and also help shut my brain down after shifts. Outsiders think I go overboard on it. Like it's some sort of obsession. It's not. I think penance is a better term.

Chapter 6

"Alex, do you have a moment?" Holly asked in the kindest possible way. I had just started my shift, and she was ready to get out of here. Part of that process involved turning over the patients she still had remaining.

"Sure, what do you have to leave me?"

"Nothing, actually. I need to talk to you about the utilization committee."

Oh, great. Exactly how I want to start my shift. Being told I order too many tests. "Yeah? What did they have to say?"

"Your imaging utilization is well above the average for our group. In fact, you order nearly twice as many CT scans as anyone else. The techs are irritated at the extra work and the radiologists are concerned about the radiation you are giving your patients."

"Did this committee happen to look into bounce back visits? Did they see which doctor has the fewest missed appendicitis cases?"

"No, that's not the focus of this committee," she admitted. Exactly. No one sits around and tries to figure out who makes the fewest errors. They just spend time looking for ways to point out which doctors are outside the averages. Funny how they never focus on the good side of the curve.

"Could it be that I don't miss much because I'm very meticulous and don't blow off my patients' complaints?"

"That's certainly one way of looking at it. But you also have to factor in the harm excess radiation can cause over time. There's not a zero risk of cancer with a CT scan."

"Right, I know. It's about one extra cancer for every four thousand CT scans. I see twenty patients a day, two hundred days a year. So I cause one extra cancer every year."

"Yes, they pointed that out. The hospital is concerned with the liability of your testing and asked me to talk to you about it."

I sighed. I really liked Holly. Her heart is in the right place and she's a great doctor. But she's here to deliver the findings of a bunch of non-clinicians who mistakenly think their work benefits patients.

"Do they have metrics on how many things I have found early, when the disease can still be cured? How many lives have I saved by detecting cancers incidentally with imaging before they were having symptoms? How much morbidity have patients avoided by diagnosing serious issues before they have a chance to become critical? Did they discuss that upgrading our old machine to a newer generation will significantly reduce the radiation exposure to our patients?"

"No, that wasn't the focus of this group."

"Tell you what. I'll be glad to change my practice pattern, but I'm going to need the hospital's help in doing so." Holly smiled at me, clearly pleased that I was taking this feedback positively and am focused on developing a plan of action. Part of me hates that I'm about to disappoint her, but not every part. "All I need is a signed letter from their attorneys indemnifying me of all malpractice risk for failure to diagnose serious issues. And I'm going to need a committee member at the bedside telling me who they think doesn't need advanced imaging. They can work as my scribe as well. That way we can document they have all relevant data to make these clinical decisions in real-time since it's their name on the chart, too."

The smile had faded from Holly's face early in my response. "I see what you're saying, and I agree with you. But I'm here to tell you the hospital is aware of this, and they're paying attention. Our group doesn't own this contract. We're here because the hospital likes the care we provide. When they stop liking us or the care we provide, we'll all stop working here."

She's right. The hospital is a business, and if they're not happy with a vendor, they'll simply go a different route. So I need to continue practicing medicine well and without missing anything, but do it by utilizing far fewer resources. Got it.

"I'll do my best to be mindful of who needs imaged, and who doesn't. I saved that unresponsive kid from a CT yesterday, actually. That's a one in four thousand risk he didn't need to take." Take that, review committee.

"Right, I heard about that. The techs complained because you entered their room during an active scan. They had already shot the scout, so he received some radiation but never got a completed scan. Had you checked the glucose before he went to CT, he could probably have avoided it entirely."

I could picture Dr. Brady laughing at me. He may as well have been in the room, pointing his finger at me and slapping his knee. Medicine is an art. It's not cut and dry. The answer isn't always obvious, especially when dealing with a sick kid and little history as to what happened, but the necessity to act immediately. Screw you, Brady.

Holly left me alone to work through the rest of my shift, just as terrified to order a CT scan on a patient as I was to not order one and miss something serious. Screw this system.

My next patient's chief complaint made me laugh out loud. "Chest pain after sneezing." He's thirty-eight years old and in room ten. The triage nurse made him a level four, the second least acute of the five triage categories she could choose from. I scanned the chart and noted a blood pressure of 210/130. That's probably why he received a level four instead of a level five.

"Hi, sir. How can I help you?" I asked, after introducing myself to the patient.

"I know it sounds stupid, but I sneezed hard and then had this weird pain in my chest. It's right here." He pointed to his sternum with his fingers curled like a claw, then moved his hand up and down his chest. "It started in the middle as a sharp pain, but now goes down a bit and into the left side of my neck."

Great, someone with ridiculously high blood pressure and now sharp chest pain radiating into his abdomen and up to his neck. That could be an aortic dissection. The same thing that took out John Ritter and Jonathan Larson. Is my patient involved in show business? Can I put that down on the indication for CT scan?

I could be sitting here in this room talking to him while his major blood vessel literally tears itself in half. It's time to lower his blood pressure and get him to CT immediately. I explained my concerns to the patient and opened his chart to enter the orders. That's when I saw it. Four prior visits this year for chest pain. I clicked onto the imaging tab and saw he had two CT scans of his chest, one in the spring and one in the summer. Both ordered by me. I clicked on the results link and found both of them were read as normal by radiology. Two doses of radiation, no clinically significant findings. Now here he is again and I have a committee looking over my shoulder. Wonderful.

I put in for the labs and intravenous medication to lower his blood pressure, along with some fentanyl for pain. Next, I selected the order for the CT angiogram and checked all the correct boxes for the indication but didn't hit enter. Do I order my third chest CT scan on this guy since Christmas? Or do I ignore the thing that could kill him and listen to the review committee?

Chapter 7

Screw it. They won't stick up for me if I miss it. I clicked the button and submitted the order. The last thing I need is our thoracic surgeon screaming at me for having missed a dissection. It starts with the consultant. Then the family. Then the administration. Then the malpractice attorney. Then the jury. So I order the test. Every time.

I dictated a quick note and then stood to go see my next patient. I hadn't even made it away from my desk before the phone rang. Caller ID showed it was the CT control room, so I picked it up before the secretary had a chance to answer. She didn't need to be in the loop.

"Lee," I said, the word cropped short by my irritation.

"Dr. Lee, this is CT. I saw your order and wanted to make sure you knew that the patient already had two CT scans of his chest this year. Are you sure you want another one?"

Of course I know, I ordered them. An aortic dissection is usually an acute finding. Just because it wasn't there on prior imaging doesn't mean it's not there today. It's like they're accusing me of checking to see if he was born with three lungs instead of two. But Holly told me the techs were in discussions with the review committee, and I can't afford to irritate anyone. Of course, they don't seem to mind irritating me with impunity.

"Yes, I'm aware, thanks. His symptoms are different today and are concerning for an aortic dissection. I could get a transesophageal ECHO instead, but our facility is not equipped to do those emergently. So, looks like a CT is the right test today." Like it was the last two times.

A huff preceded her answer. "Okay, we'll scan him again." The tech hung up without waiting for a reply. Which is good because it didn't give me a chance to give one.

The next patient was straight forward. A simple ingrown toenail. The whole encounter only took a few minutes to numb the toe, a few minutes to perform the quick procedure, and then he was on his way. Treated appropriately, without radiation, and in a timely manner. The sort of thing administration doesn't seem interested in noticing, let alone praising or rewarding.

I put his discharge papers in the rack and heard the phone rang again. CT control room. The secretary beat me to it and put them on hold while I walked back to my desk.

"It's Lee, what's up?"

"Doc, good call on that CT scan. You'd better take a look at it. He's ripped from top to bottom. I am sending the preliminary images to radiology now, but it will take some time to get the 3D reformatting done. Figured you'd like to know as early as possible."

I was stunned. He actually had it. An acute aortic dissection. I pulled up the images and scrolled through them. Sure enough, the wall of his aorta was splitting. It started just outside his heart and followed the aorta upward into the chest, then down below the diaphragm. The ascending component meant we could not treat it here at St. Luke's and the patient would need to be transferred. My job was to make that happen as quickly as possible. Fortunately, my first dose of blood pressure medication made progress on his ridiculous pressure and his pain had improved in response to the decreased force ripping his aorta apart.

"Carla, get me the trauma center on the phone. Tell them I have a type A dissection and need to talk to cardiothoracic surgery immediately. Is our helicopter here?"

"Yes, it is. They flew a heart attack out this morning, but they got back an hour ago." She began making phone calls, and I went back to speak with the patient.

"Sir, I'm afraid you have a very serious condition today. It's called an aortic dissection. Basically, your aorta is ripping apart. This needs to be treated with a surgery as soon as we can get you downtown."

"What? Surgery? Is this serious?"

"Yes, it is. You need immediate surgery, but we don't do that here at St. Luke's. I'm going to fly you downtown by helicopter. You'll likely go straight from the helipad to an operating room."

His heart rate increased the longer I spoke. The first dose of blood pressure medication was no longer adequate for his condition with a bit of anxiety added on. It was time for an arterial line and a continuous drip of medication.

Kendra grabbed the supplies for an arterial line, which I quickly placed in his wrist. Now we could monitor his blood pressure with each heartbeat and dial in the blood pressure medication quickly and tightly.

After I placed the line in his artery, Kendra handed me the end of the IV tubing to attach to it. When she leaned in, the area suddenly smelled like vanilla. Strongly. Like someone left a scented candle burning in a small room. Most staff in the ER rarely smell likely anything other than hand sanitizer. I glanced at her more closely this time. Straight blond hair pulled back behind a headband. No jewelry and very little makeup. A long-sleeve compression shirt outlined the muscles of her forearm. She's very attractive but does little to highlight that fact. The fingers of her left hand were as bare as mine. Maybe I could have done something about that in another life.

Chapter 8

Seventeen Years Ago

"Alex! Where are you?"

I crouched behind the half-open barn door and stared at my brother standing in the yard. I was out of breath and trying to recover while suppressing a laugh, which wasn't all that easy given the smoke still drifting through the barn from the burn pile. Dad burned it once a week, and today was the day.

Our barn was typical for Indiana. Large, wooden, and painted red. The bright paint has faded over the decades but still glowed a beautiful color in the right sunlight. The shingles were a light gray and mostly intact.

We claimed to live on a farm, but really, it was just a home with a barn on old farmland. We never grew much except hay, and we had chickens once for a few months. But we have a goat that we milk, more for a hobby than anything else.

"Dad heard you in the house. He said it's time to come back inside and finish your homework."

Homework? Is he serious? It's Friday night. Next week is Thanksgiving. We only have two more days of class left. I looked down at my left hand, clutching two long-neck bottles of beer. I've got more important things to focus on than homework at the moment.

My eyes scanned upward to the large stack of hay we had accumulated during the summer. We'd let a few acres grow tall before cutting, letting it dry, and then baling it.

My destination was the loft, but the ladder was on the other side of the barn door, and Luke was staring directly inside. I silently willed him to turn around, and he did, which both shocked and concerned me. Was I telekinetic, or just lucky? Maybe it's because I look almost exactly like him, just a bit shorter. People confuse us all the time, except on the basketball court or football field. My brother is much more athletic than I am. And usually more successful with the girls. My gifts were all academic, but of course, he excelled there as well.

Whatever the reason for him turning, I used the opportunity to scamper across the gap as fast as I could. I grabbed onto the ladder to slow myself down, bumping into the wall of the barn in the process. A few tools rattled on their hooks and one fell as I quickly climbed up, which was harder than usual thanks to the two open beer bottles I was cradling in my arm. I heard a metallic ping as whatever it was struck an aluminum piece on the barn door. Crap.

I pictured my brother spinning and looking for the source of the noise. He would clearly see something laying on the ground in front of the door that wasn't there five seconds ago. Busted.

Months ago, while stacking the hay, I had created a hidden room in the middle of it. I left a large bale in front of the entrance to protect my secret from anyone else who ventured up into the loft. Not that anyone other than Luke and me likely did.

I pushed the bale sideways and scooted backward into a small opening. It was hard enough work stacking bales of hay to begin with, but doing it in a way to create a hidden room was even harder. I grabbed the twine wrapped around the makeshift door and pulled it toward me to conceal the opening. Suddenly, I was alone in the short passageway leading into the somewhat larger room. I didn't dare make a noise, let alone speak.

"Alex, you're not as sneaky as you think you are," said Luke from the entrance. He waited for a moment, but I said nothing. "Look, you need to get back inside. Dad's been drinking again, and he's pretty pissed. I know it's not your fault, but don't poke the bear. It's going to be bad for both of us if you don't. Don't say anything to him, just go inside and get started."

After a few seconds, I heard him sigh and began to climb the ladder. Soon there were footsteps on the wooden flooring of the loft. The sound stopped abruptly, then was replaced with laughter that filtered through the hay bales. "You goofball. If you're going to hide from someone, don't leave a trail of water behind you."

I panicked and looked down at my hand. The beers were coated in condensation and a drop of water fell to the ground every few seconds. Busted again. I only had a few seconds until he was going to pull the bale aside and find my love shack. Stacy was supposed to be here any minute!

Chapter 9

"Nice pickup, Dr. Lee. Unfortunately, we don't do those here at St. Luke's."

Dr. Ramsey, one of the vascular surgeons. Of course, he is here today. Did the radiologist call him? "I know. I'm getting ready to fly the patient downtown."

"I looked at your chart. You nailed this one. I wouldn't have done anything different. Nice work."

I smiled at the compliment. It's nice to hear that for a change. Maybe he's one of the doctors I can start getting along with. Not that he's out here very often. "Thanks, nice of you to say. And I appreciate you looking and making sure I missed nothing."

"Sure, don't mention it. It's the least I can do for the patients here, especially given what happened that one time."

Nope, he's not one of those I can get along with. Why even go there? Time to put his card in the growing stack of jerks. I just shook my head and let it slide.

"Oh, come on, you remember the case, right? Young kid? Marfan's syndrome? He had some back pain and numbness in his leg. You put him on steroids, anti-inflammatory meds, and told him to stretch. Remember?"

Of course I remembered. A twenty-five-year-old patient walked in to see me and I diagnosed him with sciatica. He came back later that night paralyzed from the waist down. Turns out he had an aortic dissection that took out his spinal cord. Odds are he was going to be paralyzed even if I diagnosed him immediately and transferred him the moment he walked in the door. Unfortunately, he never got that chance, because he never walked again.

"It must be nice to only see people with existing diagnoses and after someone else has done the workup. Really takes the guesswork out of what to do, doesn't it?" Jerk. Get out of my ER. I stood and walked away, not bothering to wait for an answer. Do I ever walk into their offices or operating rooms and start insulting them?

"Dr. Lee, are you okay?" Carla was always worried about the staff in the ER. She's like the sorority mom, keeping us all in line.

"I'm fine. It's just that jerk of a..." I cut myself off. I didn't need to share this with Carla. It was my cross to bear. "Nevermind. I'll be okay. I appreciate your concern."

The rest of the shift was a blur of constant motion. I tried to limit the ordering of CTs and actually found an appendicitis using a bedside ultrasound. The surgeon wasn't nearly as excited as I was with my finding and requested a CT scan that confirmed appendicitis.

It's like the system is trying to make me fail. Ultimately, the patient still went to the operating room, just a bit later and after a significant dose of ionizing radiation and added expense. I put a note in the chart to reflect that I tried to avoid ordering the CT, not that the committee bothers to look into the chart and determine whether the imaging test was indicated or who requested it be done. All that mattered was the report spit out by a machine without a conscience.

I ended my shift, checked out to the night doc, and drove home in silence. My thoughts were interrupted when my gas light popped on, prompting a quick stop for fuel. A taped sign on the pump showed the card reader was not active and I needed to go inside to pay. While waiting in line, I checked out a display of car air fresheners on the counter. The bottom one said "Sweet and Popular Vanilla". How could I go wrong with that?

Once in the car, I opened the package and held it up to my nose. Not an exact match, but close enough to bring back the memory. I hung it from the rearview mirror and continued home.

It was time for a beer and to review the physiology and treatments of the cases I saw today. If I could stay awake,

I'd work my way through a journal or two in bed. This was my life.

When I was at work, I feared missing something or treating a condition wrong. When I was at home, I felt guilty if I wasn't learning from the day and trying to improve for tomorrow. Luke taught me that every time he stayed after football practice to put in extra time.

Chapter 10

I stood outside of St. Luke's, debating whether or not I wanted to go inside. I love my job, I really do. I love the patients and clinical medicine. But the administrative burden has taken the joy out of it. I was about to start a night shift and was not looking forward to it.

"Hey, are you going to make it in today? Or just stand in the parking lot?"

Kendra's voice brought me back to the present, which is great because I generally hate the past. At least the last seventeen years. Back when I had a brother. And parents.

I smiled at Kendra and inhaled deeply before replying. No vanilla smell. Dang it. Maybe my air freshener in the car had decreased my sensitivity to it. "Yeah, just enjoying the fresh air for a bit." I like Kendra. She's a good person. She respects me and doesn't join in the whispers of some of the other staff, at least that I know of. "How's your shift going? Slow Lee?" Hilarious.

"Well, don't wait too long. We need you in there helping our patients."

"I promise I'll be there on time. Just trying to sort through some things. See you on the inside." I watched her walk away, wishing I wasn't who I was. Luke was better at this than me. It seemed like he always had a girlfriend from the start of his freshman year. My mother treated them all like they were soon going to be her daughter-in-law, but they never lasted. He would get bored with them and move on to a new girl after a few months. Our school wasn't that big, but it seemed to have an unending supply of attractive women who wanted to date my brother.

I tell myself I'm ready to move on. It's been seventeen years. Emotionally I'm ready, but physically I'm not, so to speak. It's been nearly two decades, and I still can't get an erection. And I'm not even forty. Oh sure, it's no problem in the morning; when my brain is in recovery mode, and my guilt suppressed by REM sleep. The plumbing works just fine when it doesn't matter. But when I'm awake, nothing. It's like my body is mocking me. Fully alive while asleep, broken and humiliated while awake.

I'd tried all the pills. The blue one, the weekend one. I tried counseling. PTSD support groups. I think that's really what it is. The emotional impact of having caused my brother's death has ruined me. I spent my life working my way through medical school and residency in an effort to atone for my actions that day in the loft. Hoping that somehow, by dedicating my life to helping others avoid death, I could make it up to Luke and my family.

It hasn't worked yet. But enough reminiscing, time to get to work.

I found my partner waiting for me in our leather work chair. That chair is always back in our office. Everyone else uses the standard hospital-issued chairs that squeak and are unstable. But not Dr. Nicholas Park, the senior member of our group who had been here for decades. "Alex, glad you're here. It's been slow and I only have one patient to turn over."

"Okay, what do you have?" I asked, eyeing the comfortable chair. Maybe I'll use it today.

"Luciana. Thirty-year-old Hispanic lady. She doesn't speak much English but the interpreter service has been helpful. She's been here all day. Came in drunk and suicidal. Had fallen down a few stairs at home but I didn't find any significant injuries. I tried to get her admitted, but all the inpatient psych facilities are full. Hopefully she'll sober up and no longer want to kill herself."

I sighed at the report. Another difficult psych patient in an overwhelmed system with limited resources. Often patients come in drunk and suicidal, or drunkicidal, and then feel differently once they're sober. If the feelings persisted, we continued to advocate for an inpatient psych admission.

The ER cannot fix significant mental health problems. That's not our role. We stabilize acute crises and arrange for outpatient follow-up if the patient and family members believe they are safe for discharge. If not, we pursue admission, sometimes against the will of the patient.

It's tricky though. If someone truly wants to die, what's to stop them from lying and saying they were no longer suicidal? We can't go to a judge and get a seventy-two hour involuntary psych hold on every patient who comes in with vague statements of suicidality.

"That's fine. I'll talk to her again and see where her mind's at. Does she have family around?"

"Yes, a husband and a brother. The brother has been here a few times, but her husband is at work."

"Thanks for cleaning things up the department, Nick. You should get out of here." He waved as he headed for the door, walking with a slight limp and slower than when he showed up for his shift. I have no idea how he does it. Over thirty years of clinical practice and still going strong. I can't see myself making it that long. Not with the consultants I have to deal with on my hardest cases.

My shift was actually slow. I know I'm not supposed to use that word in the ER, but it was absolutely slow. I had caught up on all of my charts and only had a few active patients. It was time to check on Luciana.

I knocked and slowly entered the room where she was resting in the bed, her brother playing a game on his phone near her side.

"Hey, is she awake?" Her brother looked up and rubbed her shoulder, startling her awake. She opened her eyes wide and scanned around the room. Her right eye didn't open as far as the left, its upper lid was heavy thanks to a hematoma on her right forehead. The injury Nick was describing.

Her brother interpreted as I talked to her and assessed her current state of mind. No, she was no longer suicidal. She admitted to drinking too much and just wants to go home. She has a counselor she can call in the morning. No, she didn't feel any additional pain or injuries now that she was sober. She apologized for wasting our time and thanked me for caring for her.

I talked to her about alcohol and the risks of excessive drinking. We discussed ways to manage depression, and I provided phone numbers to call should her thoughts worsen again. She understood that we were always available if she needed a safe place to be.

Kendra grabbed the papers from me and went to discharge Luciana. As she grabbed the papers from my hand, I saw that the backs of hers were red with areas of broken skin. It was worse in the web spaces between the base of her fingers. And she smelled like vanilla again.

Luciana waved and offered a weak smile as she walked past our station on her way out to the front lobby. Good luck, I hope you conquer your demons.

"I feel so bad for her," said Kendra. "Such a pretty thing but haunted by demons she can't control. Mental health is a tough thing. It's not like a broken bone that's obvious and straightforward to fix." She reached into her pocket and removed a brightly colored plastic bag of candy. She ripped it open and took one out, the smell of sugar blending with the smell of vanilla. Suddenly I wanted a piece of cake. Kendra lifted a sugar-coated gummy candy out of the packet and tossed it into her mouth, showing me the irritated skin of the back of her hand.

"Hey, what happened to your hand? It looks pretty raw," I said.

"Oh," she said between bites of the chewy candy. "This happens every time it gets cold and they turn on the heater. The air dries out and my skin cracks. The hand sanitizer makes it so much worse. It's like pouring acid onto my hands. I'm afraid they'll look like this until March."

"That happens to me too, which is why I stopped using it. I wear gloves and wash my hands now." I lifted the back of my hand to her and pointed to a few small red areas. "It doesn't get much worse than this now."

"You should try this stuff," she said while pulling a small tooth-paste sized tube from a pocket. She flipped the lid open and walked toward me. "Do you mind?"

Was she going to put lotion on me? In front of everyone? "Sure, thanks," I said, unsure of what else to say.

She squirted some lotion on her fingers, and then gently rubbed it across the back of my hand. A strong smell of vanilla quickly followed. "The vanilla smell," I said.

"What?"

Crap. I just admitted that I knew she smelled like vanilla. I'm not supposed to be smelling people. That's creepy guy stuff. But it's not like I tried to do it or was sneaky about it. She just smelled like vanilla. Like wearing a red dress. It's just something you notice.

"The other day I smelled vanilla and didn't know what it was. Now I do." That didn't sound too creepy. She smiled and rubbed the lotion onto my hand. The sensation didn't just stimulate the nerves in my hand, it caused a tingle to go all the way up my arm and into the back of my neck. Goosebumps rose quickly on my bare forearm and were impossible to hide.

"This stuff is amazing. Do this every day for a week and those red spots will probably go gone," she said.

Okay, maybe she's my type after all. It's been seventeen years. By now, everyone is my type. "But I don't work every day this week. I'd feel bad asking you to drive all the way to my place to apply it."

She laughed exactly like I hoped she would. "Well, maybe we can find a place halfway between that serves lunch on your day off?"

Come on Alex, you're an ER doc. And a dude. You should be in control of asking someone out on a date, not her. "That sounds great."

She returned my smile and walked away, dropping the lotion back into her pocket and rubbing the excess into her fingers. I'm sure she could tell I was still watching her walk away.

"Are you finally going to go out with her, doc?" Carla didn't mind offering opinions on what was happening around her.

"Finally?"

"She talks about you all the time when you're not around. Last week someone dared her to be more aggressive. They even started calling you Blind Lee."

Really? I guess that's better than Slow Lee.

Chapter 11

Seventeen Years Ago

I could hear Alex's footsteps getting closer to the entrance of my fortress. It was only a matter of time before he pulled the bale to the side and found my lair. What fun is that? If I was going to be busted, I may as well get a laugh out of it.

I reached behind my back to set the beer down and then crawled quickly toward the entrance. I was in a crouch just behind the last bale that blocked the entrance. When my brother's steps stopped just on the other side, I sprang out, shoving the bale in front of me as I exploded from the passage.

"Boo!" I screamed, laughing as he jumped back in shock, his arms reaching out to catch the bale of hay flying at his chest. I stood up from the crouch in time to see him stumble backward away from me, quickly nearing the edge of the loft. He used a spin move I'd seen hundreds of times on the football field and nearly regained his balance until his foot caught on a loose screw in a floorboard. This sudden stop of a foot twisted him again and pitched him backward over the edge of the loft.

"Luke!" I screamed, reaching for him but finding only air as his body tumbled off the edge of the loft, his arms still clutching the bale of hay I had tossed at him. He landed with a thud on the dirt floor of the barn, a gasp escaping his chest and then a choking sound, followed by a low groan. I leaned over the edge of the loft and saw him flat on his back, the bale of hale resting on his chest. His eyes were open, but he wasn't moving. The sunlight from the barn entrance stopped just short of his body, leaving him in shadow ten feet from the door. Oh no, what have I done?

I ran to the ladder and climbed down the first few rungs before jumping the rest of the way to the ground. I landed next to Alex's left shoulder. He didn't turn to look at me but kept staring up and gasping for breath. The weight of the hay bale must be pushing against his chest and making it harder to breathe. I bent over and lifted the bale off his chest, throwing it over my shoulder like I was loading the cart during harvest season. It hit the wall of the barn next to the door and landed with a soft thud.

That's when I saw it. He wasn't struggling to breathe because he had the wind knocked out of him and a bale of hay on his chest. He was struggling because he landed on a large rake with long metal tines. The type of rake we used to sort through the ashes of the burn pile to remove metallic pieces that didn't burn. The sort of tool we stored on the wall of the barn I ran into on my way up the ladder. Their sharp tips poked out through his chest, the holes covered with bloody froth as he tried to breathe.

His eyes stared at me in shock. I wanted to scream for my parents, but the sudden, severe situation had me frozen in place. It's also not like they'd hear me, anyway. Dad was drinking in front of the TV and Mom would be in the bedroom with the door shut, reading her Bible and praying for my dad. If only she had been praying for Luke.

"Luke, I am so sorry. I'm going to go get help. Hang in there." I stood and ran to the house, ripping the screen door off its hinges and pushing the front door open so hard its handle put a hole in the wall.

I didn't bother entering the house, instead I stood in the doorway and screamed. "Luke's hurt real bad. He's in the barn! Call 911!" I was nearly back to the barn before my dad was at the door. He was running but had a hard time keeping a straight line. Not even dinner time and he was drunk, not that it was the biggest issue at the moment.

I continued my sprint until I cleared the gravel driveway that led to the barn and then dropped to a knee in a slide on the dirt floor that would have made my baseball coach proud. I stopped next to Luke and placed my hand on his chest. "Luke, I'm here," I said, but he didn't move. The bubbling around his wounds had nearly stopped. His eyes were closed. My brother was dead, and it was my fault.

"Luke!" roared my father from next to me. I hadn't heard him enter the barn. At least I don't think I did. I couldn't hear much of anything. All I could focus on was the rake tines sticking out of my brother's chest. My mind switched back and forth between the image in front of me and the memory of him falling over the edge of the loft.

I had never seen my dad cry, but he did so like it was the most natural thing in the world. He collapsed on the ground above Luke's head, an arm wrapped around his chest just below the tines, the other cradling his head. My dad, a bulky giant of a man, laid on his side in the fetal position, holding my brother and sobbing. I could never beat my dad in a physical match, but I'd crushed him emotionally. I knew my mother would be here next, and that terrified me more. She didn't deserve this. No one did but me.

I still hadn't recovered my breath from sprinting to the house and back. Actually, the longer I kneeled there, the harder it was to breathe. My vision was fading, and I slumped backwards. But I never hit the ground. My mom caught me before my head smacked the dirt floor. The relief was temporary as she dropped me once she saw Luke laying there. Both of her hands moved to hide her face, her fingers coming together and covering her nose, as if blocking her sense of smell would somehow stop this reality from existing. Her wrists quickly rotated until her fingers were covering her entire face and she dropped to her knees, softly whispering my brother's name.

What happened next was the worst thing my father ever said to me.

Chapter 12

My night shift progressed quickly, with a steady trickle of non-emergent patients. They helped to pass the time, and I was grateful for the interruption from the incessant chatter at the nursing station. I didn't watch TV and could not care less about the new Netflix show. Kendra was working a full night shift tonight, though, so I hung around and dealt with it as best I could. It was six o'clock in the morning and with only an hour to go when she ruined my empty tracking board by triaging a new patient.

"Doc, you're going to love this new one," said Kendra, a huge smile on her face.

"What is it?" Her smile could mean anything. A fun procedure, a hilarious back story to an injury, or just some ridiculous complaint in the early hours of the morning.

"Priapism. Guy gave himself a shot in the penis and has had an erection for six hours."

Six hours? That braggart. I haven't had an erection while awake in years and this jerk wants me to do something about his? "Those injections are a terrible idea. It causes this all the time." I rocked forward out of my chair and headed toward his room.

"Hey, I'm Dr. Lee. How long have you had this erection?"

"Six hours, Doc. I know if it lasts too long, that can lead to me being impotent and I can't deal with that. I'm not even forty. Can you imagine being this young and not being able to get it up? I'd rather be dead."

No, you wouldn't. Trust me. I'd considered death as an atonement for killing my brother, but it didn't seem like a fair punishment. This isn't *A Christmas Carol*. I'll carry my chains while I'm alive, thank you very much.

"Well, the best thing we can do is stick a needle in it, try to drain some blood out, and inject some medicine. That should do the trick. But you need to stop using those injections. Sure, they give you a temporary erection, but there's a risk of this happening. Our urologists don't recommend this as a treatment for erectile dysfunction."

The patient nodded back at me. "I know, I had to find some shady guy online who offered to write me a script. He even shipped me the medication out of his office."

"Let me go get some supplies. I'll be back in a few minutes and we'll get this taken care of."

I stepped out of the room and looked for Kendra. I had several jokes ready to use, but she was crouched over the EMS phone, scribbling notes on a piece of paper. I heard her last sentences before hanging up the phone. "Okay, we'll see you in room eight in five minutes. St. Luke's out."

Room eight. Infinity badness. That's not good. "What's coming in?"

"Thirtyish-year-old Hispanic female, gunshot to the chest. They'll be here in five minutes."

"What? We're not a trauma center. You need to divert them downtown," I said.

Kendra winced before replying. "I know, and I tried. But they said she lost pulses and they're doing CPR. Their protocol is to go to the closest facility if CPR is in progress."

I was pissed. And scared. "The closest *appropriate* facility. What am I supposed to do with a GSW to the chest? Even if we crack her open and miraculously fix a hole in her heart, what then?" I realized I was yelling, something uncommon for me.

"Sorry, it's not your fault. You just answered the phone." The truth was fear had overtaken me. I'm a community ER doctor. I don't do penetrating trauma. Sure, we'll get the farm accidents and blunt trauma from car accidents. Maybe an accidental shooting while cleaning a gun. But a gunshot to the chest? That's downtown trauma center stuff. Keep driving, do not get off at our exit.

We don't have many Hispanics that live near the hospital. Even fewer thirty-year-olds. Even fewer females.

"I see the lights. They're in the parking lot," said Kendra, peering out through the door to the ambulance bay.

"Ooh, it's exciting in here. I haven't been in an emergency department in quite some time."

I turned to see who said those words and quickly wished I hadn't bothered. What is he doing here? Sweater vest, bow tie, wire-rimmed glasses with a gold chain between the ends of the frame. The last thing I need is a psychiatrist. Well, maybe I need to see one, but I don't need one in the ER at the moment.

"You're probably wondering why I'm here. Well, I was collecting data on our psych cases and saw you had one last night. A girl named Luciana. Sure seems like domestic abuse to me. She'd never had a history of alcohol problems, yet she shows up drunk after falling down the stairs and sustaining a head injury. That's classic domestic violence. Did you refer her to a shelter?"

Seriously? Right now? Right when I have a trauma coming in? I saw his name badge hanging from his breast pocket. Dr. Nuñez. He shouldn't be here right now. What is he even talking about? But I had a growing sense of dread that he may be correct. I wasn't looking forward to learning who this incoming patient was.

The ambulance bay doors burst open and EMS wheeled through a stretcher covered in blood. The paramedic was giving rapid chest compressions to a woman who was clearly dead and looked incredibly familiar.

"Hey, that looks like Luciana," said Dr. Nuñez, as EMS rushed past him and into room eight. Always room eight. My stomach tightened as he said what I feared. The same woman I had discharged earlier in the evening. Now back with a gunshot wound to the chest. She said she wasn't suicidal!

The medics moved her over to our ED cot and continued CPR while giving report. "She was just here in the ER. Her brother took her home where she apparently had an argument with her husband. Neighbors heard a lot of yelling and then a single gunshot. Police arrived and found her with a wound in her chest, looks like an exit wound near her left scapula. She also has a cut on her left wrist."

Great, right through her heart. Why did they bring her to me? I can't do anything about this. No one can. "How long has she been down?"

"It's been about twenty minutes since neighbors heard the gunshot. We got on scene about five minutes after the 911 call and she had a barely palpable pulse. We scooped her up and ran out the door, but she lost pulses pretty quickly. Been doing CPR ever since. Estimated down time about fifteen minutes."

Fifteen minutes with multiple large holes in your heart. Sorry, it's time to call it. Her face was familiar to me, but a hollow stare had replaced the weak smile I remembered. The bruise to her right forehead was still there, the same as it was when I discharged her home a few hours ago. Luciana. Flat on her back, dead. And it's all my fault. Where have I heard this before?

Did she kill herself? She has a cut on her wrist and a gunshot wound to the heart. Or did someone attack her? I had to put an end to the useless resuscitation and then figure it out later. "Stop! Just stop. She's gone. There's nothing we can do for her." The team stopped chest compressions and looked at me. I saw them out of the corner of my eye because I was looking at the clock on the wall. "Time of death, six fifteen." Really, it was six o'clock, when she was shot in the heart. For some unknown reason, only coroners can establish a time of death prior to the current moment. No one is dead in a hospital until the instant a doctor declares them dead.

"Does she have family here?" I asked.

"Her brother is on the way," said a police officer who had shown up amid the chaos. "He lives with them and was the one who called it in. We don't have a location on the husband, but we're looking for him now."

"He had to have been injured, too. There was a trail of blood headed out the front door when we arrived," said the medic. They can't find the husband? What if he's on his way here to make sure she's dead?

"Relax doc, we have officers at the entrances to the hospital. No one is getting in without being searched until he's apprehended."

Is it that obvious when I'm scared? I need to work on my poker face. "Okay, let me know when the brother is here." I turned to leave the room, but took one last look at Luciana. The image that will forever be burned in my mind. The one I'll carry to my grave as the doctor who sent her back into an abusive relationship to end up dead a few hours later.

Chapter 13

I was no longer interested in enjoying the humor of my priapism patient. Now it was just another chore that stood in the way of me getting the heck out of this stupid hospital. If Kendra helped me, we could fix his condition in about ten minutes. I may have said a total of ten words the whole time I was in the room. I didn't trust my voice to hide the emotion that was building inside me. The patient didn't trust my hands much as they had a slight tremor that wasn't there the first time I talked to him.

I was a mix of anger, shame, lack of confidence, and several more self-deprecating emotions at once.

But we got through the procedure and he went home happy with a limp penis and a stern warning to not use those injections again.

The tracking board was empty now except for Luciana in room eight. Always room eight. Infinity misery and duration of angst.

"I'm going to take a break. If the coroner calls, will you just ask them to come out here? I know they will not decline the case."

Carla nodded with a face that was wrapped in empathy. I walked past her and then down the hall toward our small office. I needed to be alone. Not going to cry in front of the rest of the staff.

"Hey, can we talk about that first visit first?" The shouted words came from Dr. Nuñez, holding a clipboard over his shoulder near the nurse's station. I ignored him and stepped into the office. It's a small room with a single bed in the corner for those really slow night shifts. A desk and chair sat in the far corner along with a computer in the event we wanted to chart at the hospital instead of at home. I chose the chair and removed my hand from the door, allowing it to close automatically behind me.

But it didn't latch. Instead, it was opening again. That stupid psychiatrist! I turned to yell at him but stopped when I saw the hand wrapped around the door, pushing it open. The skin was red and inflamed. Now the room smelled like vanilla, but not sugar. Fine, I don't deserve cake, anyway.

"Hey, Dr. Lee, I wanted to talk to you about that patient. Do you mind?" Kendra whispered, her head tilted forward but still looking me in the eyes. I could see the pain in hers and I'm sure she could sense it in mine.

"I'm okay. I don't really want to talk about it, thanks. I'll be fine," I said, trying to dismiss her so that I could break down alone. Like a real man. Hurting on the inside but giving off an aura of invincibility. I'm sure Dr. Nuñez would love to dissect that while I lay on a couch someday.

She had stepped into the office by this point anyway, and the door was closing behind her. "Great, I'm glad for you. But I'm not sure I will." She huffed and rolled her eyes before turning to leave. "We'll talk later. Maybe." She turned toward the door and grabbed the handle.

"Wait, stop. I'm sorry. I was being selfish. Let's talk through this together." I stood up and held my arm out toward the chair. "Sit down, please." I stepped backward and sat on the bed, silently willing her to turn around and sit.

My telekinetic powers worked again as Kendra sat in the seat I had just made available. She sat there quietly, probably expecting me to offer some expert clinical advice on how she can deal with this. If she knew what my last seventeen years were like, maybe she'd seek counsel from someone else.

"It's not our fault," I finally said. "We didn't pull that trigger. Let's not confuse who did this."

"But I sent her home!" Kendra's eyes were open wide, and she wore her guilt clearly on her face. "I walked her out of the department and sent her to her death."

No! You will not blame yourself for someone's death. Look what it did to my life. I can't let this destroy yours as well.

"Kendra, all you did is follow my order. And all I did was follow the advice of the crisis team and the request of the patient. We cannot predict the future. We cannot keep everyone in the hospital forever just in case something bad is about to happen. Think of all the patients with chest pain we send home every day."

She looked up from the floor and our eyes met. Hers were bright green and glimmered like multi-faceted emeralds as the tears reflected the bright LED lights on the ceiling. She shook her head slowly. "I didn't even ask about the bruising. Or if she was safe."

"That's part of the standard triage questions. The nurse asks every patient that when they arrive, you know that."

"Yeah, when she was drunk and wanted to die. Do you think she would answer honestly? Did she even have the capacity to answer the questions then?"

Good point. I have no idea. I didn't see her when she first arrived. I just rechecked her before she was discharged. But I can't say that to Kendra. That won't reassure her. The truth is every nurse is going to discharge at least one patient who will go home and die in the next few days. It's just a statistical fact. Medicine is not perfect, and unusual things happen. Today was Kendra's moment, and it broke my heart. She can't let this burrow into her soul and scar her for life. I won't let it.

I leaned forward and took her hands in mine. "Kendra, we don't really know each other all that well, but that's something I hope to change soon. Believe me when I tell you, this is not something you can internalize. You did not pull the trigger. We did not put her in that relationship. We have no idea what really happened. For now, we just need to pray for her and those who loved her. Nick will be here soon and I'll see what he thought about the situation. He's been doing this a long time and I'm sure he asked her about her safety."

A loud sniff preceded a series of nods by Kendra, who then closed her eyes and exhaled slowly.

She's probably trying to figure a way out of this room without offending me. She came in here emotionally broken and looking for support; now that she's recovered she's embarrassed and wants nothing more than to flee.

"Dr. Lee, any chance we can schedule that lunch sooner rather than later?"

Before I could answer, there was a knock on the door and it swung open. I quickly released her hands and sat upright in the bed. She performed the same evasive maneuver, resulting in us both sitting up in our chairs nonchalantly when Nick Park entered the office.

"Hey Alex, I was looking for you." He glanced across from me and winced. "Oh, good morning Kendra. Sorry to interrupt you two, but I have an update on our patient."

"We know about it. We were just going over that."

"No, you don't know this. I was hoping to be here early for an administrative meeting but got stuck in traffic. Turns out a car smashed into a telephone pole and created a giant mess. I must have gotten there pretty quickly after it happened because there were only two police cars and no ambulance yet. Being the kind-hearted ER doc that I am, I pulled over to the shoulder and went to see if there was anything I could do to help."

ER doctors love to tell stories. Especially about themselves. Nick Park was no exception, other than being better at it than most.

"I got up to the scene, and the cops were just standing around, despite the driver being severely injured. He was shirtless and had a huge laceration across his chest. Blood everywhere. Guy was obviously dead, but not from the car accident."

I stared at him, waiting for the story to continue, but he just stood there like he was waiting for us to put another quarter in the machine.

"Guess who he was?" he asked.

"You said it was an update on our patient, so I'm guessing Luciana's husband?" I asked.

He clapped his hands together and pointed at me. "Yes! Hector Nuñez. Presumed person who shot his wife Luciana. Cops found a bloody knife in their bedroom. It seems like she may have gone home and stabbed him, but he had a gun close by and shot her in the chest."

"So, a double murder?" asked Kendra.

"I see it more like premeditated self-defense and a murder." She had taken enough of Hector's abuse and finally did something about it. She was just unlucky that he had a gun on him.

"Exactly what I think too." Nick looked at his watch and cleared his throat. "Hey, it's almost seven. Why don't you get out of here? I know the case well enough to talk to the coroner and I'll sign the death certificate."

I thanked Nick, who then excused himself and left us alone again. Kendra's face had softened, and she seemed much more relaxed. "What do you think about breakfast instead of lunch?"

"That sounds great. I'm starving. Let me go clock out."

I opened the door and then followed her out into the hallway. Dr. Nuñez was nowhere to be seen. I don't think I'll ever run into him again, which is fine by me. Monday-morning-quarterbacking jerk.

Chapter 14

There weren't a lot options for food near the hospital. We had a McDonald's, a gas station with pre-made egg sandwiches, and Mama Del's diner. One of them served beer twenty-four hours a day, a drink selection often offered near businesses that operate twenty-four hours a day. Hospitals are no different.

"Hey doc, about time you got here. Your friend already ordered two beers. Can I get you anything else?" The waitress smiled at me, a carefree look from a woman happy with her place in life. Surrounded by happy customers, continuing the legacy of the family-run business.

"Darlene, good to see you. I'll take a coffee, black."

"Want me to leave the pot like usual?"

"That would be great, thanks." Usually she does that to free up her time for the other customers since I drink a lot of coffee and she has better things to do than bring me refills of a free drink. Today the idea excites me because it means she'll be interrupting us less often.

Kendra sat at a table in the corner, glancing at the menu. Her side of the table had a cushioned bench seat and the other side had individual cushioned chairs. I made eye contact with her and she dropped the menu to the table in order to wave me over. She didn't need to wave. Her smiling face was enough of a tractor beam to get me over there.

"Heck of a shift, huh?" I said, sitting down across from her with my back to the rest of the restaurant. I needed nothing else to distract me from my company.

"Yes, it was. Not too busy, but boy, was it intense. How long has it been since we've had a gunshot wound to the chest?"

"I'm not sure we ever have. At least not in the few years I've been here."

She pushed a beer over toward me, but I slid it back in front of her. "Thank you, but I'm going to stick with coffee this morning. Looks like two beers for you."

"That's fine, I'll take them." She eyed me over the rim of her glass as she took her first drink. "How can you drink a pot of coffee before you go home to sleep?"

"When I'm on nights, I try to stay up a few hours before crashing. If someone works a nine-to-five job, they don't come home and go to sleep right away. They stay up for several hours, right? I think it's easier to stay up and get even more tired. Otherwise, I'll get six hours of sleep and be awake at three. Those day shifters don't get up six hours before their shift starts, right?"

"True, but I'm always so exhausted I crash if I can."

"That's because nurses work crazy twelve or sixteen-hour shifts."

"It's not that crazy. You get used to it. Plus, it gives us more days off."

"I get it. Days off are my favorite. Plus, it's fewer changeover times which are inefficient. I don't know how Nick Spark does it. He's been at this job for over thirty years. I'm not sure I'll make another ten, and I'm only thirty-three."

"Shifts like last night don't help," said Kendra.

I shook my head as I spoke. "No, they do not. We should toast to Luciana." I held my coffee cup up and she clinked it with her first pint of beer. She had chosen two pale ales from a local craft brewery. Cheap beer always did the job for me until I got into residency and started visiting craft breweries. Now the mass-produced stuff tastes like watered down garbage. She's probably had the same journey with beer as I did.

"Why do you suppose she did it?" asked Kendra. "That's a pretty violent thing to do. Stabbing someone in the chest while they slept."

"There was obviously a lot below the surface that we didn't know. I have to imagine he had been assaulting her verbally and physically for some time. She attacked him while he was asleep, but he did it while she was awake and alert. Too often victims of domestic violence can't see any way out of the situation unless one party is dead."

"She denied suicidal and homicidal intent right before I discharged her," said Kendra, staring into the space over my shoulder. She spoke the words toward me, but they were clearly meant for her own reflection.

"Of course she did. Anyone who truly wants to do something others disagree with will not admit their intentions. That's what's so difficult about treating mental health in the emergency department. There are the patients who truly are suicidal and it scares them enough to seek help. We can help them.

"Then there are people who claim to be suicidal to manipulate the system for admission and family dynamic reasons. But there're also the people whose friends or family call the police because of concerns about suicidal ideation, which the patient adamantly denies. It becomes very difficult to sort that all out. Do we go too far and place seventy-two-hour psych holds on many people who don't need it in order to catch the one who does?"

"I don't know. I just know I feel like I contributed to the death of two people and it's hard to take in." Kendra took another sip of her beer and then set the half-empty glass down. No, I'm here with her on what some would call a date. That glass is half-full.

"Let me give you some advice as someone who has taken in a lot of guilt over the years. Don't internalize this. Everything that happened here was external to us. It was going to happen whether or not we were involved."

Kendra took another drink and set her glass down hard on the table, punctuating my point. "I'll sure try. But what about you? From what I've heard, you internalize a lot of things you see."

From what she heard? Who is talking about me? "What do you mean?"

"They say you write things down a lot and then hyper-focus on specific topics for days at a time after a tough case. Are you not following your own advice?"

Now I wanted that other beer, but it wouldn't be very classy to change my mind and take it from her. I'm going to have to do this without my liquid courage. "Did you know I had a brother?"

Chapter 15

Kendra shook her head and dropped her shoulders a bit. Everyone always responds the same way when I mention my brother in the past tense. "No, I didn't. What was his name?"

"Luke. He was two years older than me. He fell off the loft in our barn and landed on a rake. Died right there on the barn floor."

Kendra recoiled back in her bench seat, but her hand reached out and held mine. "Oh no, that's terrible. I'm so sorry."

"That's not the worst of it. I had been hiding up in the loft and jumped out to scare him. He jumped backward, tripped, and fell off the loft, landing on the rake I had knocked off the wall. If I hadn't been screwing around, my brother would still be alive."

"That's terrible. I'm so sorry." Her words were nearly identical to everyone else I'd told the story to. But really, what is there to say? It's not my fault? Because obviously it is.

"Yeah, so that is the defining event in my life. It's something I wish I could change, but it's clearly not possible. The only thing I can do is try to limit death and destruction around me the best I can."

"Is that why you write things down and focus on different topics all the time?"

"Exactly. I'm an ER doc. I need to know something about everything that could walk in or be dragged through that door. It's like I'm manning a dike during a flood. If I see it start to fail, I need to shore it up with extra support. That's how I see my continuing education. If there's a bad outcome, I focus hard on that disease and physiology surrounding it, hoping that the next time I'll be able to do better."

"But you're an excellent doctor already. Is it possible you're going a bit too far and becoming obsessive with it?"

"Yes, and I admit I'm probably there. But I don't study constantly. I still go out and enjoy life a bit from time to time."

She took a sip from her second beer and continued with the questions. So many questions. "Oh yeah? Like what?"

"I like to run and lift weights. Plus, I'm a sucker for audiobooks when I'm driving."

Kendra sat up and touched my arm again. "Oh, I love books. I'm mostly into romance, but I'll read mysteries and thrillers, too."

"Good, let's talk about you for a bit. I don't enjoy being the center of attention."

"What? You're an ER doc. I thought you guys loved attention."

"No, we like to be in charge, but necessarily the center of attention."

"Fine. What do you want to know?"

Are you single? Are you interested in a relationship? Do you mind eccentric dudes who are emotionally damaged? "Tell me about your family."

"There's not much to tell, unfortunately. I have one brother, and my father died when I was young. He had an arteriovenous malformation that ruptured when he and my mother were trying to get me another sibling."

Well, that sucks. Why did I have to take the conversation there? "Oh, I'm sorry to hear that." What else is there to say?

"It's okay. It was almost twenty-five years ago."

"So you're what, twenty-six?"

"Thanks for the compliment, but I'm twenty-eight. When I'm not working, I am mostly a homebody. I take care of my mother who has health issues. I used to run, but I don't do that anymore."

"Why not? It really helps me calm down and work through my thoughts."

She took another drink from her beer and sat it down in front of her, then stared at me. What did I do? Am I supposed to talk first?

"Alex." She paused and cocked her head a bit. "May I call you Alex?" she asked

"Yes, of course. I hate the formalities some docs require in the hospital. I don't even wear a white coat. Besides, we're at a restaurant as friends."

"Well, Alex," she said, raising her eyebrows and smiling as she said my name. Yes, you may call me Alex whenever you want, as long as you keep the same look on your face. "My father had a genetic vascular issue, and I inherited it from him. I have an AVM up here," she said, pointing to the right side of her head. "I stopped rigorous exercise when I found out about it to limit the risk of rupture."

"Seriously? That's awful. I didn't realize you were facing that. Is it treatable?"

"I saw a neurosurgeon when it was diagnosed in my teens, but they said it was too dangerous to try a procedure on. There was a chance it could cause a stroke or kill me. We decided to just limit me from doing the riskiest things that are associated with rupture."

"So no running?"

"Nope. No strenuous exercise. I do a lot of yoga and that helps keep me tone and relaxed, which is good for my blood pressure. High blood pressure is bad for my AVM. Also, no caffeine, smoking, lots of Miralax, and no sex."

We'd make a magnificent pair. She isn't supposed to have sex because she might die, and I can't have sex because I'm a walking train wreck. We can do yoga together and watch TV. Honestly, that would be amazing. Maybe removing the possibility of sex from a relationship would simplify it and keep intentions pure. How many fights stem from sex, or the lack of it?

I made a mental note to look into current research on AVMs. I wanted to write it down in my notebook, but I left it in the car, and it would be too obvious anyway.

"Some of that doesn't sound too bad, I guess."

"Really? This is usually the point at which guys lose interest."

"You must hang out with the wrong guys." I filled my coffee cup and added enough cream to turn the black drink a dark brown. "What's it like living each day knowing that the AVM could rupture at any moment?"

"In a way, it's been liberating. At first I struggled with it and couldn't sleep. I was terrified of doing anything. Then the more I thought about it, I realized I should be terrified to not do anything. I could sit around and worry every day, or I could simply do my best to avoid making it mad and go enjoy my life. So that's what I do."

Oh, so it's like a mean neighbor dog. "I heard a quote one time. It was about a funeral of a very cautious person who never did anything fun. The quote said 'it's not sad that he died, it's sad that he never lived.'"

"That's pretty much my mantra. With this AVM, I never know when the end is coming, so I wake up happy every day. Just happy to be alive and appreciate life as a blessing. Plus, it helps me sort through the nonsense. I will not waste my time in a relationship if I don't think it has potential for something serious, and I don't mince words when someone asks for an opinion. I don't have time for any of that mess."

Are we in a relationship yet? Do you see the potential for something serious with me? "Tell me about your brother. What does he do?" I asked.

"He's actually a surgeon."

"Oh, that's interesting. Did you both pursue a career in health care after what happened to your father?"

"Probably. We both wanted to from a young age, but hard to say if that's what specifically started it."

"Can I get you two anything to eat? You've been drinking and talking so much I felt bad for interrupting."

"Darlene, I'd love some sausage gravy and biscuits. Thank you."

Kendra ordered a fruit plate, and we continued our conversation until the beer was out of her system and I was having a hard time staying awake. We agreed to meet again this weekend, on a rare day neither of us worked.

Chapter 16
Seventeen Years Ago

The sirens screamed loudly now, probably already at the beginning of our driveway. Not that it mattered. There was nothing anyone could do at this point. Luke was dead and we knew exactly who caused it.

My father slowly peeled himself up from the dirt floor of the barn and into a kneeling position. His eyes bored into me, suddenly able to focus despite the significant amount of whiskey circulating through his bloodstream. "What happened?" The two words came out as a groan and took twice as long to say as normal.

I had to tell the truth. My brother deserved to have the truth spoken over his lifeless body. But I didn't do it. I couldn't. So I lied. Well, at least I didn't tell the whole truth. "I'm so sorry. I was just screwing around and hiding up in the loft. I wanted to see how long it would take Luke to find me. Once he almost found me, I jumped out to scare him. I thought it would be funny, but he fell backward and landed on that rake." I pointed down at the metal spikes sticking through my brother's chest.

"And what was the rake doing on the ground with the tines up, Alex?" He pointed to the wall where several other implements hung from their appropriate hooks.

"I, I guess I knocked it off when I climbed up the ladder." It sounded so stupid to say out loud. My brother is dead because I didn't pick up a tool. My father used to remind us all the time to not leave a rake with the sharp points sticking up. We laughed about it once he'd walk away. How many times can you tell a child something before it loses importance?

My mother continued to sob and hold her face in her hands. I put my arm around her, but she jumped back like I had shocked her.

"You did this," my father said, pointing his gnarled index finger at me. His hand trembled as he extended his arm as far as he could, the muscles twitching from a blend of anger and alcohol. Never a good combination for my father. He drew himself up to his feet and stood behind my mother, wrapping one arm around her while he continued to point at me. "You killed our son!"

Then he said what I knew he was thinking. I'm glad he said it, because it's how I felt too.

"It should be you sitting there dead, not Luke!"

The first responder to arrive in the barn was Officer John Lundy. I'd known him for as long as I could remember.

He'd wave at us every time he drove by our house. I watched his face as he took in the scene.

The rest of the police and paramedics ran into the barn just in time to hear my father wish I was dead, but they were focused on Luke. I'm not sure they even heard what he said. Their assessment only lasted a few seconds until they reached the same conclusion we did. Luke was dead, and there was nothing anyone could do to change it.

Officer Lundy tried to comfort my father, but quickly found it futile. He scanned the barn and did what many people do when they don't know what to do. He started cleaning. The first thing he moved was the hay bale I had picked up from on top of Luke's chest and threw over my shoulder. He then picked up a shovel that was laying under it but paused when he saw blood on the handle. Dang it. Another thing to explain.

The next few hours seemed to take days. The whole town seemed to file through and try to comfort my parents. Our minister prayed in the barn before they took Luke's body away in a hearse. The coroner didn't feel the need to investigate the cause of death. It was pretty obvious, even for a fifteen-year-old.

Eventually, it was just me sitting alone in the barn. Darkness enveloped the interior as the sun set and the light switches remained off. Everyone else had moved inside to comfort my parents. No one was interested in comforting the kid who killed his brother. I should be relieved, I guess. I heard it was me who should be dead.

It had been thirty minutes since I had seen anyone. I think they had truly forgotten about me. Either that or they were actively ignoring me. The only sounds were birds flying in and out of the barn, and the occasional pop as the barn roof cooled and changed shape enough to stress the wood.

This was the time of night my brother and I would go roam the fields looking for varmints to shoot. A .22 rifle and a box of ammo could fill an entire afternoon with noise and fun. Now it was nearly silent, until the sound of dripping water grabbed my attention. I turned around and saw a puddle in the mud under the loft. The beers must have finally slipped off the hay and spilled. Another reminder of my foolishness. It's like Luke was slapping me on the back of the head.

It was hours since Stacy was supposed to have shown up. Maybe she did but was scared away by the commotion. Maybe it was all a setup to make me look like a fool. Either way, I'm sure going to find out next time I see her.

Chapter 17

I drove home happier than I should be, given a patient I recently discharged killed someone and then died herself. But I couldn't stop smiling. Kendra and I could have talked for hours.

I want this relationship with Kendra. No, I need it. I can't keep diving headfirst into a job that is consuming me with no healthy outlet. I need to get past the self-doubt and guilt as well. It's time to go see Dr. Francis again.

I used my phone to find his office number, and soon his secretary greeted me on the line. "Hi, thank you for calling New Hope Psychiatry, the office of Dr. Delroy Francis. How can I help you?"

This is where I had started, and stopped, my treatment a few years ago. Holly, our managing partner, suggested I see someone professionally because of how hard I was taking some of the cases. I blamed myself any time a patient did not have a good outcome, and that was not a viable long-term strategy as an ER doctor. Diseases are sneaky.

They often hide behind benign symptoms and build up impressive momentum before manifesting themselves. Our first job is to make the illness get worse slower, then stabilize. Finally, if the patient is lucky, then retreat toward remission or cure.

But sometimes it's more dependent on the disease and the patient than the doctor or treatment. Some processes are too far along to reverse. The inertia of disease too great to overcome, even with the longest lever Archimedes could find.

Dr. Francis and his team of therapists helped get me to where I could accept bad outcomes in my patients and not blame myself for them. It didn't change my desire to improve and be at the top of my game, just helped me deal with it when things got wonky.

It's time to open up to him completely. I was holding back the last time he treated me. "I need to make an appointment to see Dr. Francis regarding PTSD."

"Okay, are you a new patient, or existing?"

"Maybe both? What is your cutoff? It's been a few years since I've been there. My name is Alex Lee." I left off the 'doctor' part. I'm no one special, just a guy trying to overcome a past trauma. I see too much serious unstable mental health in the ER to dare try to get a closer appointment and bump someone who may be in an acute crisis.

"I found you, sir. You're lucky. Next month, you would have dropped off our patient list and would have had to wait for a new patient evaluation. We're months out on scheduling those. Let's see, can you make it Friday morning at 9:00 a.m.? I just had a cancellation."

"Yes, absolutely. I'll be there. Are you still in the same office?"

"Same place for ten years. Bring your ID and insurance card to the appointment and show up fifteen minutes early to fill out paperwork."

I thanked her and ended the call. Time for a quick shower and then bed. The night shift circadian rhythm disruption was finally catching up to me. If I didn't get in bed soon, I'd fall asleep on the couch or somewhere else less comfortable than my king-sized bed.

My bed felt amazing as I laid on the pillow with covers up to my shoulders, exhausted but more excited for the future than I had been in years. Why didn't I ask her out sooner? Technically, I didn't even ask her out this time, I don't think. She initiated it. But who cares? It happened, and it's going to happen again.

It will be something fun to debate on Saturday. Sleep snuck up behind me and knocked me out of my conscious thoughts of Kendra and I doing yoga together on a deserted tropical beach.

Chapter 18

What am I supposed to wear to a psychiatry appointment? I'm an ER doctor. I don't want the world to know I'm going to see a psychiatrist. How would my patients feel if I'm seeing a shrink? Would they want me taking care of them?

That's the line of thinking that kept me out of Dr. Francis's office for a while the first time. I'm not sure if it was a valid reason, or just an excuse to not go. Applications for medical licensing always ask if the applicant has mental health issues that could affect their practice of medicine. If I'm seeing a psychiatrist, I probably have to answer yes, even though my issue actually makes me a better doctor.

Strangely enough, it was a patient I saw that finally convinced me to go. He was a truck driver who had terrible sleep apnea. I walked into his room and his oxygen was in the seventies when he was asleep. Back then, you could not pass the commercial driver's license physical if you had obstructive sleep apnea. He knew he had the condition but could not get it treated because he would lose his job if he was diagnosed with it. So instead, he drove 80,000 pounds down the road for hours every day, hoping he didn't fall asleep from his untreated disorder.

Now, they have modernized the regulations and the CPAP machines are equipped with remote monitoring, so they can issue a CDL as long as the patient complies with treatment.

I compared myself to the truck driver cruising down the road with untreated sleep apnea. Would a patient prefer their ER doctor was seeing a psychiatrist to help with their issues or ignoring those issues and spiraling further down into the mental health abyss?

Traffic was tolerable today, and I arrived a few minutes early for the appointment, which means ten minutes late since I was supposed to be there early to fill out paperwork. I had just finished the last form when someone cracked a door open and called my name. Not as anonymous as it could be, but fortunately, I was the only one in the waiting room.

Dr. Francis's office is in the building's corner, allowing plenty of sunlight to enter the room through two walls of floor-to-ceiling windows. I entered his office confidently, ready to improve myself so that I could successfully manage a relationship.

"Dr. Lee, good to see you again!" His deep voice carried through the room easily, though his Jamaican accent was less noticeable than the last time I spoke with him.

"Hi Dr. Francis, it's been a few years. You look well." It was true. He still had the athletic look, and his shaved head made him appear even stronger. The reading glasses were new. He's about ten years older than me and seemed in better shape than I am now.

"Thank you. Take a seat and we'll get started." Delroy sat down in a chair next to my sofa and opened his laptop. "I looked through your old chart to refresh my memory of your situation. PTSD because of watching your brother fall to his death when you were sixteen."

"That's the gist of it. We can add broken family, abandonment issues with my parents, and a host of downstream failed relationships."

Delroy nodded as I rattled off my list of inadequacies. "Yes, you certainly have your struggles. Now that we've listed a few of them, should we see how they stack up against your accomplishments?"

"It will be a much shorter list. I went to college, medical school, residency, and now I have a job. The same stuff everyone else in my class did, but they didn't struggle like I did."

"And how do you know that? You only knew what they told you. Consider your acquaintances likes social media feeds. You don't know what's really going on with them, only the highlights they post. Grades aren't public information. Besides, does it really matter how easily something came, as long as you accomplish the goal? Who is more highly regarded in society? The one who barely tries and accomplishes his goal, or the one who overcame adversity and struggles as hard as he can to cross the finish line? Which of the two will have the crowd on their feet?"

He's right. Outwardly, I know it's true, but it's hard to internalize. It took me two years of trying to get into medical school. Once I was in, I had to spend every evening and weekend in the library just to keep my grades up. My friends all accused me of being a 'gunner', someone who was trying to get the best grades in the class and into a highly competitive residency. In reality, I was just trying to not get kicked out. That left little time for socializing and conditioned me to spend off hours reviewing my notes. Something I've held onto for my entire career.

All of that is old news and something we had discussed in the past. In order to move forward, he needs to know everything. "Dr. Francis, when I saw you last time, I wasn't entirely forthcoming with you."

He smiled at me, his perfect white teeth standing out against his dark skin. He pulled his glasses off and rubbed his eyes. "Alex, do you think anyone ever fully opens up to me? They tell me the least amount they think I need to know in order to get them to where they want to be. It's very difficult to build a level of trust with a patient to the point they divulge everything."

"I'm not going to tell you everything, but I want to get better. I've met a girl and I want to date her. To make love to her."

"Those are very normal goals, and you deserve to accomplish them. So, what is it you've been withholding from me, Alex?"

"It's about that day in the barn. In the loft. Why I was even up there in the first place." I paused, not sure I could say this out loud in front of someone else. I've been trying for seventeen years and haven't been able to do it. But I've never met anyone like Kendra, and I want this to work. So here goes.

"I wasn't planning to be alone in the loft. I was up there to meet a girl. Stacy. But she never even showed. This whole thing"—I accented the phrase by making a lasso move with my right arm—"was worthless. He died for nothing."

It sounded appropriate from my perspective, but my psychiatrist refused to allow the guilt trip. Which is good, because I'm paying him to tell me something other than what I've believed for seventeen years.

"You can't make that statement. Had Stacy shown up, and you did what teens did, and then Luke died, would that be better from the standpoint of your guilt?"

"No, of course not. I'd probably feel even more guilty because of the immediacy of it."

"Exactly. So drop that line of thinking. If Stacy had not given you that note, would you have been in the loft?"

"Not that night," I said.

"So, in a way, you also blame the girl. That is likely where your impotence issues are stemming from."

Yeah, I figured that one out already. How about you tell me why I have the other thing? "And what about the hallucinations? Whose fault are those?"

Chapter 19

"I'm sorry. What did you say? Hallucinations?"

Whoops. I hadn't planned on divulging that today. Or maybe I did but couldn't admit it to myself. Maybe this was an intentional slip up. Either way, here we go. Freud said I can't psychoanalyze myself. I should probably stop trying to do it and let the professional in the room do it. Well, the other professional.

"Yeah, so, I've had a few situations where I can see and talk to people who aren't really there. But I don't think they're hallucinations." There. I said it. I waited for Delroy to make notes in his chart, to take the information in and add to my diagnosis list.

"Wait, maybe we shouldn't call them hallucinations. They're more of a creation of my mind that I can see and talk to, but no one else is aware of."

Delroy looked at me over his glasses. "You just described a hallucination. Something that is perceived and experienced by you but isn't real."

"I just don't want you thinking I'm schizophrenic or anything. That could look bad on my record and affect my ability to practice medicine."

"But are you schizophrenic?" I'm ready for this one, Delroy. I've gone over this in my head for years. Not schizophrenic. "I don't think so. The DSM-V manual may think I am, but I'm putting an asterisk on the negative symptoms."

"Well, you clearly have hallucinations. We only need one more of the five criteria. Delusions?"

I shook my head no.

"Disorganized speech?"

Nope. Quick shake of the head.

"Grossly disorganized or catatonic behavior?"

Hah, no way. I'm one of the most organized people I know. Another head shake.

"Then let's talk about your negative symptoms. Any issues with hygiene? Lack of interest in pleasure?"

"No."

"Sleeping well? Eating well?"

"I take medicine to help me sleep, but who doesn't? I sleep fine when I'm on it."

Delroy's wrist flicked down a bit and then up on his paper. What was that, a check mark? That comment didn't need a check mark. I just don't sleep well.

"Any troubles expressing emotion? Interacting with others? Social withdrawal?"

"Well, I'm not dating, but I hang out with friends from time to time, as my schedule allows."

Delroy adjusted himself in his seat as he checked his notes. "Alex, I see what you mean about the asterisk. You're close, but there could be another diagnosis that fits more appropriately."

"What's that?"

"PTSD with dissociative subtype."

Dissociative? Is that what these characters are? Brief breaks with reality? They sure seem real. "What does that mean?"

"It means your PTSD is so severe that part of your way of dealing with it has been to create these imaginary characters around situations that caused additional stress."

I guess I'd rather have one diagnosis with a subtype than two individual diagnoses. "So, is that a good thing?"

Delroy smiled at me. "I like your optimism, Alex. I'm glad you came to see me again. You've provided me with more information that I think can help you receive the proper treatment."

"What does that treatment look like? Counseling? Meds?"

"Counseling for sure. Regarding medications, I'm not sure that would be beneficial at this point. Since these hallucinations are not causing any significant negatives in your life, I think it's fine to wait and see how therapy does first. But we can't wait too long. You're at higher risk for complications."

"Complications? Like what?" I don't like where he is going with this.

"Problems at work, relationships, financial disarray..." His words faded out before he completed the list.

"And suicide? I don't need you to be delicate with me. I need to know what you know. I want to get better."

"Fine. Yes, Alex. Suicide." I'd never kill myself. That's what crazy people do. What depressed people do. I'm neither. I'm traumatized.

"I don't see myself at risk for that, but I don't want to minimize the severity of my condition."

"Good, because it's time for psychotherapy. You need to reestablish with a therapist. I've made the diagnosis of post-traumatic stress disorder, dissociative subtype, and you need help to reprocess this event in a healthy context."

"How can I reprocess it? It already happened."

"Yes, it has. But you can change how you feel about it. You can't change the circumstances or the event itself, but you can reprogram your response to the memories."

"How do I do that?"

"There are several methods that have been successful. Hypnosis. EMDR. Even some new research is suggesting LSD as a potential, but I'm not ready to discuss that with patients yet."

"EMDR? What is that?"

"Eye movement desensitization and reprocessing. It's a relatively new technique that has shown very promising results. It uses bilateral brain stimulation while visualizing an image that has caused psychological trauma. The theory is this helps to dampen the memory and can be used to insert new thoughts and feelings about the event."

"Bilateral brain stimulation? Does this involve wires and electrodes?" I've seen electroconvulsive therapy. Leads attached to the skull and a current generator to shock the brain into submission. Yes, it's safe and effective, but not what I want to experience.

Delroy flashed me the typical smile he gives me in response to my questions. Like when a child seems overwhelmed by an extremely simple task and requires the slightest bit of parent support. Then he threw his pen at me. Well, more of a toss, but I caught it before it hit me in the chest.

"There you go. You just stimulated both hemispheres of your brain," he said.

"What? I did?" I looked down at my hands wrapped around his pen like I'm holding a frog I found in the yard.

"Yes, your eyes followed the pen, and you used each side of your brain to catch it. That's basically what we do with EMDR. Memories aren't stored in any one particular part of the brain, right? There is no memory center. That's why most cases of amnesia are psychogenic or caused by a global injury to the head. A stroke doesn't cause it."

"That's true."

"With EMDR, the therapist will have you draw up an image, an event, a feeling, something related to the traumatic experience. Then they will walk you through bilateral stimulation to lay down new beliefs or feelings around that image."

"That's seems pretty straightforward. And it works?"

"You'd be amazed."

"Okay, sign me up. I'm willing to try anything. I can't keep going like this. My job is noticing and I finally have a woman who is interested in me. I need to get past this."

"Alex, you can do this. I'll check back with you periodically, but moving forward, the therapists will handle your acute treatment. Good luck." He leaned forward and shook my hand, essentially dismissing me from his office.

Seriously? I thought I'd be seeing Delroy repeatedly over the coming months and now he's releasing me to start over with someone else? I was comfortable with Delroy and what we had discussed. Treating mental health sucks. But not as bad as not treating it, I guess.

Chapter 20

Saturday mornings are my favorite. At least the ones where I didn't work late the night before and don't have a shift scheduled for later in the day. An entire day of doing whatever I want. I could sleep in until ten, eat donuts while watching a TV show, and then run off the calories.

Saturdays also allowed me to catch up on studying the disease processes I saw earlier in the week and finish charting on my patients. It's a terrible feeling to show up Monday and have a cluttered in basket of charts to deal with.

But today isn't a typical Saturday. I have a date with an amazing woman. I hopped out of bed, skipped the donuts and TV, and cut up a plate of fresh fruit. Afterward, I put on my running shoes and headed out to run a few miles.

I hadn't gone more than a few hundred yards before Dr. Brady showed up. "Imagine running into you out here," he said. "I'll join you for a bit." Great. Exactly what I need.

"That kid did fine after we transferred him to the pediatric hospital. I read the discharge summary. Just a twenty-four observation until the glimepiride got out of his system and then he went home," I said.

"That was a near miss, though. He shouldn't have gone down to CT scan until he had a glucose checked. That's basic resuscitation. Do the DONT. Dextrose, Oxygen, Narcan, Thiamine."

I know that. The problem wasn't that I forgot it, the problem was we have immediate access to a CT scanner. Stroke alert patients actually start with a CT scan before they even get into a treatment room. Fifteen years ago, it would take twenty minutes to prepare the table and transport a patient. We had time to check all the boxes and get this stuff accomplished before CT was ready for the patient. Now, we're expected to do everything immediately, and the electronic medical record is there to time stamp it all for some non-clinical administrator to review and ding us later.

Screw Brady. He couldn't make it a single shift in the ER. "It must be nice to sit on the sidelines and judge everybody else. Do you mind if I come into your office and tell you what you're doing wrong?"

"That's not what I was doing," said Dr. Brady. "I'm trying to help patients. Dr. Ramsey and I think you're an excellent doc most of the time. You just need a little push in the right direction sometimes. That's where we come in."

I hated to admit it, but he was right. It's hard to practice solo, with no other doctors to bounce things off of. I was grateful for their help, even if it came in annoying ways. I don't consider them hallucinations. It almost seemed insulting to consider them as such. Hallucinations usually have negative connotations. And while annoying and dismissive toward me, they only show up during significant cases and help me focus.

"Alex, good morning." The greeting came from the elderly couple who lived next door to me. Our concrete patios connected with a low wall separating the two spaces. Mine was barren, theirs had several plants along it which added beauty to the space. They were a kind couple, always asking how I was doing. Always asking why I studied all the time and never had a lady friend over for dinner.

"Hi Agnes," I said. "Paul. How are you two this morning?" I paused my run to catch my breath and be neighborly. They were an adorable couple. Usually together and always happy. At least from what I could see. Delroy would probably try to tell me there's a dark underbelly they are hiding from me.

"Just fine, out for our morning exercise. What are you doing up so early on a Saturday? Do you have to go to work later?" she asked.

Am I that predictable? "No, I'm off. I actually have a date later today and I wanted to get my run in early."

"Paul," she said, slapping her husband on the shoulder. "Did you hear that? Alex has a date!" Her voice was louder than it needed to be to overcome his partial deafness. She's excited for me, and that's so adorable. It's how I'd expect my parents to react. And it's the reaction I was hoping for when I dropped the news.

My watch beeped, and the screen flashed a notification. Kendra, one hour. "She's a nurse in the ER," I said, holding my watch up. "And I need to meet her in the park in an hour. Have a great day." I jogged away, waving as I accelerated into my last lap. One mile to go.

I rarely run for time, that's not what motivates me. I run to clear my mind and stay healthy. But today I pushed it on the second lap. Kendra used to be a runner. If she asked me about my time, I wanted to impress her. Or at least disappoint her less. So I leaned forward and extended my stride length.

"So anyway, I'm glad that kid did well. Remember to check a glucose early next time, okay?"

"Yeah, got it. See you later." I sped up as much as my lungs would allow, not caring about pleasantries. It's time he found a new running partner.

I showered quickly and was out the door in fifteen minutes. Early fall in Indianapolis usually offers nice weather and today is living up to expectations. Upper seventies and sunny with a light breeze. I chose a pair of khaki shorts and a light fishing shirt with a simple print.

The type of breathable, synthetic fabric Jeff Probst would wear on a beach in a Survivor episode. My shoes are the best part. A soft woven pair of HEYDUDE shoes that matched my gray shirt.

I just hope the twenty-one-year-old patient I stole the outfit idea from a few weeks ago isn't at the same park we are. That would be embarrassing. Especially if he was still wearing the same clothes. Kendra might hurt herself from laughing so hard.

The park was nothing special, but it's where Kendra chose. I'd go sit on the side road and count cars if that's what she wanted to do. I arrived first and was the first car in the small parking lot. Kendra's Honda CRV arrived a few minutes later, and she parked right next to me. Her windows aren't tinted like mine, allowing me to see she didn't come alone. She brought a friend. An absolutely adorable one.

Chapter 21

Kendra opened the rear door and a small golden dog flung itself out of the car and sprinted at me.

"Lucy!" she yelled, to no effect. The dog was laser-focused on getting to me and trying to bite my ankles.

I picked her up, which changed her focus of attack to my face instead of my legs. "Hello to you, too."

"Sorry, she's still a puppy. She's adorable when she settles down, I promise." Kendra reached out and took the dog from me, but not without brushing against my hands. There are those goose bumps again.

"It's fine. She's adorable. Is she a golden?"

"Goldendoodle actually. A mini."

"How long have you had her?"

"She's about five months old now, but I've had her since she was eight weeks."

"Oh, she really is a mini, isn't she?" I thought she was a recently weaned based on her size.

"Yep, but she eats enough for a full-sized dog. I chose this park because it has a fenced-in area for her. I figured we could let her run and tire herself out."

Maybe I should get a dog. The puppy's energy is infectious, and it would be a pleasant distraction for me. Plus, it would force me to get out of my condo more. Agnes and Paul would probably let it out for me on days I worked. And it would give Kendra and me something else to bond over. But then mine would probably hump hers and it would get really awkward. Maybe I'll get a cat.

Kendra clipped a leash onto Lucy's collar and set her back on the ground. She took off at a run until she ran out of leash and jerked to a stop. "She's starting to figure it out, but that first run always gets her."

I know how you feel, Lucy. I'd love to run excitedly through life like you do, but I too have something I carry around my neck that holds me back.

We started walking along the path leading toward the fenced dog run, conversation coming easily as we chatted about recent cases in the hospital and some gossip about the staff in the department. Kendra was in a playful mood, and it looked great on her. "Do you want to know some nicknames you have at the hospital?"

Oh man, not sure I'm ready for this. But I trust her not be too mean. "Hit me with them."

Kendra's eyes opened wide, and she took a quick step that was more of a skip. "Okay, I'll start with the staff favorite. Vicious Lee."

"Vicious?" I couldn't say it without laughing. It wasn't close to what I was expecting to hear. "What did I do to earn that one?"

"It was an artificial hip dislocation. You were standing on top of the bed and two of us were trying to hold the patient down so you could pull harder. You were rotating the leg in and out and it went back into place with the most disgusting grinding sound imaginable."

"Oh, I remember that one. I got nauseous and sweaty because I thought I pulled the prosthetic implant right out of the femur."

"Everyone did. We took bets on how much you could deadlift after that. It was easily half the patient's weight plus two nurses."

I puffed up a bit on the inside. They noticed that? So why not call me Strong Lee? "My max is 405 pounds, but it's been a few months since I've tried for a PR. What else have you heard?"

"Well, there's Worried Lee."

That one is probably fair. We have to worry about everyone. We worry about the worst condition that could be going on. That's the mantra of emergency medicine. It's also why I order so many tests and take my time with patients. But I'd prefer Thorough Lee. It has a better connotation.

"The last one is my favorite, and the one I came up with." Her smile made me hope it would not be very mean. Kendra's too nice to come up with a mean one. Or at least tell me about it if she did.

"What is it?"

"Kind Lee."

"That's awfully nice of you. It fits me perfectly, but what did I do to earn that?"

"It was a homeless frequent flier. He comes in all the time."

"Clarence," I said. I know the man well. At least two visits a week, usually disheveled and wanting help with drinking. Then a few hours later, as the alcohol is wearing off, he's angry and walks out of the ER. Usually with pockets full of our supplies he grabs when no one is watching him. "What did I do for Clarence?"

"You changed his socks."

"That's it?"

"That's not an insignificant thing on a guy like him. It was one of the first times we worked together. You came in to evaluate him while I was still doing my assessment. You started with his feet and pulled off his socks to check his feet for wounds."

I remember that day. I didn't want to remove the socks, but it had to be done. His socks were nearly black, but likely came off the shelf as white as a cloud. Once he got them, they were subjected to all sorts of things and they stopped visiting a washing machine. The only time they got wet was when it rained or he was too drunk to not urinate on his feet.

It's poor form to miss a nasty wound simply because the patient was wearing dirty socks. "Once I took them off, I couldn't very well put them back on. I just grabbed some hospital footies instead, wrapped his socks in plastic, and threw them away."

She would not let me end the story there, which surprised me. I didn't know she knew the rest of it. "Yeah, you grabbed footies alright. Then you left the room with his feet still exposed. I had to clean his feet just so I could be in the room longer. The smell was awful. I was so mad at you."

"Sorry about that." I truly was. I hate making shifts harder on anyone else.

"Oh, I forgave you before the shift ended. When I discharged him, I noticed he was wearing fresh white socks, and you had a snazzy pair of hospital footies on."

So she did notice. Why didn't she say anything? Why has no one in the department made fun of me for that? "I didn't think anyone noticed. People love to make fun of each other in the ER, but no one has said anything about it to me."

"That's because I never told anyone. It was something I knew about you and no one else did. My little secret about how great you were. If I had told everyone else, today may not have happened."

I love what that says about how she feels. She thinks I'm a catch and something worth celebrating. It's been an eternity since anyone has expressed that feeling to me. There was a time I wanted a girl to feel that way, but she just stomped on my heart that was already ripped open.

Chapter 22

Today is my first EMDR therapy session. I'm both looking forward to and dreading it at the same time. Rehashing these memories is about the last thing I want to do. But I realize that not working through them is definitely the last thing I want to do. I need to improve. I deserve to improve. I'm going to improve.

The therapist's office was close to Dr. Francis's office, but in an older building. Psychotherapy must not reimburse as well as psychiatry. Vinyl lettering adorned the door and spelled out the names of two therapists, Trevor Starnes and Caitlyn Woodhouse. I was here to see Trevor. I hoped I could talk about impotence to a Trevor better than a Caitlyn.

I checked in at the counter and filled out another stack of papers, asking how bad I felt my life was. Why are all the questions always framed in a negative light? The worksheets made me add up my score myself, and then

I had to search the internet to find out what the scores meant. A moderate case? Severe?

The secretary escorted me toward two doors and opened the one on the left. I entered the room and took a seat in a nice leather chair. There was a matching one on the other side of a small empty table, but not much else in the room. A floor length window tried its best to provide light to a few live plants, but built-in blinds reduced the effective light considerably.

Still a few minutes until my session was about to start. May as well kill some time. I pulled out my phone and opened a medical reference app and continued the article I had been reading at home.

A minute before my appointment time, I heard the door next to my room open and close. Then mine opened, and I got my first impression of the person who would walk me through my past trauma. Mid-forties, overweight, large black glasses. He did a poor job of hiding his disinterest and had me wishing for another therapist before he even opened his mouth.

"Doctor Lee? I'm Trevor Starnes. Pleased to meet you." I halfway stood up and accepted his limp handshake before sitting back down. "Would you mind switching seats? You're actually sitting in mine."

Seriously? The seats are identical, except mine has a view of the window. I'm the one paying for this. He should have to look at the wall, not me.

"Okay, sure." I fully stood this time and looked at the door. Maybe I'll just keep walking. No, then I'd have to explain it to Kendra. She'd ask why I left and when I said 'because he made me change seats' I would be in trouble. And I wanted to get better. Maybe Trevor is a miracle worker. At least when he's in the correct chair.

"Thank you. I know it sounds petty, but the parking lot is fairly busy, and I'd rather not have my clients distracted by outside influences. There are several static images on the wall behind me you can focus on if you'd like."

Actually, that made sense. I'm glad I switched chairs and am staring at the wall now. Maybe I should give Trevor a chance. Maybe he actually knows what he's doing and I'm just being rude and prejudicial?

"I reviewed the notes that Dr. Francis sent over and we are going to use EMDR to improve your PTSD symptoms. Are you familiar with how EMDR works?"

"Sort of. It sounds like the neurolyzer from *Men in Black*, where they flash people's memories using a bright light."

Trevor's face relaxed into a warm, natural smile. "That's such a great reference. I use that to describe it to people that haven't heard of EMDR before. But we can use several techniques. Light is one, but we can also just use moving fingers, hand-held buzzers, or even have you tap yourself on the shoulders. Basically, anything that stimulates both cerebral hemispheres at the same time in an alternating fashion. Do you have a preferred method you'd like to use?"

"Not really. I've never done this, so whatever you think works best."

"I like to just start with moving my fingers. It's a very familiar image and shouldn't be very distracting. But before we get to that, I need you to describe for me the most negative image you have of the event. Which image gives you the most unease when you think back on it?"

Well, that's an easy one. It's the image I've seen almost every day of my life. I see it while I'm awake, and I relive it during my dreams. It sucks being afraid to fall asleep and also afraid to wake up. He needs to help me.

"It's my brother Luke, laying on his back, gasping for breath. The metal tines of a rake sticking through his chest. I can still see bloody froth bubbling up from the bases of them. The shocked look on his face as he stared at me, unable to speak or breathe."

He nodded and scribbled a few quick notes. "What words go best with that image to describe the negative belief you have about yourself now?"

"I'm guilty." Trevor's hand scribbled across the paper, documenting my conviction.

"And when you bring up that picture, what would you rather believe about yourself now?"

"I'm innocent. I'm normal."

"And when you bring up that picture, how true do the words I'm innocent feel to you now on a scale of one to seven, where one is completely false and seven is completely true?"

How do they feel? Like a lie. Like I'm a fraudster, trying to get something that I don't deserve. "Let's go with a two."

"When you bring up that picture and the words I'm guilty, what emotion do you feel now?"

Oh man, this isn't easy. I wish I didn't have the image at all. So, amnesia maybe? But that isn't a feeling. "Shame. Guilt. Regret." He wrote each word as I said them, then circled one. Which one got the circle? I tried to look but couldn't see his paper.

"How disturbing does that feel to you now on a scale of zero to ten, where zero is no disturbance or neutral and ten and the worst disturbance you can imagine?"

"Do you mean right now? Or when I'm picturing it?"

"Right now, as you picture your brother laying on the ground."

How do I quantify this? I'd been asking people this very question regarding pain for years. I never believed the ten out of ten people. They were clearly in pain. But to label it a ten means there's nothing I could do that would be worse than what they are experiencing. And usually that wasn't the case. Or the people who try to use a number larger than ten. The scale only goes up to ten. You're not special enough to have access to numbers higher than ten.

Ten is all you get. Use the most of it. If you say eleven, I'm going to assume it's a three.

But what is a ten out of ten on an emotional pain scale? And if I say an eight, or a seven, am I downplaying the death of my brother? Am I allowed to say it doesn't hurt as bad as it used to? Time is supposed to heal all wounds, but mine has been granulating in slowly and has developed quite the scar by now. We're well into keloid stage now. I'm hoping this therapy allows it to improve without the psychiatric equivalent of a sharp knife and a wide excision to get back to healthy tissue.

So I just picked a number out of the air. "Eight." Infinity badness. Nothing's a ten. It can always get worse, even if I can't see how.

"Where do you feel that in your body?"

Where do I feel it? In my soul. In my entire being. But that's not what he's asking. I suppose it's the crushing feeling I get in my chest, like some invisible monster has a tentacle wrapped around me and is squeezing harder and harder. "My chest."

"I'd like for you to bring up that picture and the words I'm guilty. Notice where you're feeling it in your chest and follow my fingers."

Trevor raised his right hand with his index and middle finger extended, and the thumb tucked in close. He moved his fingers back and forth in front of me twenty-four times. At least that's what I think it was. I was too busy focusing on the image and that I was guilty. I do not know if I'm remembering or simply imagining, but I'm trying.

"What are you noticing now?"

"Luke lying there, not yet dead. He was gasping for breath, trying to talk."

"Go with that." He moved his fingers again, and I made myself stop counting them. It seemed like twenty-four again. At least he's counting. "What are you noticing now?"

"It was strange. Usually when I picture the scene, I am focused on the shock and pain on his face, or the metal sticking through his chest. This time I let my mind wander across his whole body and to the surrounding area a bit. It was less distressing to focus on the rest of the scene instead of just him. I didn't feel my heart race as much as it usually does."

"Go with that." There go the fingers again. But I didn't focus on them this time, I focused on Luke. "What are you noticing now?"

"Usually I just focus on the wound, like I'm punishing myself and trying to feel bad on purpose. But this was different. Like I'm giving myself permission to move on from the injury and focus on the situation surrounding it."

"Go with that." Trevor's hand raised up and did something while I drifted back to the barn. "What are you noticing now?"

"My chest. I feel like I'm struggling to breathe." The monster is back, squeezing for all it was worth.

"Go with that." More hand movements, but I was picturing my dad kneeling next to Luke. "What are you noticing now?"

"A tightness in my chest, some anxiety. I had moved from looking at Luke to staring at my father."

"Go with that." I wasn't waiting for his fingers to move anymore before jumping into the memory. I remembered what my dad yelled at me, and it pissed me off. He screamed at me, telling me it's my fault that Luke was dead. Back when it happened, I just stood there. Too in shock and submissive to my father to respond. Since then, I've replayed this scene with hundreds of variations of new dialog. I explained why it wasn't all my fault. I didn't leave a screw sticking up on a floorboard. It wasn't my responsibility to keep the loft floor in good repair. Maybe if he hadn't been drinking all the time, he would have noticed the screw was loose.

"What are you noticing now?"

"I'm a little mad."

"Go with that." Follow the moving fingers. Focus, Alex. "What are you noticing now?"

"What kind of parent says something like that to his child? It was obviously an accident."

"Go with that." Fingers again. I bet his shoulder muscles are in shape. "What are you noticing now?"

"Perhaps it was because of his drinking or he was projecting. Maybe it was easier to have someone else to blame. Like it gave him something to focus on other than it just being an accident."

"Go with that." Twenty-four more, back and forth. Why couldn't my dad have pulled the family together then instead of lashing out at me?

"What are you noticing now?"

"I was thinking about how I wish he had handled it. In the moment, maybe just grieve without assigning blame. He could have just asked what happened and sorted out the blame later, when we knew the entire story. It was a jerk move to scream that at me."

"Go with that." Trevor's fingers moved again, like they always do. It's like they are my guide on this journey through my psyche. Focus on the fingers, they will show the way. "What are you noticing now?"

"It's not my fault. Accidents happen. My dad didn't mean what he said but was reacting in the moment."

"Go with that." He waved his fingers twenty-four more times. "What are you noticing now?"

"My dad told me he loves me and that nothing will ever change that. It was like he knew nothing he could say would make me feel worse than I already did."

"When you bring up the original memory, how disturbing does it feel to you now on a scale of zero to ten?"

Here it is. Am I going to be honest? If I said a zero, I could fake my way through it and never have to come back. But then I wouldn't get better, and Kendra may slip through my grasp. "I'd like to say a zero, but I'm probably at a three."

"It's okay to feel that way. It's a very traumatic moment in your life. Our goal is to get you to the point you can recall those events without the associated disturbing emotions that come along with it. We are about out of time for the session, so it's time to wrap up. How are you feeling about what we covered today?"

"Better than I expected to. Usually I'm pretty worked up when I go back that deep, but today I feel pretty normal." I wasn't just telling him what he wanted to hear. I legitimately felt okay. Which is strange because usually it ends with me mad and wanting to self-sabotage with alcohol or other destructive behaviors.

"I believe we are going to meet again next week. In the meantime, I want you to concentrate on those positive emotions. I want you to keep a journal with you and keep track of emotions and other thoughts that come to you regarding these memories."

"I'll do my best. Thanks, see you next week."

I exited Trevor's office, feeling better than I did when I walked in. It was time to do something I haven't done in a while. I wonder if she still has the same phone number.

Chapter 23

"Alex? Is that you?"

"Yes Mom, it's me. How are you?" I was still sitting in my car at Trevor's office. I knew if I drove away, I'd probably find an excuse to not make the call. Then I'd admit that to him next time and feel like a little child. So I dialed her number. Of course it was the same one. She probably still kept her newspaper subscription as well.

"Oh my gosh, I am fine. Thank you so much for calling. Is everything okay?" I could hear the worry in her voice. She's probably wondering why I chose to call today. Surely I must be dying.

"Yeah, everything is fine. How about on your end? It's been a while since we talked last." That's an understatement. It's been at least a year, maybe two.

"Well, your father's health could be better. He's not getting out of the house much anymore. Even just the doctor visits take all his energy for the day. Oh, and he's not drinking much anymore. Just a beer every now and then."

I'm glad he quit, but it's probably too late already. He'd hit it hard for decades by now. "That's good, I guess." It was already getting awkward and we're only a minute into the call.

"Do you want to speak with him? He's out on the front porch swing."

No, let's not go there yet. Baby steps. "I don't think I'm ready for that, yet. I just wanted to check in and let you know that I'm seeing someone."

I could hear the gasp through the phone. Come on, Mom. Is it that surprising? I know you've always wanted grandkids, but that's still a long way off, though you don't need to hear the physiologic limitation for that one. And that's not who I was talking about, either.

"You are? Who is she?"

"Well, she's a nurse at the hospital. Her name's Kendra and we just started dating. What I meant to say was I'm seeing a therapist. He's helping me work through what happened with Luke, Dad, and everything around it. I want to reconnect with him and spend more time with you. I'm just not there yet."

"I understand. This has been tough on all of us, especially your father."

Especially Dad? How can you say that? He just sits around and drinks himself into oblivion. Or at least he used to, when he was healthy enough. How about me? I'm in the prime of my life and am struggling at work because of my paranoia. I've never really even dated. "With all due respect, I think it's been harder on others than him. When's the last time you did anything for yourself, Mom?"

"Oh, I don't need to do too much. There's so much around the house to keep me busy."

Yeah, like taking care of Dad and all the things he's supposed to be doing. The car was becoming hotter despite the late season, or I was simply becoming uncomfortable because of the conversation. "Look, Mom. I need to get going. It's been good talking to you."

"You too, Alex. Uhm..." she started to speak and then paused. I knew what was coming. She wants me to come home. No thanks. Not interested. She probably wouldn't leave him along long enough to meet me at a restaurant, anyway. But she persisted and showed more courage than I did by continuing. This time, her voice was soft and trembled. "Do you think you'd be able to make it back home soon?"

Could I make it? Of course. I only live an hour away. Do I want to? Yes, but not yet. Give me time. Trevor still has more layers to sort through. It may not be a good idea to go back right now. It might even set my progress back. "Sometime, Mom. I work a lot coming up and I'm just not ready to talk to Dad yet. Soon, though. I promise." Lying to myself did not bother me. It was the lie to her that made me sick to my stomach.

Chapter 24

"Doc, an ambulance is on the way in with a stroke patient. They're in the window for tPA and should be here in a few minutes."

"Thanks, Carla. Let me know when they're here." Wonderful. A stroke alert. Easily the most actively monitored complaint in the hospital. For every person involved in direct patient care, there are probably three looking over our shoulder and critiquing the care provided.

Medical treatment of stroke is not a complicated decision tree. The problem is deciding whether to administer 'clot-buster' medications in an attempt to improve functional outcome six months later. The most nebulous of endpoints for a critical decision that must be made in minutes.

These patients take a minimum of thirty minutes of direct time to sort through the diagnosis, interpret tests, speak with family and consultants, and determine a treatment plan. Which meant I had better hit the bathroom now.

Unfortunately, I had just closed the door when I heard our EMS doors open. Must be the stroke patient. I sighed and opened the bathroom door. It's only another thirty minutes, and the administrative clock was ticking for the tracked metrics on stroke treatment.

I walked past both resuscitation rooms, but they were empty. "Carla, where's the possible stroke patient?"

"They went straight to CT. I think they'll be in room seven when they come back."

Great, straight to CT scan. No assessment by a doc. Protocol says we must get an immediate head CT on all stroke patients, so off to the scanner they go with an order for imaging entered by protocol.

The patient was on the scanner table when I entered the CT room. She had a nurse on each side by her hip and the radiology tech stood at the top, adjusting her head in a device to hold it still. The patient was not on a monitor. Protocol says they don't need to be on a monitor. It only delays the time to obtain the CT scan.

The hospital is reviewing me for excessive imaging, but their policies are stopping me from evaluating this patient prior to scanning. Lovely.

I went into the control room and leaned against a desk while the scan started.

The paramedic followed me into the room. "Doc, the patient's daughter called us for left facial droop and left arm weakness. She had a stroke six months ago and these are the same symptoms she had then."

"Heart rate and blood pressure okay?" I asked.

"Blood pressure was only eighty when we got there. She's got a liter of fluid going, but we haven't rechecked in. Glucose was one twenty."

Very low blood pressure. Strokes usually lead to high blood pressure as the brain tries to send blood to itself. Low blood pressure may indicate an illness that is reproducing the prior stroke symptoms due to suppression of the brain's ability to compensate for prior insults.

I scanned the images as they appeared and found no hemorrhage or blood clot obstructing a major vessel. It was time to decide whether to administer the clot-busting medication. I let the nurses handle the trip back to the ER and went to find her family to discuss our options. I still hadn't gotten a chance to examine the patient. The funny part is my exam isn't part of the algorithm. I'm supposed to magically sneak in a detailed neuro exam during all of the chaos.

"Hi, ma'am. I'm Dr. Alex Lee. I'm the ER doctor taking care of your mother. Were you with her today when this happened?"

"Yes, thank you. I have been with her for the last few days. She's been too weak to care for herself, so I'm splitting time with my brother. We're doing what we can to keep her independent."

"That's great. I wish more people would take the effort to do the same for their families. What did you notice this afternoon?"

"She hadn't eaten much all day and only had one glass of water. She fell asleep in the recliner around 2:00 p.m. and then woke up at three, confused. When she woke up, she seemed scared, like she had a bad dream. That's when I saw her face drooping again. I asked her to raise her arms up and that's when I saw her right arm was weak. She tried to talk, but it was gibberish. Since these are the exact symptoms she had last time she had a stroke, I called 9-1-1 right away. I know there's only so much time to give that medicine to break up the clots. She didn't get it last time and I'm still trying to settle with the hospital, but my lawyer thinks we'll end up having to sue."

Of course. Let's make the stakes even higher. It's like she's trying to summon some hallucination from the depths of my psyche. Mentioning a planned lawsuit during a visit is never a great way to improve the patient experience.

"Well, we need to be certain she's actually having a stroke before we consider giving that medication. There's about a five percent chance it could cause a severe disability or even death if we give it to her."

"Have you seen her? She can't talk, her face is drooping, and she can't lift her right arm. She's right-handed. I'm no doctor, but those are stroke symptoms."

"Yes, I've seen her, but I haven't gotten the chance to examine her yet. She was taken directly to CT and should be back momentarily. I agree those are stroke symptoms, but it's possible they have come back because of an illness. You mentioned she hadn't been doing well for a few weeks, and the medic said her blood pressure was very low. It's possible an illness is affecting her brain globally, and that is bringing back her old stroke symptoms."

"But it's also possible she's having a stroke, right? She didn't get treated last time and she never fully recovered."

The sound of a bed rolling down the hallway preceded the patient arriving back in the room. I did a detailed but expedited neuro exam. I could feel her daughter's eyes on me the entire time, almost daring me to screw something up. The patient was clearly symptomatic in a way that fit with an anatomic distribution of stroke, but her blood pressure is still in the eighties. It makes more sense that this is an illness bringing back her stroke symptoms rather than a new stroke in the same spot.

"I agree with you, she is definitely having stroke-like symptoms. The question is whether we think it's cause by a stroke or an illness. As I'm sure you're aware, there's the statement that 'time is brain' and if we're going to give the clot-busting medications, it should happen quickly. She doesn't have any reason we cannot give them to her. We need to decide whether we think this is a stroke and the symptoms are bad enough that we should risk the complications of the clot-busters."

Chapter 25

"Well you're the doctor. Is she having a stroke? She just had two CT scans. Won't that tell you?" There was no animosity in the question, and it was a very appropriate one to ask. The problem was I couldn't answer it definitively and could feel the angst rising inside. She's already threatening to sue over a prior stroke where the hospital did not administer the clot-buster medication. Now I'm not convinced she's having a stroke and am considering not giving the medication because I don't want to put her at risk with no potential benefit. But if I don't give the medication and this turns out to be another stroke, she will likely have a worse outcome and I'll be named in a lawsuit. And no, the imaging will not say with certainty whether this is a stroke.

"When I look at your mother as a whole, my best guess is this is not another stroke. Strokes are generally not like heart attacks. It's very unusual to have another stroke with the same symptoms as the last one because of how the anatomy works. To have similar symptoms, she would need a clot or another reason for decreased blood flow in the exact same place in the exact same blood vessel as she had last time. Strokes are like a high-stakes game of Plinko. Most strokes are from a small blood clot traveling to the brain, and there are numerous branch points where that clot can travel before lodging. Unless she has a focal vascular abnormality, the odds of a repeat stroke in the same area of brain causing the same symptoms is fairly low."

Her daughter seemed to follow my logic, which explained the confused look on her face. "So you don't want to give her the medication? She can't talk and can't move her right arm. Did I mention she's right-handed? How is she supposed to manage on her own? I'm not even sure she could safely eat. Would she need a feeding tube?"

All valid concerns, and ones I don't have definitive answers for.

"Doc, her temp is one hundred and three," said the nurse.

"Okay, thank you. Let's start fluids and antibiotics for now." I turned back toward the patient's daughter to continue our discussion. "She has a high fever and low blood pressure. I can tell you that if this was my mother, I would not give her the clot-busters. Strokes don't cause high fevers and low blood pressure, but those two can bring back prior stroke symptoms, especially in the elderly.

If you wanted to hedge a bit, we could start the fluids and antibiotics and then get her down for a quick MRI. If that shows a stroke, then I think it's appropriate to treat her then. It will add a delay but may save her an unnecessary risk of death."

"How often do you see your mother? Are you helping her with an existing disability from a hospital who screwed up her care last time?" She broke down in tears as the emotion of the situation overwhelmed her. I didn't feel the need to answer her questions as they seemed rhetorical. She didn't say the last question out loud, but I'm guessing that's the one she started crying over. 'What if she doesn't improve, and this is her new normal?'

"Treatment of stroke is not as straightforward as it seems. There are a lot of tough decisions with significant consequences that must be weighed. If you want her to get the clot-busters, I will order them. My recommendation would be let's accept a bit of a delay to get the MRI and treat her infection in the meantime."

Her daughter was standing at the side of the bed, wiping saliva from the corner of her mouth. "Fine. Let's do that. I just hope you're right."

"Me too." I spoke with the MRI tech who took the interruption in his schedule in stride and agreed to have his machine ready in ten minutes. It's actually incredible that a patient can show up to a small community hospital and within thirty minutes undergo three advanced imaging studies using two different machines, see a doctor, get an IV, fluids, and antibiotics. I decided against pointing this out to the patient's daughter. She's probably not in the mood to appreciate how amazing her access to care is.

I stepped out of the room and nearly ran into Dr. Thatcher. He was leaning against the wall and sipping coffee without a care in the world. Strange behavior for a neurologist who was standing outside the room of a potential stroke patient.

"What? Nothing to say?" I asked.

"Nope. I've been listening and watched your exam through the curtain. I agree with you. I wouldn't give her thrombolytics either. Fingers crossed the MRI is negative."

"Doctor Lee, can I sneak past?"

I stepped sideways to make room for the nurse to get past me. She continued toward the drug dispensing machine to grab the antibiotics. Two liters of fluid dripped in quickly, one through each IV catheter. I'm hopeful the fluids and antibiotics will be finished by the time the MRI is complete. If the Tylenol can bring her fever down, it's possible she'll look a lot better by then. Or she'll have a positive MRI, we'll administer the clot-buster, and I'll get reprimanded by the hospital for the delay in stroke management.

Maybe Dr. Thatcher will go to bat for me in front of the patient care committee if it comes to that. Or perhaps

I shouldn't share the fact that I have hallucinations. I'm guessing the hospital administration would frown on that.

Chapter 26

Today is my second session with Trevor. I'd prefer to not work in the hospital on the day of a session, but I'm scheduled every day this week and I don't want to put it off. I need to get better. I just can't get broken down to where I can't focus on my patients. We'll need to wrap up in time and get back to a decent level of function.

I smiled at the secretary and another man in the waiting room, then took a seat, knowing the door would open right on time for my session. Three minutes to go.

Kendra would be proud of me for facing my fears and trying to get past them. I want to tell her, but I want to make sure it's working first. What if I tell her and then she feels guilty she's not pursuing treatment for her AVM? I accept her who for who she is, but I don't accept myself for who I am at the moment. I can be better. And I will be better.

That is, if Trevor ever opens the door, kicks out his last patient, and starts our second session. I flicked my wrist enough for my smart watch to display the time. 11:03 a.m. Come on Trevor, three minutes late? You were very insistent last time that sessions started and ended on time. What is this?

Two minutes later, I knocked on the glass at the secretary's desk. "Excuse me, can you confirm I have an eleven o'clock appointment with Trevor? My name is Alex Lee."

"Yes, sir, we have you down. He's just running a little late with this client. Please be patient."

I turned and sat down. 11:05 a.m. I pulled out my phone and did a map search for 'EMDR therapy' in my area. Two results showed up. Trevor, and another one very close! I clicked on the icon and it brought up Caitlyn Woodhouse. The other name next to Trevor's on the front door.

I sighed audibly and put my phone away. I'd just have to wait. Once I resigned myself to my fate, the door opened and Trevor followed a woman out. She was a bit younger than me and seemed very well put together. The type of person who makes everyone jealous on social media. Probably a perfect family, perfect job, and clearly very beautiful. She wiped a last stubborn tear from each eye.

"Sorry about that, Trevor. I had forgotten about some of those things that came up during our session. Or repressed them I guess."

The man in the waiting room stood up and put his arm around her. "Trevor, thanks for helping her through this.

I don't know if she told you, but her headaches have gone away. You're a lifesaver."

The woman turned to me as they walked past and made me feel even worse about my selfishness. "I'm sorry if you're his next client. He likes to be on time. I'll try to finish early next week."

"It's no problem at all. Have a great day." I said the words with a smile for her and her husband. The same guy who watched me impatiently double check my appointment and sigh loudly just a minute ago.

Trevor pointed toward his office, ushering me inside. "Sorry about that. You're an ER doctor though, right? You're probably pretty used to the delays in patient care that arise once in a while. I have my lunch after this, so you'll still have your entire hour for the appointment. I'll just eat faster." The sincerity of his smile was the last piece of luggage for my guilt trip.

"Sounds good, thanks." I entered his office and took my usual seat. I guess I have a usual seat now, it's my second visit. Sometimes it only takes a few sessions to complete treatment, so am I about to be halfway done? It doesn't seem possible.

"Okay Alex, how did you do since our last visit? Did you write anything down in your journal?"

"No, actually I didn't. I'm not one to journal much." Other than documenting concepts I need to improve for with patient care. "I noticed I had less anxiety when dealing with some of my sicker patients. The hallucinations seemed less annoying, but there really wasn't anything I was concerned about missing or reminded me of a critical case I'd had before. That's when they usually show up the most."

"Good. Let's get started. What is causing you the most disturbance right now?"

Jumping right in. Only have an hour, and some of that is coming out of his lunch break.

"I want to have a successful romantic relationship. The impotence thing is still a problem, and I don't want to self-sabotage my relationship with Kendra. In the past, I usually screw things up almost on purpose so that the relationship ends before it becomes serious. It hurts less to end it early."

"What is the most disturbing image or feeling you associate with that?"

"I'm sure it's because I was in the barn to meet a girl. If I hadn't been meeting her, this wouldn't have happened. It's as if any new relationship begins that chain of events and I'm afraid it will lead to someone being harmed."

"What negative words come to mind when you imagine the scenario of meeting a girl in the loft?"

"Selfish. Reckless. Stupid."

Trevor wrote the words as I spoke them. Or at least I assume that's what he wrote. I still can't see the sheet of paper. "And when you think about that, what would you rather believe about yourself now?"

"Typical teenager. Innocence."

More quick notes. "On a scale of one to seven, how true do those words feel in relation to that memory? Seven would be them feeling entirely true."

"Probably a two."

"That image of going to meet the girl in the barn, how disturbing is it right now, on a scale of one to ten?"

I hate these scales. The worst is the Wong-Baker faces scale. Two people got their names associated with smiley faces. I'd wanted to make one for constipation. It would be both diagnostic and guide therapy. The higher the number, the more strain the face would show. As the number got higher, the corresponding therapy would become more aggressive.

Trevor was still looking at me. "Sorry, probably a seven. If something goes wrong with Kendra, it would be a ten. But right now, I'm sitting at a solid seven."

"So that seven, that high-level disturbance. Where do you notice it in your body?"

"Maybe in my stomach? I get a sense of dread whenever I think about trying to pursue someone. Like a mild nausea."

"I want you to bring up that image of meeting the girl in the loft, and the words selfish, reckless, stupid. Notice where you're feeling it in your stomach and follow my fingers." Trevor lifted his fingers like he was going to send me away with a holy benediction, then began moving them back and forth. "What did you notice?"

"The same. Like if I hadn't been up there with her, this wouldn't have happened. Luke would have been fine."

"Go with that." The fingers moved again, and I leaped backward in time. I tried to let my mind wander, but it kept going back to earlier that day. Back to when we were still at school. "What did you notice?"

"I was back in school the day it happened. We were in a passing period and Luke's friends stopped to harass me in the hallway. That's when Stacy put the note in my pocket to meet her in the barn later. It's frustrating because I was just trying to get to my next class, but they stopped me and then she shoved the note in my pocket. I didn't actively do anything to set all this in motion."

"What are you noticing now?"

"Annoyance. Like I'm a victim too."

"Go with that." I watch his fingers move back and forth across my vision, but emotionally, I'm back in school. This time it's with the knowledge of what was going to happen later that night. What was I supposed to have done? Run after her in the hallway? Stand her up? Go to her house and explain why it wasn't a good idea? Any kid my age would have done exactly what I did that day. Including Luke. The fingers stopped. "What did you notice?"

"That I did nothing wrong by going to meet her. Any of my friends would have done the same, just like any typical teenage boy." Woah. I actually felt that way now. What is the term he uses to feel good about something? Positive cognition?

"When you bring up the memory of going to meet Stacy, on a scale of zero to ten, how disturbing is that idea now?"

Can I say this? It really feels like a one or a two. It wasn't my fault I was up in the loft that day. But it's felt like a ten for years. I can't just let it go. "Let's say a two. I feel a lot better about it, but it's not all the way gone."

"Where do you notice it in your body?"

"In my throat. It's not in my stomach anymore. It seems like it moved up a bit. Like that nervous feeling you get in your throat sometimes."

"Okay, go with that." Trevor's fingers began moving, slowly ticking back and forth on their way to twenty-four. I have been holding on to this feeling for so long it's hard to let it go. It was down deep inside me, at my core. Now I'm realizing it was okay to have been there. Luke would have done the same thing. It's okay to let this one go. Trevor's fingers stopped and then he brought his arm back down to the table. "What do you notice now?"

"Peace. I think I'm at a zero on the disturbance scale. Luke would have made fun of me for days if he knew I had a chance to meet a girl in the loft and didn't do it."

"When you bring up that memory with the words innocence and typical teenager, how strongly do you believe them as they apply to this memory? A one means not at all, and a seven means they feel completely true."

It's easy to answer this time, but I still pause. How did we get here? He just asked me a few questions and waved his fingers back and forth. But we're here nonetheless. "I'm a seven."

I said it out loud and believed it. I truly feel that it wasn't wrong to want to meet her up there.

"Wonderful. Now, close your eyes and focus on that memory, along with your positive words. Innocence. Typical teenager. I want you to scan your body while repeating those words to yourself. Do you feel tension or tightness anywhere?"

No, I truly don't. It's okay to feel this way. "No, I'm good."

"You've made significant progress today, Alex. How do you feel about that?"

"Proud. Confident. Hopeful."

"That's great, Alex. Congratulations." Trevor was smiling at me, clearly happy for me, and likely a bit proud of himself, as well. He glanced sideways at his clock. "We still have ten minutes left in the appointment. That's not enough time to dive into another session, but I want to give you some homework for the week. Pay attention to any thoughts that come to mind regarding this memory or the emotions around it. If you have negative feelings, try to repeat the positive ones you mentioned today. Keep a log of these moments and we'll talk about them next time."

He's still going to get his full lunch hour since we ended early. But I don't care. He deserves it. He should get a catered lunch by some industry rep like the medical specialists get. Not the ER, of course. No one cares to buy us lunch or sell us anything. We're at the mercy of the hospital formulary and insurance coverages. But who would sponsor Trevor's lunch? It's amazing how some of the best work can be done without millions of dollars in technology. Just good old-fashioned clinical acumen and reasoning performed by a trained specialist.

If only that extended to the emergency department. Now the expectation is to perform all the tests the patient desires. I'm like a fast-food worker. Listen to the order, enter it, and try to complete it before the customer complains.

"Okay, I will. Thanks for today, Trevor. I'm feeling better and can't wait to come back next week. Take care." I leaned forward and shook his hand before heading back to the lobby. He stayed seated and jotted down a few more notes as I left.

The secretary was not at her desk, so I couldn't offer a smile and a wave to ease my still-guilty conscience. Noon. Three hours until I had to be at work. Just enough time for a run and a shower. I'm going to try for three miles today.

Chapter 27
Seventeen Years Ago

I don't want to go to school today. It's only been a week since Luke died and three days since the funeral. Mom let me stay home a few more days after that, but I still wasn't in the mood to listen to teachers or see anyone else. I know how they are going to look at me. The whispers. The stares. The judgment. There's that kid who killed his brother.

But my mom wouldn't listen. She said it was the best thing for me. She said being alone won't help anything. I think she just wanted to get me out of the house because Dad was cycling between major depression and blind rage. His coping mechanisms were to double his alcohol intake, never leave the house, and pretend he had no children.

The last thing I wanted to do now was disobey my mother and lose the last connection to a parent I had, so I grabbed my backpack and headed for the bus stop. I'd get on just before Stacy and plan to sit in the row just ahead of where she normally sits. She'll have no choice but to explain herself for standing me up and setting all this in motion.

I had thought about what I was going to say to her since that night. Rehearsed so many lines while staring at myself in the mirror. At first, they were tearful and filled with rage and spite. It was her fault I was up there, and she never even showed up. After the funeral, the thoughts tamed down and were focused on trying to lay a guilt trip on her. The more blame I place on her, the less I was at fault. Anything to ease my conscience. But I decided that wasn't fair either. I didn't even know why she stood me up, but I intended to find out.

The bus jerked to a stop and brought me back to the present. Stacy's stop. Fitting that it jerked at this stop. It's the jerk's stop, after all. She was the second one to climb on the bus and took the seat immediately behind me. Game on.

"Hey Alex, I'm so sorry to hear about Luke. How are you doing?" Her eyes were soft, and she wore an empathic frown on her face. She was sitting forward in her seat and leaning close to me.

I didn't expect this response and was too stunned to say anything substantive. "Yeah, I'm fine."

"My family and I were at his funeral. I made the flower arrangement myself from my mom's garden. I hope you liked it."

My mother actually pointed that out. She still has them on our kitchen counter. "Oh, that's nice. I didn't notice, though." A bouquet will not make up for how I feel about this. Process your guilt however you want, but don't expect to earn forgiveness with such a simple thing as flowers.

Her eyes squinted at that comment, and she leaned back in her seat. "Well, I'm sorry for what happened. I'm here if you ever want to talk about it. We're praying for your family."

"What's with him?" said her friend in a soft whisper.

"He's just hurting. He doesn't mean it. I'll try to talk to him again next week."

But next week never happened. I didn't want it to. That was the last time I ever found Stacy Griffin attractive. It turns out school was only a fifteen-minute bike ride from my house. Shorter if it was raining and I wanted to get there quicker. That's the time I learned it's easier to ignore a problem than deal with it in the moment. If only I could go back and teach myself a different coping mechanism.

Chapter 28

"Hey, be careful!" said Kendra, jumping forward as her bucket of golf balls tipped and spilled across the grass.

"Sorry, I didn't mean to do that. But it wasn't entirely my fault."

"What? You shanked a shot that went behind me and knocked over my bucket of balls. How is that anyone else's fault?" She asked the question while posing like a cover model for a ladies' golf magazine. She was leaning on the grip of her seven-iron with her right hand, and her left was resting on her hip. She looked amazing. The cold air hadn't scared her away from wearing form-fitting jeans, and that's why I chose the spot behind her.

"You're the one who wanted to go hit balls. I told you I'm terrible at it."

"But you're a doctor. Don't you guys learn to play in medical school? I thought it was required as part of your training."

"See what happens when you stereotype? You about get whacked in the backside with a golf ball."

"Whatever. You hit the ball off the toe of the club, and that's why it came straight at me. Try to keep your swing arc even, so the club is in the same position when it hits the ball." She used her club to pull a ball into position and then lined up in her stance. "Like this," she said as she wound up in a slow backswing, and then accelerated through the ball. A soft whoosh was all I heard as the club face struck the ball and picked it up cleanly off the grass.

"Oh, just hit a perfect shot? Got it," I said. "Tell you what, why don't we switch positions? That way, you're behind my back where it's safe." I didn't wait for a response and used my nine-iron to hook her the pocket in her jeans and pull her toward me.

"But if we switch places, you won't be able to keep checking me out every time I swing." She tossed her club on the ground next to my feet and inched her way toward me as I pulled more with the club.

"Safety first. I don't want to put you in danger from my innocent gawking." She was now only a foot away.

"Innocent? Is that the type of gawking you were doing?" Her right arm moved on top of my left shoulder and curled behind my head.

"Mostly, yes." I dropped my club to the ground and pulled her in closer.

"Most Lee? I don't think that works as a nickname. Next time you gawk, drop the innocent part, okay?"

Her lips muted my reply, which was fine by me. Now was not the time for mindless chatter, it was time for happiness. To live in the moment. To forget about the nonsense of the hospital and the struggles with my family. Kendra is my future, and I love how that looks, feels, and… tastes?

I pulled back from the kiss and smiled at her while my hands roamed across her pockets. "Easy there, big guy, we're here to golf."

"I thought so too, but you're holding back on me. I want what you have." My hands continued exploring until I felt what I wanted. I squeezed and heard the crinkle from her left front pocket. Her eyes popped open, and her smiled faded away. A classic look of guilt. I reached into her pocket and removed a mostly empty small package of sour patch kids.

"I can explain, I promise," she said, shaking her head back and forth.

"Hang on, candy first." I popped a yellow one into my mouth and then replaced the package into her pocket.

"I never know when you might want a kiss, and the last thing I want is to do it with bad breath. So, from time to time, I'll eat a piece of candy. If I shared them with you, I'd have fewer for me and then you may have an awful experience when you kiss me. So, it's not entirely my fault."

I laughed at the absurdity of it. She used my line and turned it back around on me. I leaned down and pulled her in for a tight hug. "Please don't ever change. I love you exactly how you are."

Woah. I said it. Out loud. And in her presence! I'd said it to myself dozens of times while thinking about her. I'd typed it in texts but deleted it before sending. But here it is. At the driving range. Why didn't I just leave it as the three words? I tried to hide it in a longer sentence. Such a chicken.

"I love you too, Alex." Neither of us relaxed our grip until I moved my hand back toward her front pocket. She pulled her left arm from behind me and caught my wrist before I could reach the bag of candy. "Hey now, the rest are mine. I need to be prepared for any kisses that might follow this one."

I wish I had my notebook with me. I need to remember to buy a five-pound bag of sour patch kids. Or gummy bears. But I'd have to let go of Kendra to write it down, and that's not something I ever want to do.

Chapter 29
Six Months Later

My sessions with Trevor are still going great. We've been able to back them off considerably and I'm only going once a month now. The creations of my mind, or 'hallucinations' as Delroy calls them, have mostly stopped. When I'm stressed with a critical patient, I'll still see them from time to time, but nowhere as bad as it used to be.

I'm not taking the sleeping pills anymore either. I thought it was going to be easy to come off them, but I was wrong. So wrong. It's like suddenly changing your entire bedtime routine but adding a chemical dependency component to it as well. I had strange withdrawal symptoms. Dizziness, palpitations, vivid dreams, insomnia, but I fought through all of them. I knew I was getting better and couldn't rely on sleeping pills my entire life.

Today is another eight-hour shift. Easter Sunday. I was lucky enough to pull the day shift, when half the world remembers about church and finds their way to a pew before stuffing themselves with three days' worth of food. ER volumes are always down significantly during the usual celebration times of major holidays, as if emergencies don't happen when people are more interested in traditions or television marathons. It highlights the truth many ER visits are more an urgency or convenience than a genuine emergency.

I obviously wasn't going home for a family meal, so I told Holly I'd work the shift. Let everyone else enjoy their family gatherings. Kendra got together with her family on Palm Sunday, so she's here working with me today. I'm the sucker though. She's getting double her usual rate as it's a major holiday, whereas I'm still making the same. Insurance companies don't let us charge them more simply because we provided care on one of the most celebrated holidays of the year.

It's okay though, the staff brought in a full buffet spread of food and I'm filling the significant down time with repeated trips to the break room to check on the buffet.

"These cheesy potatoes are fantastic," I said.

"Thanks, they're an old family recipe," said Kendra. "We make them pretty much any time we get together."

"If there's any left, will you bring them over for dinner tomorrow?"

"How about I just bring the ingredients and make a fresh batch at your place?"

"New patient, room seven!" Kendra's hand dropped to her communication device to dampen the audio, but the mood was already ruined. I stuffed a last bite into my mouth and followed Kendra back into the main department.

An EMS crew stood in the hallway outside room five, but that wasn't the room announced on the device. There must be someone else here. At least it wasn't in room eight.

"Get off me!" I heard the shout before I could see the patient. Two security officers were already in the room, holding the patient down on the bed.

"What's the deal with him?" I asked.

"Not sure, Doc. A car dropped him off out front and then he started attacking people."

The patient looked to be in his twenties and was sweating profusely. The officers had his chest and arms secured to the bed, but he was flailing his legs up and trying to kick anyone he could reach. We're a small department and don't have enough extra hands to deal with severely violent patients on a normal day, let alone a holiday. That's where medications come in handy.

"Can we give him haloperidol?" asked Kendra. Great idea.

"Yeah, give him ten milligrams intramuscular along with two milligrams of lorazepam." This guy was up and clearly needed to be put down. Psychosis? Intoxication? Demon possession? All three were just as likely at this point, but we needed to get him under control.

Kendra stepped out to get the meds while I did a quick assessment. His heart was racing along, likely at least one hundred and fifty beats a minute. His skin was hot and sweaty, he had massively dilated pupils, and his forearms and face were covered with deep ulcers in various states of healing. The classic appearance of methamphetamine abuse.

Meth frequently causes paranoia and psychosis along with hallucinations, to the point patients often believe they are infested with parasites. Naturally, a person who saw a parasite crawling under their skin may try to dig it out with their fingernails, a pen, knife, or any sharp object they had access to. Our patient today had all the classic features of meth abuse and acute intoxication.

"I've got the meds. Hold him still and I'll inject him," said Kendra.

The officers redoubled their efforts to hold him still while I leaned on his thighs to control his legs. Kendra cleaned an area on his left thigh with an alcohol swab at the same time the patient started spitting at all of us. I took a direct hit to my left cheek and reflexively lifted an arm to wipe it off, which gave the patient the opening he was looking for.

The now-freed leg flexed at the hip and then extended the knee, launching the foot straight into Kendra's head.

I knew where the foot was going to land but wasn't in a position to intervene. I had to stand there and watch my girlfriend take a foot to the head from an agitated patient. I imagined the pressure wave radiate through her skull, into her brain, and through the AVM. She dropped the syringe onto the bed and stumbled backward, dropping to the ground and holding her head.

"Kendra!" I yelled, torn between letting go of the patient to tend to her and dropping my elbow into the guy's throat. Instead, I grabbed the syringe and plunged it into the thigh I was holding, delivering both medications deep into the quadriceps muscle. I withdrew the needle, extended the safety to cover the sharp end, and tossed it into the sink.

Kendra was sitting on the floor, something she normally refuses to come anywhere near with anything other than her shoes. She actually lays down sheets to stop children from crawling around on the disgusting floor. Now she seemed too stunned to care where she was lying.

"Are you okay?" I asked.

"My head hurts. He kicked me."

"I know, I saw it." And he kicked you with the leg I released to clean my face off. Had I just sat there for another ten seconds, you would have been fine. Once again, I caused harm to someone I care about. "We need to get you checked in as a patient. I'll order a head CT for you and do a complete neuro exam."

I stood up and looked around the room at our skeleton holiday crew. The officers were holding the patient down but appeared less stressed as the medications began to kick in. Another nurse was placing him on the cardiac and respiratory monitor. Why was everyone paying more attention to this jerk of a patient than to one of our own team members?

"Can you walk? If not, I'll get a wheelchair and take you into an empty room. We need to get you to CT."

Kendra held her left hand out to me, her right still held against her skull. "Alex, relax. I'm okay. I just have a headache and some nausea. I don't need a CT scan. Just give me a minute. It's probably just a concussion."

"He kicked you directly over your AVM. We need to get a CT scan immediately."

The nurse working on the patient paused and looked at Kendra with a look of concern. "You have an AVM?"

Uh oh. She didn't tell her coworkers about that? Whoops.

Kendra moved her hand enough so that I could see her glaring at me. "Yes, it's nothing. I'm fine. I'll get up in a minute."

I left the room and returned a few seconds later with a wheelchair. I locked the wheels and helped her climb into it before rushing her out into the first open room.

"Alex, seriously. Calm down," she said. "You're being ridiculous."

I'm not being ridiculous. I'm being cautious and doting. How can she say that? "You just had a head injury and have a known AVM. I need to evaluate you."

"Don't I have any say in this? I'm an adult, you know." She's becoming irritable, a classic early sign of a traumatic brain injury!

"I'm going to call CT and make sure they're ready for you. Be right back."

I tried to leave the room, but her left hand grabbed my wrist and held me in place. "Hey, you have to stop this. Take a breath. You're actually making me feel worse. I don't feel that bad, just a bit nauseous. They can't run a CT on me yet, I'm not even registered. And what good is a CT scan thirty seconds after an injury? It could be too early to see any bleeding even if it was going to happen, right?"

She made a good point. Maybe I am rushing things. Maybe her irritability is because I'm acting like a fool, not because of her head injury. The last thing I need is another hallucination following me around. I need to calm down.

"Alex, sit down. Close your eyes and just breathe." I obeyed my patient's command and was rewarded with a loosened grip on my wrist and her hand sliding down into mine. "I'm going to be fine. You didn't make him kick me. Stop blaming yourself."

How is it possible that Kendra was kicked in the head and I'm the one being comforted? By her. I pictured

Trevor telling me to calm down and asking me to hold a positive image in my mind. Instantly, I was walking with Kendra and Lucy in the park and I began to feel better.

"You're really feeling okay?" I asked.

She squeezed my hand and nodded. "Yeah. I'll take you up on that CT scan, but you should go check on the guy you gave all those medications to. He may be pretty sedated. Make sure he's breathing okay."

"Fine, I will." I let go of her hand and stood up to leave the room. *She wants me to check on the person who kicked her in the head. I love this woman so much.*

"Hey, did you give the injection in the area I cleaned?"

"No, I just used the leg by me. We had to get him calmed down before he hurt someone else. It'll be fine."

I found the patient heavily sedated and no longer actively restrained by our security team. Restraints made from thick fabric secured his wrists to the bed, and he now had an IV established. I ordered a few tests on him before tracking down the registration tech and asking that she check Kendra in as a patient. The CT techs weren't thrilled I was adding new patients and CT orders, but I'd been better lately so they can take their concerns and shove them up their gantry.

Chapter 30

"Doc, the CT is up if you want to look at it. I don't see anything new." The tech was pleasant on the phone and was giving me a friendly heads up because she knew I was worried. It felt good to be part of the team. Except for the part where I caused my girlfriend to get kicked in the head.

I entered Kendra's dark room to check on her. She was resting with her eyes closed, so I quietly logged onto the computer and pulled up her head CT. I agreed with the tech, there did not appear to be any acute blood. The AVM was barely noticeable on this non-contrasted study. There had to be a way to get past this diagnosis. She deserves to live without fear of a sudden brain hemorrhage.

"You know, watching a girl sleep is kinda creepy." Her eyelids remained closed when she said it, but the corners of her mouth turned up slightly.

Does she know I always sniff the air after she walks by? Vanilla, every time. That seems more creepy than watching someone sleep. "I agree. But watching a woman sleep is actually quite romantic, if done properly." I pulled the stool over by her bed and sat down. "How are you feeling?"

"Better. Just a mild headache. They gave me some Tylenol a bit ago. I think I can finish my shift."

"No, you don't need to do that. The charge nurse already reached out and has someone coming in to cover you. They are offering an incentive on top of the holiday pay. It only took one phone call to get someone to come in."

"One? That's got to be a record. Usually we ignore the calls when it's the hospital calling."

"When I see the phone ring, I always want to say I just had two beers and I can't come in, but I can't leave my partners hanging. Just like yours didn't."

"Together everyone achieves more, right? You know what I want?" she asked.

"What's that?"

"I want to lie on your couch and watch TV all day tomorrow. You can bring me chocolate and sugary snacks. Like sour patch kids. Do you have an electric blanket?"

No, but I bet Target does. "I'm sure I can find one around somewhere. That sounds like a perfect day. Do you think you can drive home? I don't mind giving you a ride when my shift ends. You can sleep in this room for a bit and we'll get your car later."

"Nah, I'll be fine to drive. Alex, thanks for taking care of me. You're very sweet."

And you're very worth it. "Not a problem. I'm going to check on your assailant and make sure I don't need to intubate him after the massive dose of sedatives we gave him."

The agitated patient was still sleeping soundly thanks to the stiff dose I gave him. His vital signs looked better and his heart rate slowed down to just over a hundred beats a minute. How does a person show up with acute agitation due to methamphetamines on Easter, of all days? He'd been here for hours and no family or friends had shown up or called to check on him. He probably burned all the bridges in his life. We'll likely never know who dumped him out of the car at our triage desk, either. The sad reality of the life of an addict.

Sometime tomorrow he'll be awake and alert with no recollection of what happened. The hospital will probably encourage Kendra to not press charges against him, and he'll go back to using drugs after declining our offer of counseling. I need to talk to Holly. We need readily available spit masks for when this happens again, and adequate staffing even if it is a national holiday. She can't do anything about the second thing, but maybe this will spur administration to act.

I checked on Kendra one more time and was surprised to find her standing next to the bed. She had pulled off the monitor leads and was working to remove the wrist band. I held out my trauma shears, and she slid the band between the blades.

"Thanks. I'm feeling a lot better. Just going to go home and crash. Pick me up tomorrow morning?"

"Of course. And sorry for spilling your secret about the AVM. That wasn't my place to say that. I got caught up in the moment and wasn't thinking."

"Don't worry about it. Not a big deal. It's just a part of me. They'll have to accept it just like I have."

I walked her out to her car to make sure she still felt well enough to drive. Reassured, I headed back into the hospital to complete my shift, confident her mother would call me if there was a problem.

Chapter 31

Relationships with counselors and therapists are extremely one sided. Trevor knows some of my deepest secrets, and I don't even know what he likes to eat for lunch. That makes it difficult to purchase lunch for their office as a thank you for the help they have given me. It's probably considered inappropriate or unethical to give them cash, so here I am with a gift certificate to a popular restaurant in town that offers delivery.

I tapped on the glass at the reception desk and made eye contact with the office secretary. She hesitated a moment and then wheeled over and opened the glass.

"Hi, I'm Alex Lee, here for the eleven o'clock appointment with Trevor." I held out an envelope and handed it through the window. "This is a thank-you gift for the work you all are doing for me and the community."

"Well, how sweet of you. Thank you kindly." Kind Lee. That's me.

"You're welcome." I took a seat across from the man I embarrassed myself in front of months ago and gave him a quick nod of acknowledgment. This time Trevor's door opened right on time and the same woman walked out, smiling and happy. Nicely done Trevor.

"Alex, you ready?"

I answered with a smile and a brisk walk into his office. Been ready since I walked out last time.

"How have you been?"

Every time it's getting easier to dump my feelings out on the floor in front of him without worrying about how he will react. "There was some drama at work. A drunk and belligerent patient kicked my girlfriend in the head. She has an abnormal blood vessel in her brain and I lost control of myself. I wanted to break the guy in half."

"That's understandable. Assaults on healthcare workers are becoming a bigger problem every year. We feel it in the mental health world as well. How did you end up handling it?"

"I sedated him heavily and then evaluated her as a patient. She was okay, but I got pretty manic about evaluating her and not wanting to miss anything."

"And did you get any of your hallucinations? Or, excuse me." He glanced down at his notebook and read the line. "Creations of your mind that you can see and talk to, but no one else is aware of."

Zing. How does he stay so prepared with such little time between patients? "No, I didn't, actually. Those haven't shown up much at all. And when they do, it's more of a collegial interaction than insulting."

"So their inherent negativity has gone away? Interesting."

"Yes. And I'm grateful for it."

"Alex, you have made a lot of progress with the EMDR sessions. How do you feel about taking a break today from that and trying a standard therapy session? Instead of EMDR, we can discuss aspects of your life that are currently troubling you."

"That's fine. I don't really have friends and I don't talk to my family, so it would be good to talk about some things."

"Since you brought it up, where are things at with your family? Have you tried to reconnect yet?"

"Yes, I called her several months ago. I keep telling myself that I'll call again to set up a time to go home, but I haven't had time to do it yet."

"You haven't had time to make a phone call? In the last few months?" He had the faintest of smiles on his face, as if he knew where this logical progression was going to end up. Stupid Socratic method. He was right. It's a stupid excuse.

"Fine. Yes, I've had time. No, I didn't call her."

"Why not?"

That's the million-dollar question. It wouldn't take long. I know she'd be home and would probably answer right away. Even so, I haven't called. "I guess I'm nervous about how it will be received. What if my dad answers and rips into me?"

"What if it's the answer to her prayers, and she wants you to come over right away? Which reaction do you think a mother who has already lost one child is more likely to have?"

He's right, of course. "I think it would make her extremely happy. And before you get a chance to say it, yes, I want my mother to be extremely happy. Maybe I'm too prideful. I feel like I'm owed an apology."

"By your mother? Or your father?"

"Mainly my dad. Mom just got dragged into it and our relationship suffered because of it."

"The great thing about this whole situation is that you have the power to change it. I'd like you to consider going home to see them."

"I'll talk to Kendra about it. She's coming over for dinner tonight. Things are going well with her and I'm feeling secure in the relationship. I've met her mother. Maybe she should meet mine." That last sentence earned me a smile and a nod from Trevor.

"What else is bothering you?" he asked.

"I didn't react well when Kendra got kicked in the head by a patient. I blamed myself because I let go of his leg to wipe spit off my face. Then he kicked her with that same leg I had been holding."

"What reaction did you have that you feel bad about?"

"I wanted to break the guy. Punish him for what he did to the person I love. But he's my patient. Obviously I can't think that way."

"Thinking that way and acting that way are different."

"Sure they are, but I had this flash of rage that I hadn't felt before. If we had been alone in the room, I'm not sure what I would have done."

"Do you have a history of rage or impulse control problems?"

"No. No worse than anyone else. I'm usually pretty even keel."

"So why do you blame yourself for feeling that way when your girlfriend was assaulted? You controlled your behavior, tended to her, and continued to treat your patient. Isn't that the definition of self-control?"

"Yeah, I suppose it is." I hope he truly believes these things he says, because they always tend to make me feel better. Except when he tells me to call my parents.

We talked for the rest of the session about my job satisfaction and my relationship with Kendra. Before leaving, I promised to ask Kendra to help me reconcile with my family. After dinner. And wine.

Chapter 32

The last six months with Kendra have been amazing. I wish I had been ready to have a relationship like this a decade ago, but it doesn't matter now. I have the rest of my life to focus on. A life with less guilt and self-sabotage.

We're to the point that our dates aren't really defined times to schedule and arrange. It's just assumed that we will spend most of our time together outside of work. Sure, we still do specific things like take her dog for walks, go to movies, and the occasional weekend trip, but we usually stay close to home. Am I officially old? I don't feel old. I feel like I've got an entire life to go out and lead.

Kendra worked a twelve-hour shift today but I was off. I'm envious of her twelve-hour work schedule as it allows for more days off, but I'm not sure that I could make serious decisions for twelve hours straight. My mind is shot after only six hours on busy shifts.

I had a bottle of wine opened and properly aerated by the time she knocked once and entered my condo. A slight chill followed her in the doorway, but the heat of her body overpowered it. Goosebumps on top of goosebumps.

I handed her a stemless glass of wine and cleared a spot next to me on the couch. "I only have one more EMDR session left with Trevor. Can you believe that?"

"That's great, Alex. You're such a different person now. Your self-confidence is really showing at the hospital. Supposedly, it makes you more of 'a catch'. At least that's what the other nurses are telling me."

"Oh, you're talking about me with the other nurses, are you?"

"Yes, and it feels great. Before they'd just complain about you. Now, some of them seem jealous that we're together."

"As well they should be. I'm definitely a catch." I clinked my wine glass against hers and placed it against my lips, inhaling the aroma of the wine before taking a sip.

"That's a perfect example. You would never have made that comment six months ago. You would have told me how you're broken and not worth dating. That I should go find someone worthy of me."

"I chose the more difficult option. I decided to make myself worthy of you. Well, I had some help. Trevor and Delroy played a big role in identifying my problems and helping me get past them."

"So this EMDR thing is really helping? It sounds like voodoo to me."

She wasn't wrong. I thought that at first, too. Maybe there is some placebo component, but it's working better than anything else has worked before, so I'm going to roll with it. Trevor is a miracle worker.

"I know it does, but you can't argue with success. I'm telling you, I feel so much better about what happened. It's like I can finally accept it wasn't all my fault and I was part of an unfortunate accident. Deep down, I think I always knew that, but I wouldn't allow myself to believe it. Our misbeliefs can hold us back significantly in life."

"Is it making you forget? Or just think differently about the past?"

"I'm definitely not forgetting. But it's helping me put different emotions around it. There is nothing that's going to change the past. All I can do is react differently to it in the present."

She adjusted herself on the couch next to me, now sitting with her right leg folded underneath and pressed against my thigh. "What do they actually do? Can you show me what a session is like?" She took a drink from her glass and snuggled back into the couch cushions like a prestigious patron settling into her stage box at a performance.

"I can try, but I'm no expert. This can bring up some pretty rough feelings that you need to be ready to deal with. Are you sure you want to try?"

"Sure. Why not?"

"Fine. You'd need to think of an event that triggered negative feelings and hold that image in your head while we talk about it."

"Okay, let me think for a minute."

Her head tilted to the right and her eyes deviated up and to the left. The classic thinking pose. What if she comes up with something serious and I screw it up? Trevor always spends time at the end for closure and preparing for the next session. I don't know how to do that properly. I can't screw with her psyche. Do no harm.

"Got it!" Her excitement caused her body to elevate off the couch, making our wine rock back and forth. The large, deep glass kept everything inside. I love her eagerness for life.

"What did you come up with?" Hopefully, nothing too serious.

"Remember the other day when you said you were going to take me to a fine Italian restaurant, and then we ended up eating takeout pizza? I can still picture that neon sign over the door, the one with the piece of pizza that flies toward the guy's mouth before disappearing inside. Then I hear him mocking me with an internal dialog."

Is she serious? That caused distress? I meant to get reservations but forgot about it until the day we were supposed to go. When I called, they were fully booked, so I took her to our local pizza place. I thought it was a cute date. Like we were in high school. Young love.

"I didn't say a fine Italian restaurant. I said 'fine, Italian restaurant it is' at the end of our debate about where to go. Pizza is Italian."

Her laughter reassured me she was joking. "Well played. But I don't buy that for a moment. What happens next after I have identified an issue I want help with?"

"I'd ask you to come in and sit on my couch."

She looked side to side and nodded. "Done. What's next?"

"We talk about what's going to happen, what to do if you become anxious or stressed about recalling the memory. I'd ask you how intense these feelings that you have are, so we know when we're making progress. Then I'd have you focus on the scene while performing bilateral stimulation techniques until the feelings aren't as intense. Then we'd identify some positive beliefs that you want to associate with the memory and do more bilateral stimulation until those feelings take hold."

"And you're sure this is helping you?"

"Absolutely. I'm not as obsessed with missing something in the ER. I'm also not taking my sleeping pill anymore." There's something else that's improving also, but I wanted to show her that, not ruin the surprise by telling her.

She took a sip of wine and then sat up straight, looking at me. "Let's go."

I took her through the process as best I could. There was a mix of laughter and serious moments as we tried to reprogram her to believe my restaurant selection was adorable rather than disappointing.

She finished her glass of wine and leaned forward, wrapping her arms around me. "I do feel better about it now. You're a miracle worker." Her lips were against my neck as she spoke and her chest pressed tight against mine. I looked for somewhere to set my wineglass down but found none, so I held her with one arm. I was starting to feel normal again. Very normal. Time for a joke.

"What's crazy is this is how Trevor and I end each session, too."

She laughed and pushed back away from me. "Why do you always have to ruin the mood?"

"I just wanted you to get the full experience. Oh, and speaking of mood, something else is getting better as well."

"Yeah? What's that."

I stood up quickly and leaned backward with my hands on my hips, head turned to the right like I was posing for a picture at the top of a mountain. My sweatpants and boxer jocks did their best to keep me modest, but there was no mistaking the prominent bulge in front.

"Hey, congratulations! That's huge!"

"Aw stop, you flatter me. I know we're not there in our relationship, but I'm pretty much average."

She rolled her eyes and let out another adorable laugh. "I meant it's a huge accomplishment." She paused a moment and then continued. "And a compliment. Is that really your first, uh, episode in seventeen years?"

"While I'm awake and around a woman? Yes. It randomly started working again about a month ago, but this is the first time it has with you here." I strutted around the room like a kid holding a sparkler on the Fourth of July. "Do you know what this means? We can have sex!"

"No, it doesn't. It means you can have sex. Remember? I still have the AVM and gave up sex because I don't want to die?"

"Come on, that's ridiculous. There are different levels of sex. We don't need to be like the scenes in Jerry Maguire or Thomas Crown Affair. It can just be like swinging in a hammock in the slightest breeze."

Kendra rose from the couch and walked toward my kitchen. "I'm glad you're doing better, I really am." She sat her wineglass down on the kitchen table and picked up her purse, pulling her arm through the strap. "But I'm not. I can't talk my way through my abnormal anatomy. No one can wave their fingers in front of my face and make me no longer at risk of dying."

By now, she was headed toward the front door. "Maybe next session you can talk about respecting boundaries and how to not ruin an evening."

I was too stunned to speak as the door closed behind her. My lack of an erection had ruined several relationships and ultimately led me to stop dating. Now I can finally have one again and it caused my girlfriend to walk out on me. I looked down at my pants, now laying evenly across my pelvis. The sparkler was out. The show was over. I got burned.

"Come on!" I screamed. "You idiot!" Once I acknowledged my actions, I ran to the front door in time to see her taillights as she drove away. I tried to call, but she sent it to voice mail after a single ring. I can take a hint.

I stood in the kitchen next to a now empty wine bottle, debating whether to open the next one. No, that's not the right thing to do. I saw a medical reference book on the counter and considered reading up on something to distract myself but ruled that out as well. I'm not going to regress into my old ways of dealing with emotions. Trevor would shake his head at me if I did that. I dropped my head to my chest and sighed, the burden of my own stupidity too great to keep my head up.

That's when I saw them. My running shoes by the back door. I laced them up and headed out.

Chapter 33

Eleven Years Ago

"I think that's everything, Mom. Even if it's not, I can't fit anything else in the car."

She had been crying for at least an hour, but still helped me load up my car. My dad stayed in the family room watching football and drinking beer. It didn't matter that I am heading to medical school today. Nothing I did mattered to him.

"You know, he really is proud of you. He just can't bring himself to say it."

"He doesn't need to use words to tell me how he feels, Mom. I can read it loud and clear. It's fine though. I'm doing this for you and Luke. I'm going to become a doctor and try to stop people from dying." I turned my head toward the family room. "Maybe I'll even help a few alcoholics along the way." I said the last line louder than I needed to, but I was trying to compete with the football announcer in the other room.

"Are you sure you don't need anything else? I can send you money or ship you anything you need."

"Mom, I'm fine. I'm twenty-two years old and about to start medical school. I can take care of myself. The student loans include money to live on."

"And enough for gas money to drive home for Christmas?"

Come on, Mom. I lived at home through college. That was awkward enough. Once I pull out of this driveway, I'm not planning on coming back while Dad's here. "Maybe, we'll see. If you come to visit, I'll sleep on the couch and you can have my bed. Colorado is beautiful every day of the year."

She smiled at me and nodded. "I'd like that very much. I'll see if I can find time to get away for a few days." Her quick glance toward the family room told me that would not happen.

I leaned down and kissed her on the cheek. "Take care, Mom. I'll call you when I get out there." She followed me out the front door and let the screen door slap closed behind her. I climbed into my car and pressed down the clutch, wiggled the gear shift to ensure it was in neutral, then fired up the engine. The tiny four-cylinder Civic started immediately and purred like it had for every one of its last two hundred thousand miles.

I looked in the rearview mirror to make sure I was clear and then shifted into reverse. When I looked out the windshield one last time, I saw something I didn't expect to. My dad was there, holding a small box. My right foot was already on the gas and my left was easing up on the clutch, but I shifted back into neutral and pulled up the parking brake. I didn't want to, but I felt obligated to. They raised me to respect my elders, or at least give the appearance that I did.

He walked to the driver's side, so I cranked the window down to see what he wanted. He extended his arm and handed me the small box he was holding. "I bought this as a Christmas gift for Luke. I figure he'd want you to have it instead of it just sitting in his room on a shelf."

I wasn't prepared for this. Not for my dad talking to me before I left or the gift he had purchased for Luke's graduation. Luke was a senior when he died and had just barely broken the rushing record for our high school.

At the beginning of his senior year, it seemed like he was going to need two seasons to get enough yards in for the record. But he wanted it so badly. He'd spent the summer running sprints across the property, dodging cones, and doing burpees in the middle of runs. He even gave me a whistle and told me to blow it at random times. When I did, he would make a cut and go a different direction, all while maintaining a full sprint. He knew what he wanted and would stop at nothing to get it.

Fortunately, our quarterback that year was terrible, so the coach switched to a run-based offense. That meant

Luke got the ball almost every play. By the end of some games, he could barely walk, but the yards kept piling up like the payout of a slot machine. If we hadn't made it to sectionals, he would have come up short. He only beat the old record two yards. Six feet. As far as I am tall. But he did it, and my dad was so proud of him.

"Don't open it until you get out there. Good luck, Alex." My dad nodded at me and then went back inside, not even waiting to see me drive away. I waved at Mom and then backed out of the driveway, pointed my car west, and drove for the next seventeen hours.

I'm glad he didn't say 'make me proud'. I hate that phrase. It's not a child's responsibility to make a parent proud of them. It's the parent's duty to be proud of a child. He could have said 'I'm proud of you'. That would have meant something. But he didn't. And I think I know why.

Colorado Springs held my future. Indianapolis contained my past. One I was trying hard to run away from.

Chapter 34

I didn't sleep much at all last night. After Kendra left, I went for a run, but couldn't stop thinking about her and what a jerk I was. Our relationship had been working the way it was. We were in love and drew closer every month. Until little Alex showed up after seventeen years like some drunken estranged family member and ruined everything.

No, that's not fair. He didn't ruin it; I did. The excitement for life that I used to feel was coming back, and I lost control of it. I was making progress, but she is still facing the same obstacles. The same thing happened when Viagra came out and changed the dynamics of so many relationships. Trevor is my Viagra. That fat, balding, myopic miracle worker has rekindled my flame. What is a proper appreciation gift for that situation?

I need to get Kendra an apology gift and apologize to her as soon as I get to the hospital. She can't refuse to talk to me there, it's literally a requirement for her job. I pulled out my phone to call her again and saw the call log. Ten unanswered outbound calls, all to her. Not a single incoming one. I sighed and put the phone away. What's the use? This is something I should do in person, anyway.

I skipped the continuing education audio program I usually listened to on the way in to work and instead focused on what I was going to say to her. Sorry. I was a jerk. You deserve to be treated better. I'd be content to never make love to you.

Trevor's face popped into my head. Staring at me through thick-rimmed glasses. I could read the disappointment in his expression. I'm going to have to talk to him about my erection and what I did with it. Such a fool. I feel like a kid who waited sixteen years to get his driver's license and then wrecked his car pulling out of the driveway.

An ambulance pulled into the bay at the same time I exited my car in the physician parking lot. The medic saw me walking toward them and waved me over. "We're gonna need you, Doc. She doesn't look very good."

"What happened?" I asked, hurrying toward them.

"She was at home and had a sudden headache, then collapsed. Her smart watch called us when it detected the fall, which is fortunate because no one else heard it. Her family was confused when we showed up at the door."

Kendra! I could see her laying on the stretcher. Maroon scrubs today, running shoes. No! She probably spent last night crying after what I did, and that raised her blood pressure enough to blow the AVM. What was I thinking?!

I ran the few remaining steps to the gurney until I could see her face. Brown hair! Kendra's a blond. A wave of relief washed over me, replaced quickly by a wave of guilt. I shouldn't feel relief. It's the worst day of this patient's life. She has plenty of people who care about her too. We need to get her inside and figure out what happened.

"Which room do you want us in, Doc?"

"Room seven if it's available," I said, using my badge to open the door for the EMS crew. I jogged ahead of them to prepare myself for what needed to be done.

"We've got a critical patient. Which trauma room is open?" I yelled. A nurse stepped out from behind a counter and pointed at room eight. Of course. I looked into room seven as I jogged past. A disheveled man lay sprawled out on the bed, a hospital gown trying its hardest to keep him decent. "Clarence? Again? Come on, man. You gotta stop drinking. You're killing yourself."

I directed the medics into room eight. Of course, it was room eight.

"Get RT down here. We're going to have to intubate her and then go straight to CT." I turned around toward the secretary's desk. "Carla, can you check on the availability of our helicopter?" We're a small community hospital. Whatever caused her to suddenly lose consciousness likely cannot be managed here.

The medics wheeled her into the room, followed quickly by Rosanne. "You should call Kendra too. We're going to need another set of hands," I said.

"Sorry Doc, she called in today. Said she wasn't feeling well. Looks like it's just us."

What? She never misses work. She felt fine yesterday. Didn't even have a headache or feel off at all. Well, until I ruined our relationship.

I examined the patient quickly and found that she couldn't move the right side of her body. She was breathing, but irregularly and exhaling in deep sighs through flaccid lips. She needed her airway protected before we went to CT.

After the nurse pushed the medications I ordered to sedate and paralyze her, I passed a breathing tube into her trachea. Once I confirmed proper placement, we unlocked the bed and headed toward the CT scanner. I nearly ran into Holly, who was standing in the hallway outside the room.

"Heck of a case to start your shift with, Alex. Are you turning into a black cloud? This poor woman's only twenty-eight."

"Unfortunate Lee. But I'm going to make sure she gets to twenty-nine. Do me a favor, get a page out to neurosurgery, would you? I think she's got a ruptured aneurysm or some other spontaneous bleed. We can always apologize if the CT is negative."

Holly nodded and turned to Carla to relay my request. Three minutes later, the CT tech groaned as the initial images scrolled by on the monitor.

"She's got a huge bleed on the left side, doc."

Of course she does. That's the only thing that explained this. "Let's get an angiogram, too. Maybe there's something they can repair."

I left the CT suite and returned to the ER. I hadn't even set my bag down at the workstation yet, and there were likely other patients to see. And Holly probably wanted to leave.

"Carla, is the helicopter here? We need to get her out of here."

"Yes, they were just waiting for confirmation of the flight request. Should I tell them it's a go?"

"Yeah, and I need that neurosurgeon on the phone immediately. She needs the trauma center and I can't send her until I have an accepting doc."

Carla reached for her phone to call the transport crew, but it chipped the briefest ring before she picked it up. "St. Luke's Emergency Department." She motioned me over with her other hand. "Yes, thanks for calling back so quickly. Let me get Dr. Lee for you."

I leaned across the counter and grabbed the phone from Carla. "Hi, are you with neurosurgery?"

"Yes, this is Dr. Patrick Vaughn. How can I help?"

Chapter 35

I gave him a quick summary of the patient and waited for the inevitable flurry of questions that often follow these consults.

"You said she's only twenty-nine? Is there a vessel to go after?"

"Uh... hang on, scanning those images now." I said the words into the phone but toward Holly, who was reviewing the images on her computer. She gave me a thumbs up.

"Alex, she's got an aneurysm in the anterior cerebral artery. Maybe 3mm."

"I'm told she has about a 3mm aneurysm on the ACA. Is that something you can intervene on?"

He didn't even hesitate. "We're sure going to give it a try. How quickly can you get the patient here?"

"The helicopter is spinning up now. I'm going to give her hypertonic saline to reduce the ICP and then we'll load her up. She should be to you within an hour."

"Very well. I'll have the OR team in place when she arrives. Make sure you send the images over the cloud system so I can review them."

"Will do, thanks Dr. Vaughn. Good luck."

"Hey, before I let you go, is my sister working there today?"

His sister? Dr. Vaughn? Kendra Vaughn? Kendra has a mashed-up bunch of blood vessels in her brain and her brother is a neurosurgeon? Why did she never mention that?

"No, not today. She was supposed to work but called off. She's an excellent nurse who I really love working with."

"I bet you do. Aren't you the ER doc she's dating? Alex is it?"

Yes, well, I was yesterday. I'm not sure I am today. This is a lot to take in, especially while caring for a critical patient. "Yes, I am. Your sister is an amazing woman, but I need to get going. The patient is on her way back from CT and I need to get her ready to fly out of here."

"Sounds good Alex. Nice to talk with you. Maybe we'll meet in person soon and I can give you an update on how the patient did."

"I'd like that, thanks. Take care." I'd like that because it would mean Kendra didn't dump me for being an idiot. I handed the phone back to Carla, who was giving me a sideways glance.

"There's no patient coming back from CT. Is that doctor Kendra's brother?"

"Yeah, can you believe it? What are the odds? Her brother is a neurosurgeon."

"I am surprised she hadn't told you yet. She's so proud of him. Why would she not mention it?"

Because she has a ticking time bomb in her brain and didn't want to talk about it with me. "No idea. I'll ask next time I see her."

"You sure got off the phone quickly when he asked about her, and she called in to work today. Did you screw something up?"

Absolute Lee. "We did not end well yesterday. I've tried to call, but she's not answering."

Carla shook her head and sighed. "Figure this out, Doc. She's a terrific woman."

Of course she's right. I need to figure this out. But how can I do that when she won't answer her phone and doesn't show up to work? Am I supposed to just show up at her house with flowers and yell at her from the sidewalk?

"Hey Alex, do you have a moment?" It was Holly, still dressed in scrubs. She's probably going to give me an award for ordering fewer tests and speeding up my patient care. I should include Trevor and Delroy in my speech, but that would tell everyone I'm seeing a shrink and therapist. Maybe I'll just thank them myself.

"Sure, as long as it's good news. What's up?"

"Two things actually. The first is definitely good news. You are now within the normal distribution of radiology imaging, and your door-to-disposition times are much better. The hospital administration is much happier about that."

"And what about bounce-backs? I haven't heard of any significant misses, have you?"

"No, you're doing fine. Keep it up."

Who doesn't enjoy hearing positive feedback like that? Especially from someone I admire. But there's that second thing she had to talk about. "What's the other thing?"

"Someone filed a complaint about your care the other day." I could see the awkwardness in her face as she gave me the news.

"They called you to complain about me?" I asked.

"No, worse than that. They called the hospital administrator to complain about you."

What? Who would do that? I have my occasional dust up with patients and families like everyone does, but nothing had stood out for months. What's this about? "I don't understand. What did they say happened?"

"A medic saw you restrain a patient rather aggressively and then give a large dose of a sedative into a muscle without cleaning the skin first. The person thought you should have been more gentle and placed the patient at risk of an infection by not sterilizing the skin first."

I could feel myself losing control of my emotions. It had to have been the medic I passed coming out of the break room while finishing the last of the cheesy potatoes. "You're telling me there was a medic watching our team struggle with a violent patient and they didn't offer to help, but took it upon themselves to complain to our hospital administrator about how we handled it?"

"Yeah, that's pretty much what happened. I didn't realize you were struggling to restrain a patient. That was on Easter, wasn't it?"

"Yep. When the hospital scheduled us short handed because they expected volumes to be low. Then we get a violent patient and don't have enough staff to manage him safely. Why couldn't this medic have stepped up and held an arm or a leg for us? Kendra got kicked in the head by this guy after he spit on me. Can I file a complaint against the medic?"

Holly smiled at me. "I wish, but that's not how it works. Did you clean the skin before giving the injection?"

"No, I didn't. I had no extra hands, our staff was being injured, and we had to put him down right away. Besides, he injects meth all over his body. One extra injection site will not cause any problems."

"I agree with you, but it's the appearance that matters to the hospital. They asked me to write up a formal report about it and then present to the board meeting next month. I wanted to hear your side of things before I wrote it up. Sounds like you did nothing wrong, and I would have done the same thing."

"Thanks, Holly. That means a lot. Let the board know that if they want to discipline me for this case, they can just hire another doc because I'll quit on the spot. I will not let patients abuse our staff and then get punished thanks to onlookers who could have helped but didn't."

"If it comes to that, I'll write you a glowing recommendation for your next job."

Holly headed down the hall toward the exit. I don't know how she does it. I have a hard enough time just being an ER doc and treating patients. I can't imagine adding administrative nonsense to that.

Chapter 36

I've got a few hours to kill before my shift this afternoon. Usually, I'd stop by Kendra's place if she was around, but that's not really an option right now. The longer I brooded in my condo, the deeper the pull of self-pity became. I needed to get out of here.

Running was out of the question this morning, but a brilliant idea popped into my head. Trevor needs to hear about my improvements at work and the issue with Kendra. Maybe I can catch him between patients. He's going to be so happy to hear about my progress, but I need help with how to talk to Kendra about it. I have to be ready in case she takes me back.

I drove to his office with my window partially down, enjoying the unusually warm weather for this early in spring. The window was slightly open, but I had the heater on. Who wants recycled air when they're on a mission? I wanted the feel of fresh air hitting me in the face and lifting me up. What significant events happened while sitting cooped up in a room?

The parking lot was fairly full, but I squeezed my car between a Mercedes and a Honda right in front of Trevor's suite. It was two minutes after the hour. Stupid traffic. He may be in the next room already, but maybe he's running late. I can't wait fifty-eight minutes to talk to him. Maybe he's on a lunch break in the back.

I was approaching the door when I saw someone reach for the handle on the inside. It was a blonde woman whose face was looking down at her phone. Kendra! What is she doing here? I pivoted left and used a few quick steps to put some distance between myself and the door before I heard it open behind me. My head was down and shoulders scrunched up against my ears, willing myself to become invisible.

How could she do this? Trevor is helping me overcome so many problems. I'm finally to a point I can sleep without medication and be awake without constantly blaming myself for my brother's death. I'm getting erections again. I'm a more functional doctor in the hospital. I don't think the former has anything to do with the latter, but it's worth considering. Sure, we had a fight, but she can't interject herself here. We're not married. She's not even listed on my privacy release form.

An engine fired up behind me, followed quickly by tires rolling on asphalt. I rotated my body back toward the building as the vehicle drove behind me. I took a quick look over my shoulder in time to see her CRV leaving the lot. The nerve of her! Trevor better not have said anything to her other than 'I can't divulge confidential patient information.'

I strode back toward the office and ripped the door open, my actions powered by righteous indignation. Sliding glass windows blocked my access to the registration staff, but I knocked loudly enough to get the attention of a worker in the back. "Hey, why was that woman here? What did you tell her?"

That must have gotten the lady's attention because she rushed up to the window and slid it open. "I'm sorry. What did you say?"

"I asked what you told that woman who just left."

Her face took on an angry look rather than the sheepish and apologetic one I was expecting. "Sir, that is none of your business. You're a doctor. You should know I can't divulge confidential patient information."

"But she's not a patient, she's my girlfriend! If she was–" The opening of the front door cut my sentence off. I turned to see who was interrupting me and was face to face with Kendra for the first time since our fight.

"Oh, Alex. Hi," she said, looking away from me quickly.

"Kendra, what are you doing here?"

"I left my driver's license and insurance card. I realized it after I pulled away and came back for them. What are you doing here today?"

"What? You're a patient here? Since when?"

Kendra looked behind me at a woman sitting in a waiting room chair, desperately trying to act like she wasn't paying attention. "Do you mind if we go someplace else and talk?"

Yes, I would love that. And then you can explain yourself to me. You can… No. You don't need to do that. I need to apologize. Check your ego, Alex.

I apologized to the woman behind the counter for my earlier behavior. She shook her head at me and turned toward Kendra without acknowledging me. Kendra leaned in and took her documents from her, and then we both left the office.

"Maybe I should ask what you're doing here. Today isn't your therapy day," she said, once we were outside.

Well, this is embarrassing. I'm supposed to be this tough guy ER doctor, her knight in shining armor. Ready to protect her against anything that should happen. But I can't tell her I drove out here to tell a fat bald guy he helped me get an erection. So, I lied.

"Trevor asks me to check in from time to time and let him know how I'm doing. Given what happened recently, I figured that was worth an update."

"Why? What just happened recently?"

"You know, when you were over and left mad."

"Because you..." She wanted me to say it out loud. Admit what I did. Prove to her I know how I screwed up. I'm not a freaking child! But I did sort of act like one.

I sighed and turned away from her briefly. I couldn't just come out and say it. It had to look like I'd contemplated and it and am embarrassed by how I behaved. That was easy, because it was true. "Acted like a fool. I let my excitement get away from me and turned into a jerk."

"Yes, you did. Thank you for admitting it."

"I wanted to admit it so many times since then, but you wouldn't answer your phone, and you called off work yesterday."

"Can you blame me? I just needed some time. I had so many sick days I was losing them, anyway. So, mental health day. I needed some me time."

I looked at her again. Something was different. "Did you get your hair done? It looks great."

"Yes, I did. Every spring, I add some red highlights. Like my head is getting ready for summer. I rarely do it this early, but I wanted the pick me up."

"It looks good on you." And then we both stopped talking. This is the first time we'd run out of things to say, but I suspect she's like me right now. Plenty of things to say, but not sure she wanted to say them.

"Do you want to get some food? I still have some time before my shift. I know a little diner by the hospital we could eat at."

She smiled at me and nodded. "I'd like that. Meet you there?"

"It's a date." I clapped my hands and jumped in the air a little as I turned toward my car.

Chapter 37

Darlene's face lit up when she saw us walk into the restaurant. "Well, look who it is! Should I get a pitcher of coffee and two beers?"

"How about coffee and water to start with today?" I don't want alcohol clouding my judgment, I've got some serious apologizing to do. And I never drink within eight hours of a shift.

Darlene winked and headed back behind the counter as we took our seats at the same table we used the first time. I took my usual seat across the table from her.

"It's good to see you," I said.

"Same. I tried to stay mad at you, but all I wanted to do was call or text."

"So, why didn't you?"

"Because you were a jerk, and I wanted you to know I was mad at you."

"Mission accomplished. And I know I was a jerk. We had a great thing going and then I tried to change the trajectory. I don't need sex."

Darlene picked a terrible time to bring the drinks. "Maybe you don't, but I sure do, sweetie. My old man hit the jackpot when he married me."

Kendra and I couldn't hold back our laughter. "Is that why you're so happy all the time?" I asked.

"A lady never tells," she said as she walked away. But judging by Kendra's additional laugh, I'm guessing I missed a signal when she was behind me.

"Well, that was awkward," I said.

"Oh, come on, she's sweet. And funny."

"What I was trying to say is that I like us for us. I forgot about your AVM and what that meant for your life. I promise to do better in the future."

"So, I should give you another chance?"

Yes, of course. I'd give you a million. But you'll never need them. Maybe I'll take your extra chances since I burn through them quickly. "Yes. I'm like a three-year-old at a bowling alley. I take forever to start, and you know I'm going to screw up badly. A lot. But if you put some bumpers in place, eventually I'll end up where I'm supposed to be."

"Am I the bumpers?"

"Yes. And the ramp to help me throw the ball."

"Fine, I can be all of those for you. But should we keep score?"

"Absolutely not. Let's never keep score in our relationship."

She leaned across the table and kissed me. "Deal."

"So, now that we're back on track, why were you at the therapist's office?"

She sighed and took a drink from her glass. "Diving right in, I see."

"It caught me by surprise. I thought you were there spying on me, trying to see what I was talking about. It never occurred to me you might be there as a patient."

"You really think I'd go to all the trouble of spying on you? If I wanted to know, I'd just ask."

"Do you not want to know?"

"Of course I do, but I don't feel I should ask. I'm respecting your privacy." She took another drink and looked at me while she did it. "I assume you'd do the same for me."

Busted. Okay, fine. New tactic. I stood up and worked my way around the table and took a seat next to her on the bench.

"Absolutely. When you're ready to share, I'm ready to listen." I put my hand on her back and rubbed up and down along her spine. My index finger dipped between the bony ridges as I went. I leaned in closer and felt the prominence of her hip bone, and then moved back to her spine.

As soon as my hand returned to the middle and rubbed again, she quickly twisted away from me. "Hey, are you sizing me up for a lumbar puncture? I felt you touch the top of my hip and then go back to my spine. You're wondering how easy it would be to stick a needle in there, aren't you?"

Busted. Again. What could I do but laugh? "Guilty. But to be fair, I feel you running your fingers along the veins on my hands and forearms. Don't tell me you're not thinking the same thing about IV access."

This made us both laugh at the absurdity of our lives. It felt great to share a joyful moment with her. I need to stop being a jerk. Where's my notebook? I need to write that down. The truth is, I stopped carrying my notebook. I didn't need it anymore. It was just another crutch.

She recovered enough to speak first. "I can't stand patients who have no veins. They're usually morbidly obese, too. It makes no sense. If your body is twice the normal size, shouldn't your veins be twice the normal size to match? It's ridiculous how often we need to use ultrasound to place a line now."

"Well, technically, you're interested in the cross-sectional area of the vein. Remember, that is πr^2, so the area should be the square of the radius, not double."

That earned me a slap on the shoulder. "You dork. Just agree with me and move on."

Fine. "I thought about you the other day at work."

"Really? What happened?"

"When I got there, EMS was unloading a woman on their stretcher who had your same body type. They said she had a sudden headache and then collapsed. She was wearing scrubs."

Kendra's eyes widened. "And you thought it was me?"

"I did. For a brief second. I ran over to them but saw she had different colored hair. We intubated her and then went to CT which showed a ruptured aneurysm."

"That's my exact fear. How did she do?"

"I don't know yet. We flew her downtown, where the neurosurgeon was going to decide how to repair it. He seemed like a very capable guy."

"Good." Her demeanor had changed, and this word came out slower and almost like a question. Not that she was questioning whether it was good, but like there was another question she was keeping inside her head. Time to answer it for her.

"Yeah, guess what his name was?"

"Cutty McBrainerson?" She knew what was coming. I had to applaud her effort at a humorous distraction.

"Maybe among his friends. But professionally, he goes by Dr. Vaughn."

"Oh, interesting. What a great name. Several strong consonants, a last name that just fades off the tongue."

"Right? I thought so, too. He asked if his sister was working in the department that day and then asked if I happened to be the ER doctor dating her."

She nodded but focused on taking a drink of water instead of answering. I joined her as we let the words float uncomfortably for a while.

"You're probably wondering why I didn't mention my brother is a neurosurgeon when I told you about the AVM."

"The thought crossed my mind, but I figured you had your reasons. I'm just curious."

"I didn't think it was relevant because I wasn't going to have anything done about it."

I get it. Some things are easier to avoid than talk about. It's been the story of my life. But I don't want that for anyone else. "Did he go into neurosurgery because of your father, or because of you?"

"He's never said. We talked about my AVM a few times, but he doesn't want to operate on it. He would have to go through a lot of healthy brain tissue to get to it, and he's afraid I'd end up with personality changes or stroke-like weakness."

"What about an endovascular approach? Could they coil it from inside the artery?"

"That technique wasn't very far along when I was diagnosed, so we never really considered it back then. I've done some reading on it and it can be done, but the success rate depends on the anatomy. It also has a higher risk of bleeding afterward than an open surgical approach. My brother used to bring it up all the time, but he hasn't said anything in the last few years. Maybe it's because I bite his head off every time he mentions it."

"Why?"

"I don't know. That's what I'm hoping to figure out with Caitlyn and therapy. I'm sure some of it has to do with my father's death. Probably also worried about putting guilt on my brother if something happens to me after the procedure."

"But what if something happens to you because you didn't have the procedure in the first place? What if you end up like my patient the other day?"

She leaned her head against me and squeezed my knee with her right hand. "That's why I live every day in the moment and am thrilled when I wake up the next morning. The first thing I do is stretch both arms and legs to make sure they all work. Then I smile, happy that I'm functional for another day. Maybe I'll talk to him about the vascular approach again. It's way less invasive and shouldn't affect healthy brain tissue, assuming they put the coil in the right place. If they screw it up, I'd have a massive irreversible stroke."

Truly a rock and a hard place. So many reasons to not undergo the procedure. I didn't know whether to encourage her to have it done or to skip it. If I encourage her to have the procedure, she may think I'm being selfish and just wanting her to be able to have sex. With me. She's enjoying life now, but every day is another round of Russian roulette, wondering if today's the day the vessel bursts.

So I do the only thing I can think of that is safe. I put my arm around her and squeezed. "I'm sorry you're facing that. Let me know if you ever want to talk about it again." And then I left it alone.

Chapter 38
Nine Years Ago

Medical school was hard. Ridiculously hard. They couldn't just show us what a syphilis rash looked like and tell us to use penicillin to treat it. They had to explain what a spirochete was, how it lived, how it reproduced, how it was transmitted, and how penicillin worked. We couldn't just learn general concepts about microbiology, we had to memorize dozens of facts about scores of bacteria and regurgitate them back onto a sheet of paper that had more white space than ink. It wasn't even multiple choice.

In reality, we knew we would look up what to do when it came time for clinical practice, but they wanted us to prove we could memorize it. Microbiology was one of those weed out classes. You could either do what they wanted, or you couldn't. And I was showing them I couldn't. A score of seventy percent is the cutoff to pass the class, and I was sitting in the upper sixties with the final exam tomorrow.

It's covering some new material, but also everything I already proved I didn't learn the first time.

Luke was the one who wanted to go to medical school. He had the natural ability and intelligence to do it. That's why he was such a good running back. He could memorize the playbook in a single night and remembered which side a particular defender favored. He would have crushed medical school. I'm barely scraping by.

"Hey Alex, some of us are going out for drinks in an hour. You up for a study break?"

"Thanks Glenn, but I'm going to hang here and keep at it. That test tomorrow is freaking me out."

"No worries. Hang in there, buddy. See you in class in the morning."

Glenn meant well. He and the others were always inviting me to go do things with them, but usually I declined. The last thing I needed was guilt over a good time when I received my next poor grade. I stayed at the library for a few more hours until my stomach was distracting me from studying. Fortunately, I live in an apartment across the street from the library, so I left my books on a table and walked home to eat. I brought a stack of note cards to review as I walked. Time between destinations is still time, and I couldn't afford to waste a minute.

Dinner tonight was macaroni and cheese, the deluxe version. I used to eat the plain cardboard box version in college but switched to the deluxe in medical school. Yes, it cost more money, but I was going to be a doctor. I could afford it. My financial adviser had me write 'max' on the requested loan amount every year.

At least that's what I thought the first time I classed up my grocery list. Now that I'm in danger of failing, it seemed like a ridiculous splurge that I may end up trying to pay back over the next thirty years of student loan payments. Tonight, I made two batches and put one in a plastic container to take back to the library with me. I grabbed a bag of chips and a jar of instant coffee as well. I'm going to have to study all night if I wanted a chance to pass microbiology.

Pulling an all-nighter is like running a marathon. You have to rest before it or the built-up fatigue can affect your performance. If I was too tired to recall the information, I'd be screwed.

I had a last-minute thought to grab my bathroom kit as well. Who wants to take a test without having brushed their teeth in twenty-four hours? Sleep is one thing, but hygiene is another. I stopped in front of my dresser on the way out of my bedroom. Sitting there on top was a small white box my dad had given me the day I left for medical school. The gift he had bought for Luke. I dropped my supplies onto my bed and picked up the box instead.

An elastic cord made of golden material wrapped around the box, holding it closed. I had wanted to open it several times but always chickened out. I was afraid whatever the box contained would distract me for a while and I needed to focus on my studies. Now I hoped it contained some magical talisman that would help me pass this test and stay in medical school.

I pulled off the golden tie and lifted the lid, revealing the contents inside. Inside the box was a black felt pad supporting a gold rope necklace. A football with the number eight engraved on it hung from a small loop in the middle. Luke's number. Eight.

Dad bought him a necklace to commemorate his high school football career, but never got the chance to give it to him. I wondered how long he held onto that necklace, just waiting for Christmas to come so he could give it to him. I don't know why, but the thought of the gift being so close yet never received caused me to break down into uncontrollable sobbing. Maybe it was the necklace alone, or perhaps the necklace mixed with the realization tonight was my last night in medical school. Either way, the tears didn't stop for almost an hour. Sixty minutes of time I could have been studying. This is exactly why I had never opened the box.

I had dialed my parents' number many times over the last few weeks, but always hung up before putting in the final digit. Now I wanted to share the moment. To break down the wall that Luke's death built between us. But I chickened out and didn't do it. I used the test as an excuse and prepared to head back to the library.

As I lifted the chain out of the box and undid the clasp, I saw an inscription on the back of the football. I turned it over and held it up, tilting it until the light caught the engraving well enough to read. '5436 yards, none of them easy'.

That last part was true. Luke could do what seemed impossible. He ran for that many yards, with eleven guys on the opposite team trying to stop him on every play. He'd either score a touchdown or get knocked down at the end of every play. And as long as there was time on the clock, he'd get back into the huddle and try to do it again.

I reached behind my head and secured the clasp on the chain. The football hung down on the front of my neck. At first it was cold, then my body warmed it and I couldn't feel it anymore. It was a part of me.

All I have to do is learn twelve to fifteen facts about a hundred viruses, bacteria, and fungi. Unlike Luke, there is no one trying to stop me. And I'm close. Really close. I've been working as hard as I can to learn this stuff and I'm so close. But so are many people who fail out of programs. There has to be a cutoff somewhere.

I grabbed my snacks and headed back to the library. It was 8:00 p.m. Twelve hours before my test. Half a day to learn random facts about tiny microbes that can't even be seen without magnification.

But now I've got Luke on my side. I've done the math. All I need is a seventy-five percent to pass and move on to third year where I start my clinical rotations. I've been getting upper seventies on the practice exams. I can do this. Between Luke's necklace, coffee, and my guilt, I'm going to get there.

And I did. I got an eighty-one. Exactly six more than I needed. Six. Two yards. The same margin Luke got his record by. I found my magical talisman. Thanks, Dad.

Chapter 39

I was falling asleep when my phone vibrated, and the screen illuminated the room. It was set to 'do not disturb' mode and I only gave one person an exclusion. I rolled over and grabbed it from the table next to my bed.

Kendra: Hey, are you busy Friday morning?

Busy? Nope. I'm off Friday and if I had anything scheduled, I'd back out of it instantly.

Me: No, wide open. What's up?
Kendra: I have an appointment with a neurosurgeon. I'd like you to be there.

Woah. She didn't tell me about that. I thought she wasn't looking into options on this AVM.

> *Me: Yes, I'll be there. Drive together or meet there?*
> *Kendra: Pick me up at 8*
> *Me: Okay. Are you up? Can I call?*
> *Kendra: ring, ring*

I scooted backward in bed so the pillow was under my back, and I was sitting up a bit before dialing her number.

"I thought you'd be asleep," she said.

"I thought I would be too. You just caught me. Where did this appointment come from?"

Obviously, she didn't just find out about the appointment at ten o'clock at night, two days before the scheduled time.

"I've been working with Caitlyn, and she encouraged me to have another opinion about the AVM and treatment options. She said part of dealing with an ongoing stressor is having the most knowledge about it that I can. I checked, and it had been over ten years since I've even had an angiogram."

"Yeah? That seems like a long time."

"Well, now it's only been eight hours."

That caused me to sit upright in bed. Any thought of sleep vaporized. "Oh, wow. You really are moving forward on this, aren't you?"

"I needed to know if I'm making the right decision by not treating it. And that can't happen without information."

"I'm following. I'd be glad to go with you to the meeting. Will your brother be there as well?"

"He'd better be. He's the surgeon I'm meeting with. He said he'll have Dr. Kumar there also, one of their interventional neuroradiology partners. If a vascular approach is the better option, Dr. Kumar would be the one to perform it."

"That's amazing, Kendra. I'm excited, but also nervous for you. This could be life changing."

"And lifesaving. I'll let you get back to sleep. See you at eight?"

"I'll be there."

***

It took forever for Friday to arrive, even though it was only a day and a half after the phone call. I was up at five-thirty, got a quick run in, and was at Kendra's by 7:45 a.m. I skipped my Jeff Probst attire for slightly more formal clothing. The sort of thing you'd wear to a church service in Florida in the middle of summer.

I knocked on the door, knowing the real-life doorbell would be more effective than the digital one. Right on cue,

Lucy started barking as loud as she could. Well, it was more like yipping. But it was loud enough to get Kendra to the door.

"Good morning," I said, trying to be as chipper as possible.

It was not reciprocated as Kendra rolled her eyes and pulled the door open for me. That's not the response I was expecting.

"Hey, are you okay? What's going on?" I asked.

"This is a huge deal for me. I've been ignoring the bullet aimed right at my head for over ten years, and now I'm about to spend an hour talking about it with two people who may be able to help me dodge it. I just can't feel excited. I'm nervous as can be."

"I can see that. What can I do to help?"

"Take Lucy outside before we go and lock the car door so I can't jump out before we get there."

There it is. Her humor is coming back after that flash of annoyance, born of her fear of the unknown.

Kendra's mother sat at the kitchen table, eating a bowl of cereal. "Tell Patrick I said hello and remind him he hasn't come to visit me in a while." Her voice was slow and uneven, a persistent symptom from the stroke that relegated her to transport via a wheelchair most of the time.

"Good morning, Mary. How are you feeling?" I asked.

"Good. Thanks for asking. Thank you for going with her today. We've both been a wreck thinking about this coming up. I've made my thoughts known very plainly. You may wish to be more subtle." She winked at me and continued to eat.

Lucy peed as soon as she reached grass and then marched into her crate once we were back inside. Kendra dropped a treat through the top and then we headed for my car.

My phone said it would take forty-five minutes to get there, which gave us plenty of time to talk about everything except the upcoming appointment.

I parked outside the impressive offices of University Brain and Spine. Their office doubled as an outpatient surgery center and the parking lot was nearly full. I should have been a neurosurgeon. A busy ER parking lot is a bad sign. But in the outpatient world, it meant a thriving office with a schedule full of patients who would most likely pay their bill.

I hopped out of the car and tried to make it around to Kendra's door before she opened it. I missed it by half a second but was able to close it for her.

She dipped her head and leaned into me, pushing me against my car. "Alex, I'm afraid they're going to tell me there's nothing they can do."

I wanted to say I understood, but I can't say that, because I have no idea what she is feeling. So I just squeezed her hand in mine.

"But I'm also afraid they might tell me there's something they can do."

I smiled at her and gave her hand another squeeze. "Well then, let's just get it over with and see what they have to say. Do you know which floor it's on?"

"Second, I think."

She was correct. Dr. Patrick Vaughn, MD. Suite 201. Kendra checked in with the secretary and, after passing the insurance card and driver's license back and forth, was told to sit and wait for her name to be called.

"No giant stack of paperwork to fill out?" I asked.

"I did it online last night when I couldn't sleep." She pulled her phone out and started scrolling through Facebook. I wasn't about to interrupt her and bring her mind back to the neurosurgeon's office, so I did the same thing. My medical reference apps were feeling neglected.

"Kendra Vaughn?" A nurse leaning out past a door called Kendra's name, and we followed her through it. The nurse performed a quick check of vital signs and then escorted us to an exam room. "The doctor will be with you soon," she said, and then left us alone in the room. We took seats in the two four-legged chairs, leaving the stool open for Patrick.

"Do you think she knows you're his sister?" I asked.

"I doubt it. They probably see so many patients a day, it's hard to even focus on the name in front of you. It's just a piece of information, no different from an address or an allergy."

"Are you speaking from experience?"

"If I came up to you on a shift and asked if Alice could have more pain medication, what would your response be?"

Hospitals like to claim patients are more than just a number. It's true, of course, but it's the numbers that keep everything in order. "I'd ask what room the patient was in because I'd have no idea what their first names were."

"Exactly."

Chapter 40

A quick series of knocks grabbed our attention right before the door opened and Kendra's brother walked into the room. His aura screamed neurosurgeon. Dressed in a tailored suit, wire-rimmed glasses, perfect hair. He probably didn't struggle in medical school like I did. He just decided to do it and then eleven years later he's a neurosurgeon.

He hugged Kendra warmly and then turned to face me. "Alex? Patrick Vaughn," he said, holding his hand out toward me. I shook it as hard as I dared, trying to be on the impressive side of the line between too weak and too forceful.

"Yes, good to meet you. Thanks for working her in so quickly," I said.

"Are you kidding? I'd meet Kendra at two in the morning if I had to. I've been wanting to have this discussion for a decade. I could barely sleep last night after

I reviewed your images." He looked around the door and yelled into the hallway. "Anil, you still here?"

"Let me pull up the angiogram you had done and I'll show you what I found." He sat down on the stool and pushed over toward the computer on the counter. After a tap with his ID badge to unlock the screen, he pulled up her images in the radiology software.

Another man walked in then, tall and dark-skinned. Another handsome, well put-together dude. Is it a prerequisite for working here? "Guys, this is my partner, Anil Kumar. He's one of our interventional neuroradiologists. He does amazing work." Anil shook our hands, and we completed the introductions.

"I think you've treated a few of my stroke patients. I work out at St. Luke's and we fly out the large-vessel occlusion strokes for clot retrieval."

"Okay, right. I recognize your name now." He turned toward the computer monitor where Patrick was scrolling through images. "He's going to show you what we're considering."

Patrick scrolled to an image that represented a thin slice through her brain. It was a two-dimensional image of a three-dimensional organ, but showed what we needed to see.

He circled his finger around a cluster of blood vessels, clearly different from the surrounding brain tissue. "This is your arteriovenous malformation. It's not insignificant, but it's also not the largest one we've treated. The good news is it only has one feeder vessel on the arterial side, right here." He pointed at a white line coming out of the AVM and merging with the other cerebral blood vessels.

Dr. Kumar continued the explanation. "With that single feeder vessel, I can use coils of wire to eradicate the blood supply to the AVM. If it goes well, I can massively reduce, or even eliminate, the blood flow to the abnormal vessels. It could nearly normalize your risk of intracranial hemorrhage to that of the standard population."

"How much of a hedge is 'nearly normalize'?" I asked, earning a nod from Kendra.

"It's a guess, but I'd say maybe one to two percent higher than background risk."

"And where am I at right now?" said Kendra.

Her brother fielded this question. "With an AVM of your size, the annualized risk of rupture somewhere between two and four percent."

"That's not all that different," said Kendra, sighing and slouching her shoulders. "Is it even worth the risk if the benefit is so small?"

"No, Kendra. The risk of rupture is two to four percent *per year*. So as we sit here today, you have a twenty to forty percent risk of rupture in the next ten years. And forty to eighty percent in twenty years. A ruptured AVM carries about a forty percent immediate mortality rate, with most patients that live through it experiencing significant disabling neurologic consequences."

"But it's possible it might never rupture?" she asked.

Dr. Kumar looked at Patrick and they both shared a sigh. Her brother voiced what they were both thinking. "It's possible, but that's the exception. If you are healthy and should otherwise have a normal life expectancy, odds are the AVM will rupture at some point."

"And then I'm facing the forty percent mortality risk and even higher risk of severe disability?"

This time, they both nodded.

"What is the actual procedure and recovery like? Will I be out of work for a while?"

"We do this in a very advanced procedure lab with fluoroscopy so we can see where the catheter is at all times. I'll gain access in the femoral artery and then navigate a wire up into the affected blood vessel. Once there, I'll deploy small platinum wires into the feeder vessel for the AVM. This causes the artery to spasm on the foreign material and hopefully close off entirely."

"Is it just one wire?" asked Kendra.

"It depends on how successful it is, but usually we deploy several wires in order to get the best result."

"What about glue? Is that an option?" I asked.

Patrick smiled and nodded. "You've been doing some research on your own, I see."

Dr. Kumar answered. "It's off-label and not something I'd want to start with. Currently we use cyanoacrylate, basically the same stuff you repair lacerations with, as a rescue method if there is an active leak after a different procedure."

"Am I awake during it? I'm not sure I want to feel a catheter wiggling through my brain."

"And I can't have you moving during it, either. I'll have an anesthesiologist present who will provide sedation for you."

"And what about the risks?"

"Good question Kendra. I like that you're looking for as much information as possible. The major complications we worry about are rupture of the blood vessel because of my catheter or the coil and stroke. It's possible the coil can go somewhere other than where I release it, whether from device failure or other reasons. But the overall risk of complications is low. I'd estimate for your procedure it would be around one to three percent."

"So I have a one to three percent chance of a stroke or hemorrhage from the procedure? And if I bleed, there's a forty percent risk I die?"

"Yes, that's true. But remember, you have a two to four percent annual risk of that happening already. Your risk every year is higher than the procedural risk of what we're discussing."

That is a brilliant point. "So, you're saying this is safer than not treating it?"

"Exactly. Nothing is without risk. The question is, how do you want to view life? Limit additional risk and hope the bomb doesn't go off? Or try to defuse it." Dr. Kumar leaned back against the wall and let that comment hang in the air.

Kendra's brother leaned forward and squeezed her knee. "Look, you don't need to decide right now. Go home, think about it. Pray about it. If you decide to move forward, we'll need a few more tests to prepare for the procedure, but we can probably schedule it within a few weeks of your decision?" He looked at his partner for confirmation.

"Yes, I'm sure we can. I'll make myself available for you."

"Okay, I've got some thinking to do. Thank you both for meeting with me." Kendra stood up and hugged her brother and then shook hands with Dr. Kumar. I exchanged handshakes and then followed her out of the room.

Chapter 41

We left the medical building carrying the weight of the decision she had to make.

"Is it too early for a drink?"

I glanced at the clock on my dash. Not even ten o'clock yet. "I drink at 8:00 a.m. after a night shift. There's no forbidden time."

"Alex, it's okay to tell me not to do something. I need you to be giving good advice right about now."

She's right, of course. But I can't make this decision for her. I can't be the one to suggest she undergo something that puts her at risk, even if not undergoing it carries even more. This has to be her decision.

"Then yes, it's too early to drink. And you should make this decision with a clear head, not one clouded by alcohol." I paused a moment before continuing. "How was that? Better?"

"Yes, thanks. Listen, if this was just about me, I'd do it in a heartbeat. But this affects two people."

We've really grown close, but we're not engaged and haven't spoken directly about marriage. It's sweet of her to feel this way about the decision, but she can't base it on me. Fortunately, she continued speaking before I could make my point.

"I also take care of my mom. What happens if I die during the procedure or have a massive stroke? Who's going to take care of her?"

"Your brother is a neurosurgeon. I'm sure he can arrange care for her. And I'd take care of you." I meant what I said, but it came across as a bit more forward than we'd talked about before.

"You?" She looked at me with a shocked face and then turned to look out the window. "We're not even married. I wouldn't be your problem."

"Hey, you'd never be a problem. If you hadn't come along, I may never have gotten back into counseling. I'd still be the same impotent doctor, hallucinating my way through shifts and ordering way too many tests. I was actually getting worse, and it was only a matter of time until Holly would be told to fire me."

"Former Lee," she said with a bit of a laugh.

"You guys just love making fun of my name, don't you?" I teased, hoping to lighten the mood.

"Well, can you blame us? Your name is perfect for it."

"Would you like it if I did the same with yours?"

"Go ahead. I'd actually like to see what you come up with."

Nuts. I had nothing prepared. How can I change Kendra? Spendra? Nothing useful came to mind. Vaughn? Vaunted? That'll have to do.

"When someone misses an IV, I'll say their skills are vaunted." Hah.

Kendra broke into a full laugh at that one. "What does that even mean?"

"Vaunted? Praised excessively. But I'm turning it around to mean they're terrible."

"Oh, I get it. So I'd say something like 'your insult game is vaunted'. I forgot I'm dating an older guy who's not as cool and hip as I am."

Ouch. "Older? Yeah, five years older. That doesn't really count."

"Well, either way, I'm glad you were with me today. Thanks for coming."

"There's nowhere else I'd rather be." It's a cliché, but perfectly accurate. "But I get to pick our next date activity. Yours aren't very much fun."

"I can't argue with that, but I'm glad you could meet my brother. I could tell he liked you."

"Oh yeah? How could you tell? Do you guys have a secret look or something?"

"He whispered it in my ear right before we left. We Vaughns are known for our subtle ways." She turned to face me and dropped the joking tone. "I'm going to talk to my mom tonight, but what do you think I should do?"

How is this even a debate? Just schedule it for tomorrow! "From what I heard, it sounds like not having the procedure is more dangerous every year than going through it once. If it's successful, you wouldn't be much different from me. At least from a risk of spontaneous brain hemorrhage."

"If. That's the magic word. I know it sounds like a straightforward decision based on what we heard, but it just doesn't feel like it. It's like I'm standing in a relatively safe place for the moment, and I'm supposed to make a jump that two percent of people fail just because it's a bit safer on the other side."

"Not 'a bit safer'. A lot safer. If you do nothing, you have between a forty-four and eighty-eight percent chance of this rupturing by the time you're fifty. If you have the procedure, it drops to about three percent and you can start doing the things you've been avoiding. Running, drinking, smoking, sex..."

"But I don't want to do all of those things anymore," she said. The selfish side of me hoped she was referring to smoking.

"I agree. You shouldn't smoke. It's bad for you. Seriously though, imagine being able to lift your mother when she needs it and not worrying about your brain exploding. It's obviously your decision to make, and I'll be here no matter what you decide."

"But what if the procedure causes a massive stroke and I can't even get out of bed on my own?"

I smiled at her. So concerned about the worst that can happen instead of focusing on the positives. We make a perfect couple. "Then we'll finally catch up on our Netflix list, and you won't be able to complain about what I make for dinner."

I dropped her off at her apartment, and we promised to talk again later. Surely her mother was going to talk her into having the procedure.

***

Kendra: You awake?
Me: No, sleeping
Kendra: So you're dreaming about me?
Me: Always. What are you doing up?
Kendra: Can't sleep. Mom and I talked. I'm going to have the procedure.

That got my attention. I jumped out of bed and called her. This wasn't a time for texting.

"Hello?" she said.

"You're going to have it done? That's wonderful. I think you made the right decision. Anything you need, I'm here for you."

"Thank you. My mom told me to tell you she said 'hi'."

"Is she still up also?"

"Yeah, we're eating ice cream and talking about Dad."

"When are you going to have the procedure?"

"I have a week off in two weeks. I'm going to call Patrick when I wake up and see if he can get it scheduled then. They own the building and he's a senior partner in the group, so hopefully he can make it happen. I'd like to be off for a few days before going back to work."

"Yeah, that makes sense. If I'm working, I'll get the shift covered so I can be there."

"I'd like that. But you can't be in the procedure room. You have to hang out in the waiting room like everyone else."

"Of course. I wouldn't have much of a clue what they're doing in there, anyway. I can hang with your mother and entertain her during it."

"She'd love that. She's been wanting to spend some time grilling you without my presence. Listen, I'm going to try to sleep. I'll let you know when the procedure date is. Love you."

"Love you, too. I think you've made the right decision. Sleep well."

I hung up and tossed the phone onto the bed but was too excited to follow it onto the mattress. She's taking the next step! It's possible in a few weeks we could both be fairly normal!

I was still awake two hours later. Is Kendra sleeping? Should I text her? No, if she was asleep, and I woke her with a text, she'd be irritated at me. She needs to sleep to be rested for her procedure.

Chapter 42

Kendra: I talked to Patrick. We scheduled the procedure for June 3rd at 8 a.m. Are you free?
Me: Yes, I'm free. I'll be there. Want me to drive?
Kendra: Yeah, thanks.
Me: It's a date. Tell your mom to get her questions for me ready
Kendra: She already has a list. I'm not joking. Pick me up at 5:30a?
Me: I'll be there early

The last few months have been the most fun I've ever had at work. Residency was fun because everything was new, but life as an attending isn't always as glorious as it sounds. When patients or families are upset or a complication happens, I'm the one that hears about it. Usually very loudly.

Since Trevor has been helping me, I enjoy my time at the hospital so much more. The CT techs are starting to warm up to me and even offer me cookies when I'm down there checking on a patient. The only round things they offered me before were sets of angry eyes glaring at me.

The doctor-patient relationship is complex enough as it is, but with emergency medicine, I only have a few seconds to build trust with the patient and family. They need to immediately trust that I am competent and they can rely on my judgment and evaluation of their condition.

Today I walked into work smiling and ready to tackle whatever medical disaster society chose to cough up into our facility today. Holly was sitting at the physician work area, spinning a pen on her finger. "Hey Alex, the hospital chose a date for the meeting about your case with the violent patient. I need you here at 9:00 a.m. on June 3rd."

Of course you do. But sorry, I'm not available. I've got more important things to do. I'll quit before I miss her procedure date. I'm an ER doctor and can move anywhere in the country. I could find another job in ten minutes. Of course, that means the hospital can also replace me in the blink of an eye.

"Actually, I can't make it on the third. I've got somewhere I need to be."

"Alex, this is the hospital administration and nursing director. You need to be there. We chose a date that you weren't scheduled in the department."

"I understand, but I'm not available and won't be there. I do have a life outside the hospital, just like everyone else does. I'm happy to discuss possible dates with them, but I won't be summoned. Once I get settled in I'll give them a call and sort it out."

"Please be diplomatic. They're just doing their job."

I flashed Holly my most disarming smile. "I'm always diplomatic. I'll let you know. Let's get you out of here, do you have anything to turn over?"

"No, I'm good. There are two waiting to be seen that just got here, but everyone else is admitted or discharged. Have a good shift."

The first thing I did was log into the computer system and see why both patients were there. The first patient presented for nasal congestion and the other complained of vomiting and diarrhea. Two more people here for convenience and not an emergency. No one requires my immediate attention, which is great because I have a phone call I need to make.

"Hi, St. Luke's Medical Staff Office."

"Hello, this is Doctor Alex Lee. Is the chief of staff available?"

"Yes, he just got out of a meeting. Let me get him for you."

I tapped my finger on the desk, trying to unload the nervous energy building up inside me. I really didn't want to quit and get a different job. I liked it here. They tolerated my quirks, and I understood the system. And my girlfriend works here.

"Hello Alex, how can I help you?"

"Tom, thanks for taking my call. I heard you wanted to meet to discuss an issue we had with a violent patient who was assaulting our staff. Thank you for taking this on. We were woefully understaffed on Easter and did not have adequate personnel to manage an acutely agitated and violent patient. I need help convincing the CEO and CNO that we can't run skeleton crew in the ER because we never know what's going to come in the door."

"Yes, about that. Those are certainly valid concerns that I will send up the chain, but there's also the issue with the medic who witnessed what happened."

"Right, another huge problem. I need to know who that was so that I can talk with his chief. He watched us struggling with a violent patient and did not step up to help us control the situation, but instead chose to sit on the sidelines and watch. He put the patient at risk of injury and also led to one of our nurses sustaining a significant head injury."

I could tell he wasn't prepared for my take on things. Dr. Tom Abbott is a good guy, but he's mainly an administrator now. He doesn't do much bedside care anymore and certainly not on patients with excited delirium.

"Alex, as you know, we have a policy of allowing anonymous reporting of concerns, and—"

Nope, not going there. I'm in charge of this conversation. Trevor has helped me gain the confidence to take the lead. Time to interrupt. "And I appreciate that. I'd hate for my complaint to come back and make it awkward when he brings patients to our department, so thanks for keeping my name out of it. Plus, I don't think his local firehouse would appreciate knowing he let members of a medical team flounder in a dangerous situation without stepping up to help. It's best we keep this close to the vest."

His silence was exactly what I wanted to hear. This time, I didn't ease the tension by breaking the awkward pause. He blinked first.

"Tell you what, I'll talk to them about your concerns and get back to you."

"Sounds great, thanks. I'm available pretty much any time I'm not on shift, except June 3rd. Let me know if you need my help to follow up on any of these issues."

We agreed to talk again soon and ended the call amicably. With that out of the way, it was time to exclude some emergent causes of nasal congestion and diarrhea.

Chapter 43

Procedure Day

My alarm went off at 4:30 a.m., so I smacked my wrist to shut it off and then checked my time. Nine-minute mile. Not bad. One more mile to go, and it's time to speed up the pace. This procedure is going to go well and Kendra is going to run again. She's got the runner's build, whereas I'm built like a linebacker. If I'm going to keep up, I need to push.

I made it back to my condo eight minutes and thirty seconds later. Nausea crept up and my mouth watered in preparation for the stomach contents that were on their way up, but they never arrived. Thanks to Trevor, I enjoyed that run with no hallucinations and didn't even run into any neighbors. Maybe I should stay up all night worrying and run at four o'clock more often.

I put a bagel in the toaster oven and set the timer for four minutes. I was nearly back to the kitchen when I heard the timer ding. Rats. I thought I could shower and get back before it finished.

The bagel went down quickly as I got dressed and headed for my car.

> *Me: Just leaving, did you sleep much last night?*
> *Kendra: Not much. I want coffee but I'm not allowed to have anything.*
> *Me: Don't worry, I brought enough for both of us. You can have yours after the procedure. See you soon.*

The short drive to Kendra's was uneventful, other than still sweating from the run. I had the air conditioner on full blast and leaned forward to keep the back of my shirt dry. Maybe I should have spent a few more minutes in the cold shower.

Kendra's mother wanted to be at the hospital for the procedure, and it was up to Kendra and me to get her there. I was looking forward to spending some time with her mother and see if I could learn some stories of what she was like as a child.

I knocked on Kendra's apartment door at 5:20 a.m. Ten minutes early, but that's much better than ten minutes late. She opened the door almost immediately, much quicker than I expected.

"Hey, good morning. I'm getting our bags ready to go." She kissed me on the cheek and pointed to a stack of bags next to the door. I waited for Lucy to come at me like a missile, but she never did. Kendra must have gotten a sitter for her.

"This is an outpatient procedure, right?" I asked.

"Yes, but I'm not sure how long it will take, or if it will even get started on time. I packed an overnight bag for myself and some supplies for my mother."

"I can take care of myself!" shouted Kendra's mother from the kitchen.

"Good morning, Mary," I said, stepping around Kendra and addressing her mother in the kitchen. "Looks like we'll be spending some time together this morning while we wait."

"That's right. I've been looking forward to it. I bought a brand-new book of crossword puzzles that we do in case we run out of things to talk about."

"Mom, just promise me you'll try to use a filter." Kendra turned toward me and continued. "Ever since the stroke, she has lost a lot of her inhibitions. She just says whatever comes to mind. Sometimes it's pretty funny, other times it can be embarrassing."

"And sometimes I just do what I want and blame the stroke," said Mary with a wink.

Kendra pushed her mother's wheelchair into the kitchen and began transferring her into it.

"Here, let me help you," I said, taking a step toward the chair.

Kendra brushed my arm away and rotated her body in front of me like she was boxing me out for a rebound. "Why? Are you trying to learn how to do it in case this procedure gives me a stroke?" She didn't even look at me when she spoke.

Woah, where did that come from? "Hey, I was just trying to help. This procedure is going to go fine. Your brother wouldn't work with people who aren't capable."

"Kendra, apologize to him this instant. You're just nervous. Don't take it out on poor Alex."

"Whatever, sorry. You guys can manage. I'll be in the car." She turned and strode toward the front door, where she picked up the two bags and continued toward the car. She left the front door wide open.

I stayed facing the door and spoke loud enough for my voice to carry out to the car. "Poor Kendra. I can't imagine what she's going through right now. She needs a nice vacation after this is over."

"Yes, she does," said Mary in a low voice. "The last few days have been... tough. She's not sleeping well and not really eating. I see her looking in the mirror a lot. I think she's afraid of ending up like me."

And there it is. There's a low risk of complications, but it's not a zero risk. She's facing the risk of a massive hemorrhagic stroke if she does nothing and a smaller risk if she has the procedure. Either way, she's walking toward a potentially unfavorable outcome.

"It's hard to say I'd do anything for Kendra when there's so much I can't even do for myself," said Mary.

"You're showing her how to keep on living, no matter what life throws your way. I don't hear you complaining about your disabilities. You just roll with them and enjoy life, regardless."

"Did you just make a wheelchair joke?"

Did I? What did I say? I played back my words until I figured it out. Roll with it. Oh, man. "I'm sorry, that's not what I meant."

Mary laughed and swatted my arm. "Relax, will you? It's fine. Most people are afraid to interact with me. It's like they think they'll catch a disability or something. Just treat me like you would anyone else."

These Vaughn women are tough. "That, I can do. Let's get out to the car."

I held the wheelchair stable as Mary scooted sideways off the kitchen chair. We reversed the process to get her into the car and then I folded her chair and loaded it into the cargo area of my car.

The sun was just brightening the sky when we pulled out of her apartment complex and headed toward the medical facility. No one had spoken since we started the trip and the silence was becoming awkward.

"So, Alex," said Mary from the back seat. "Kendra tells me your penis works again. Once her AVM is fixed, are you going to help get me some grandbabies?"

"Mom!" yelled Kendra as she spun around to admonish her mother with her words and an icy glare. The nasty look didn't have any effect on Mary, who was laughing as hard as she could.

"What? Should I have used my filter on that one? I couldn't take how quiet it was in here. I know you're nervous, honey, but I am so optimistic and happy for you. Let's choose to be happy. You are about to walk through the door of a room you've been trapped inside for years. Trust me, you need to enjoy life while you can. You never know when something's going to happen."

I tried to shrink down into my seat and concentrate on the road. Maybe if I stayed still and didn't breathe, no one would notice me. I could reach for the seat controls and probably lower my seat another inch or two.

Kendra sighed and her whole body relaxed in one motion. "You're right. Sorry guys, I've been so nervous about this for the last few days. Alex, sorry about sharing the intimate details. Clearly I need to confide in my friends who actually have a filter." She said the words with a smile and a rub of her mother's knee.

It was time for me to break my silence. "But aren't most of your friends people who work at the hospital? I have enough nicknames around that place. I don't need any more."

"That could be fun, though. I'll have to think of a new one for you."

"Ooh, is this where we take an adverb and turn it into a nickname?" asked Mary.

"Mary, you too?" I asked. "You're supposed to be on my side."

Chapter 44

We arrived at the building at six o'clock, right as someone was unlocking the patient entrance door. I pulled into the drop-off area and Kendra helped me get her mother into her wheelchair. She pushed Mary inside while I parked the car. I resisted the urge to park in the spaces labeled 'physician parking' and took a spot in the regular parking area.

A small excavator blocked the sidewalk on one side of the door. Orange construction fencing separated the area being worked on. A large section of grass was missing around the backhoe and a pile of dirt sat on four by eight sheets of plywood covering more of the grass next to it.

By the time I got inside, her brother Patrick was there, talking to Kendra and her mother. "Good morning, Alex. Thanks for bringing them today." We shook hands, and then he turned back to Kendra.

"You look great today. I'm so glad you've decided to get this fixed. Dr. Kumar is in back, said he got a great night's sleep and he's very hopeful about your procedure. If all goes well, he should be done by about 9:30 a.m."

"Mom, you hang here with Alex, and I'll take Kendra back to the preoperative holding area. You can get changed, and then the nurses will get you prepped for the procedure. He'll probably use the femoral artery for access, but we'll also prep your wrist just in case."

I stepped forward and wrapped Kendra in a tight hug. "I'm yours and will be here no matter what. I'll be praying for you."

She kissed me on the lips and then leaned back in my arms. "You'll still be with me even when I'm leaving you in the dust on runs?"

"I can't wait. Good luck." She turned out of my grasp but held my hand until we were fully stretched apart. Her fingers extended to maintain contact as long as possible, mimicking Michelangelo's "The Creation of Adam".

"Let's go stake our claim," said Mary. "This place is going to be crawling with family members soon, and I want the best seat in the house." I stepped behind her chair and pushed her in the direction she pointed.

We settled in at a round table and prepared for a few hours of anxious waiting. The deep grumble of a diesel engine drew my attention as the once-idle backhoe began digging in the trench.

***

By nine o'clock, my anxiety was spiking. I knew this was likely around the critical time of the procedure. Surely by now they had accessed the vessel feeding the AVM and had mapped out the approach. Dr. Kumar may have already deployed a coil or two.

Mary was deep into a crossword puzzle. "Alex, what's an eleven-letter word that most people pronounce incorrectly?"

An eleven-letter word? I have no idea. This is the oddest question yet. "Sorry, no idea."

"Incorrectly. Come on, that wasn't even a hard one. If you're going to be giving me grandbabies, you need to work on your dad jokes."

"Clearly," I said, shaking my head, but smiling.

"There it is. Today's nickname. Clear Lee."

I opened my mouth to reply but jumped in my chair instead and twisted to the right. A loud explosion came from a metal panel on the wall, along with a puff of smoke. Instantly the lights in the building turned off and all background noise stopped, except for the nervous chatter of people in the waiting room. A few seconds later, several lights turned back on and the construction worker from the excavator ran into the front of the building through a door he manually pulled open.

"I think I hit a power line with my bucket. Did anyone notice anything?"

"Just a big explosion, puff of smoke, and then blackness," I said, standing up. "You may have killed power to the entire building."

"Looks like the backup generator is working. I'll get our engineering team out here to take a look," he said.

Kendra's in the middle of her procedure, and this guy kills power! Was all the equipment plugged in to the proper outlets for generator power? Did the anesthesia machine or imaging equipment cycle power? I'd seen ventilators shut down suddenly because they were not plugged into the red generator-supplied outlets. The door they took Kendra through was close. I could probably find her operating room in thirty seconds.

As the minutes ticked by, my apprehension grew. I worked through the relaxation techniques Trevor taught me for recovery between EMDR sessions but couldn't stop pacing and staring at the door. I'm an ER doctor. We get activated when there's concern for something serious. And we're right smack in the middle of serious at this very moment.

"Alex, it's okay. Relax," said Mary. "They have backup power. Everything will be fine."

Will it be? The registration staff did not seem concerned as they gathered together and shared some nervous excitement. Their computers were not on backup power, which meant there was nothing to do but gossip. No one ran through the hallways and no code blue alarms sounded overhead.

Maybe it will be fine. Before I could worry myself into action, the door opened and Kendra's brother walked toward us.

"Sorry about that. We've never lost power before, but fortunately the backup system came online quickly." He took a breath and spread his hands out quickly before continuing. "Anyway, I have good news. Her procedure went well, and she's in the recovery room already. She had just arrived there when the power cycled. I'd have come out sooner, but I had to help check on all the active cases."

"Thank you, Patrick. Is she awake? Can we see her?" asked Mary.

"She's still waking up from the anesthesia. We'll get you back soon, but not yet."

Now I really wanted to rush back there. I'd rather break down crying happy tears in a private room than in front of all these strangers out here. At least the power is out, and it's darker than usual.

"That's fantastic news," I said. "Your partner was able to stop all the blood flow through the AVM?"

Patrick smiled as he pulled out his phone. "Yes. Do you want to see the video?"

I walked next to Mary as Patrick flipped his phone around to show us two video clips. The first was a black and white view of her brain with a catheter sitting in a blood vessel. Suddenly, the vessel turned black as the surgeon injected dye. Then it spread out into a blur as the AVM distributed the dye through the mess of blood vessels.

"That was before the embolization. Now look at this one."

The next video was similar, but a few black wires rested in front of the catheter. Another puff of dye filled the feeder vessel but was distributed away through other vessels and none of it went into the AVM. Total success!

"That's incredible. So, is this considered a cure?" I asked.

"As close to one as is possible. When she's fully awake, I'll do a complete neurological exam on her to ensure she did not have a stroke during the procedure, but I don't expect to find anything. I think she can look forward to a life without concern for a spontaneous brain hemorrhage."

That's when I lost it. I was already nervous during the procedure, then I became panicked when the power failed. Now I just learned she's likely free of this sword of Damocles and couldn't hold back the emotion any longer. Tears poured out of my eyes, but Mary covered the sound of my sobs with the volume of her own.

We'd been hoping and praying for this result for weeks and now it's here. "Patrick, thank you so much. I don't even know what to say."

"You don't need to say anything. You're showing me all I need to know about who my sister is dating. And you're very welcome." He shook my hand before leaning down and hugging his mom.

As happy as I was for Kendra, I felt guilty about crying over it. I rarely cried when a patient died, but it happened from time to time if it was a child or a difficult social situation. But here I am, crying for someone living. Such is the emotional roller coaster of emergency medicine.

Chapter 45

Patrick led us back to see Kendra, and we found her in a small recovery room, sitting up and sipping water through a flexible straw. She held the cup in her left hand and waved at us with her right when we came into view. She smiled around the straw, and another wave of emotion crashed into me.

She just used both arms and flashed us a symmetric smile when she recognized us with her vision. No sign of a massive hemispheric stroke.

"Hey, guys. I heard it went well," she said with a normal inflection in her voice. Fluent speech. Another great sign of intact neurologic function.

"We heard that too. So happy for you," I said as I pushed her mom up next to her bed. "How do you feel?"

"Sleepy, but overall good. Except I can't move my left leg."

My joy instantly turned to panic. What? Why not? This was a right sided AVM, if treatment caused a stroke it would cause left sided weakness!

"That's right, Dr. Kumar is left-handed, so he put the access sheath in her left femoral artery. She needs to lie flat for a few more hours to reduce the risk of bleeding from the access site."

I sighed loudly and shook my head. "Oh my gosh, I thought you meant you physically couldn't do it because something happened during the procedure."

"Sorry, I wanted to show you I still had my sense of humor. Patrick told me not to do that to you, but I couldn't resist." Her face was relaxed from the remnants of anesthesia combined with the resolution of anxiety about her procedure. Now she just looked calm and happy. And ornery.

"I'm going to have to get you back for that, you know," I said. "But I'll let you recover for a few weeks first."

"So everything went well? She's... fixed?" asked Mary with a weak and faltering voice.

"Mom, I wasn't broken."

Patrick leaned over and rubbed his mother's leg. "Yes, Mom. She's going to be just fine."

"So, she's not going to end up like me?" It was Mary's turn to be overcome by emotion as her biggest fear crumbled away. Patrick consoled her as I stood aside and watched this beautiful family interact. Why couldn't mine be like this? Supportive. Speaking freely to each other.

After a few minutes, her mother could speak again. "When can she go home?"

"Assuming the access site looks good, she should be able to leave by around four o'clock. No lifting anything heavy for a few days."

"Not even Lucy?" asked Kendra.

"Nope. She's too heavy, and I'd be careful about dog claws on your lap with the recent arterial access. Dr. Kumar will be in to talk with you all after he finishes his next case." Patrick sat down in a chair and leaned back, settling in to wait on his partner.

"Don't you have to get ready for a case or office patients?" asked Kendra.

"Are you kidding me? I cleared my calendar once you scheduled your procedure. I've got nothing but time for you, sis."

That's it. I need to call my dad. It's been too long. I want this type of relationship with my family again. At least what's left of it. Once Kendra has recovered and is back at work, I'm going to ask her to help me make that happen.

I'll start with a phone call to him, then plan a visit back home. My mom deserves to be as happy as Mary is right now. It's beyond time to swallow my pride and just go see him.

"Patrick, when can I go on my first run?"

"Let's hear what Kumar says, but I'm guessing about ten days."

Ten days? That's not nearly enough time. I've been running longer distances and at a quicker pace, but I'm not ready to go up against her yet.

"Can you make it a month? I'm not quite in shape enough yet. I need more time before she's allowed to race me."

"Better watch out, Alex. She used to run me down when we were playing. I could run a basketball court, but she'd blow past me on any kind of distance run."

"I don't mind if she beats me. I can't wait to watch her do all the things she's been avoiding for half her life." But I'm not just going to watch. I'm going to help her do all of them. There's one thing in particular I'm hoping to help her with, but I can't say that in front of her mom and brother.

A soft knock on the door drew our attention toward the entrance to her room. The neurointerventional radiologist poked his head around the curtain and then entered when he saw she was awake.

"How is she doing?"

"I feel good," said Kendra. "My brother said that things went well?"

"Yes, they did. The coils did their thing, and then I reinforced the area with a bit of cyanoacrylate glue.

Between the two, I was able to completely isolate the AVM from its arterial feeder vessel."

"Can you explain that differently for us non-medical people?" asked Mary.

"Sure, sorry. I put a platinum wire in the artery, and it reduced the blood flow significantly. Like shoving a stick in a drain. Some blood was still getting through, so I used a medical grade superglue to fill in the gaps. The result is no blood flow into the AVM and essentially a normal blood cerebral anatomy."

"I showed them the video. You did great work, my friend." Patrick smiled at his colleague.

"Thank you. It's amazing what we can do with a needle and modern techniques. Not everything requires a scalpel and bone drill. So much better for these types of situations."

"Hey, I do my best work with a scalpel and bone drill," said Patrick, grinning.

Dr. Kumar gave a quick summary of the recovery process and confirmed that she can start running in about ten days. The wound should heal sooner than that, but best to not increase pressure on the vessels until more time passed.

Kendra spoke up and asked we all wanted answered. "Does that mean I can stop worrying about it rupturing and go live my life?" There it was. The whole reason she went through this procedure and faced an immediate risk of stroke and disability.

"Yes, absolutely. You should have about the same risk of spontaneous hemorrhage as anyone else walking around. If you continue living a healthy lifestyle and watch your blood pressure, you should have no restrictions on what you do in life."

Kendra already looked relaxed from the anesthesia, still metabolizing its way out of her system, but somehow she relaxed even further. "That's great. It seems inadequate to say, but thank you."

"Dr. Kumar, they're ready for you in room three," said a voice from the hallway.

"You're very welcome. I'll make sure to stop in and say hello at your follow-up appointment with Patrick. My next case is ready to go. Do you have questions for me?"

Kendra shook her head at which point Dr. Kumar waved and left the room.

"Busy guy," I said.

"Yeah, he's been a great addition to our group. We have enough work for him to do twice as many cases, but he refuses to work sixteen hours a day."

"I don't blame him. I don't enjoy working sixteen hours in two days," I said.

"I usually work three twelves in a row," said Kendra.

"To be fair, they're not quite in a row. I work a thirty-six-hour shift every time I'm on call," said Patrick, tweaking his sister a bit.

"Why does medicine try to destroy the people who work in it?" asked Mary. "Who will be there to take care of the sick when everyone has burned out and quit the profession?"

Great question. It's one I haven't yet come up with an answer to. A glance at my watch confirmed we had another five hours of small talk until Kendra could leave. Time to switch the conversation to something more relaxing.

"Does Lucy know her walks are about to get a lot faster?"

Kendra grinned and snuggled herself into her pillow. "I haven't told her yet. I hope her little legs can keep up. It's nap time for me. See you guys soon."

My stomach reminded me that breakfast was a long time ago, and I excused myself to grab some food. I needed to keep my strength up to sit in this chair a few more hours.

Chapter 46

The next ten days went by quickly. Kendra had removed herself from the schedule while she recovered from the procedure, so we had ample time for walks and hanging out together.

Today was post-op day ten. The day they cleared her to run again. I met her and Lucy at the same park we used for our first date. But this time we were going to run around the entire thing.

Lucy tried to run to me but stopped short before the leash pulled on her collar. She was learning. I hoped she didn't have the endurance to run hard the whole time. I wouldn't mind a break once in a while on this run. For Kendra, of course. I wanted her to ease into it. And maybe not make me look too bad.

"Are you ready?" I asked.

"I think so. I've been thinking about this day for a long time. Guess who went shopping yesterday," she said, spinning around slowly to show off her calf-length leggings and new shoes. A hair band covered in donuts pulled her hair back tight.

"Very nice. And the outfit is great, too."

She laughed and smacked my arm playfully. "Okay, let's go." Kendra set out at an easy jog, her steps light and silent as I plodded along next to her. Lucy was in front, pulling on her leash as we ran along the asphalt path around the perimeter of the park.

"Tomorrow is my first shift back," she said. "I hope it goes well."

"It'll go fine. You should be nice and relaxed after this mini vacation."

"Vacation? Is that what you call it when someone shoves a catheter in your groin and fills your brain with metal and glue?"

"Any time I don't work a few days in a row, I consider it a vacation. There have been a few shifts where I'd consider undergoing that procedure to get a few days off afterward."

Kendra laughed at my attempted humor. "Well, you work tomorrow, so vacation is over. May as well speed up." She leaned forward and pulled away from my side. Lucy's leash dragged on the ground for a few moments until she noticed the lack of resistance, causing her to speed up as well.

I lengthened my stride and caught up to her ten seconds later. We were doing at least an eight-minute mile. I had maybe ten minutes left at this speed. Talking is going to be hard. Better get it over with now. "I think it's time to call my dad and get back home to see him. Watching your family come together around your procedure has really made me want to reconcile with mine."

"That's great, Alex. I'll go with you. We can bring Lucy along, too. Dogs are great icebreakers. If it gets weird, we'll just focus on the dog for a minute."

"That would be awesome, thanks. Let's get you back to work first and then I'll set it up. My mom will be thrilled. She always wanted me to date, but it never worked out."

"Have you told her about us?"

"Yes, but it's been about six months."

"Well, she's going to be thrilled to hear from you. You met my mom. It's only fair I get to meet yours."

Lucy was no longer tugging on the leash and had dropped back to run next to Kendra. Come on, Lucy, throw in the towel. Please.

"Yep," I said, gasping a bit after speaking the single word.

"What's the matter, Alex? Getting winded?"

"No," I sputtered.

We'd covered about a mile and a half, but much faster than I was used to. How is she in this good of shape her first day out?

Suddenly, she jerked to a stop with her right arm pulled behind her. I stopped and turned around to check on her and saw Lucy sitting down on the path. "Come on, girl.

Let's go," said Kendra, tugging lightly on the leash. Lucy responded by laying down. She was done. Good girl.

"Rats, looks like we'll have to take a break," I said, leaning over and resting my hands on my knees. "How are you able to run this fast your first day back? Have you been secretly training?"

"What do you mean? This is a slow jog. Give me about a month and I'll actually be running."

I walked over to Lucy and disconnected her leash. I picked her up, and she thanked me with a bunch of quick licks to my face.

"She likes to be carried," said Kendra.

"I see that. I think she also likes the taste of sweat. Maybe you need to get her a salt lick." We started walking along the path back toward the car at a much more enjoyable pace. After a minute, I put Lucy down and she was kind enough to walk along beside us.

"What are you making me for dinner tonight? I need something good before my first shift back," asked Kendra.

"I was thinking steaks on the grill."

"Perfect. I'll need a small leftover box for Lucy."

"No, you won't. Just bring her over." And maybe just move the rest of your stuff to my place while you're at it.

Chapter 47

Today's is Kendra's first day back at work and I can't wait to see her there. That's probably why I woke up so early, even before my alarm went off. That gave me enough time to get a quick run in and shower before heading to the hospital.

I made it to the physician's work area a few minutes early and found the overhead lights off. Holly was slumped down in her chair, eyes closed and breathing evenly. "How long has she been asleep?" I asked Carla.

"About thirty minutes. I shut the light out to see if she can get some better rest. I guess they had a busy night."

Good. I love hearing how busy the department was when I'm not there. Revenue is great, especially when I'm not the one generating it.

"Doc, who are the flowers for?" asked Carla.

"Oh, these? Today is Kendra's first day back after her procedure. I figured she might like some flowers."

"Pretty sure any woman would. Those are beautiful."

They really were. I am fantastic with flowers. I ask the florist to choose what they think would look best, and it usually works out perfectly.

"That's very sweet of you. We all pitched in and bought pizza for lunch, so don't go get your grilled cheese today."

Oh, I'm still going to get my grilled cheese. Now that I'm running more, I'm able to eat more. In fact, I'm already hungry again. The cafeteria has the best grilled cheese. Texas toast style bread that they rub with melted butter and slow cook on a flat top. A squirt of ketchup completes the presentation.

I set the flowers down on top of the counter by the nurses' workstation. She can't miss them. And neither can all the other nurses. I can hear it now. Romantic Lee.

"Well, those are pretty. What's the special occasion?" I recognized the voice and the vanilla smell. And the fingers rubbing across my back.

"They're for you in honor of coming back to work," I said, holding back my desire to kiss her in front of everyone. "I'd kiss you, but I don't want this place to turn into Grey's Anatomy."

"You don't think it already is? Have you ever been in the supply closet?"

"All the time, just not with anyone else. Why, have you?" I asked, picking up the flowers and pulling them away from her.

"No, I'm joking. And give me back the flowers." She reached across to pull them back onto the counter and then leaned over them, inhaling deeply. "They smell amazing."

"I told the florist I wanted the flowers to remind me of you."

Kendra rolled her eyes at me but smiled as she walked toward the nursing pre-shift huddle. I checked on Holly, who was now awake and logging out of her computer. "I have nothing to leave you. Though I spoke with Tom Abbott about you yesterday."

Ah, the Chief Medical Officer of the hospital. "What did he have to say? Still wanting to meet with me about the complaint?"

"No. He said you made a very compelling argument on your phone call and he handled the complaint personally. It helped that Kendra got kicked in the head and the staff reported her injury to the hospital."

Excuse me? It helped that the patient assaulted my girlfriend? "I'm sorry, what?"

"Maybe that came out wrong. It wasn't a good thing she got assaulted, but security attested to the fact we were short staffed that day. It's one thing to talk to them about what could happen, but when they're faced with actual consequences, it's harder to ignore."

"Yeah, I guess so. They like to preach about preventative medicine but refuse to do anything to prevent the problems we all see coming."

"Funny how when it's their money on the line, their recommendations change, eh?"

"Yep. Now go home and get some sleep. We can try to fix the system when you wake up."

Holly sighed as she stood up. "Fine. Empty board. Just the way you like it. Remember who your favorite partner is."

"I never forget that. But don't tell Nick. He'll get his feelings hurt."

"Hah. Whatever feelings that guy had are buried under tens of thousands of patient encounters. He seems immune to anything now. Makes me jealous."

Not me. I still want to feel the world and its emotions when I retire. I offered a weak nod and took over the workstation. My inbox of incomplete charts was calling my name. Now is the perfect time to catch up before the patients woke up and realized how much pain they were in.

"Hey, we need help out front! Bring a stretcher!" The shout came from the triage nurse who had leaned inside the door before running out the front entrance.

Most of the team ran toward the entrance, while Kendra went for the code bed. The department keeps a stretcher with a backboard and resuscitation bag ready at all times to respond to codes or sick people in the front entrance, or anywhere else in the hospital.

I grabbed a pair of gloves and followed Kendra through the double doors. It's usually a drug overdose. Downtown, it might be a stabbing or gunshot wound, but this is a community hospital. Maybe someone delivered a baby in the car on the way to the hospital.

The scene in the circle drive was chaotic, but quiet. Everyone knew what needed to be done first and then prioritized the tasks from there. The ER staff has been around the block a few times. Several nurses were leaning into a car and supporting someone in the front passenger seat. Kendra pushed the bed as close as she could, but the patient was going to have to be lifted to get on the cot.

I pulled my gloves on and threaded my way to the passenger door. I touched a nurse on the shoulder and switched places with her, supporting the patient's shoulder with my hip.

"Hi, Alex." The voice came from inside the car and took me by surprise. Why does the driver know my name? And the voice was familiar. I turned and looked directly at a woman I hadn't seen in years.

"Mom?" My heart sank along with my gaze until I was looking at someone who resembled my dad. But much older, and much less alive than I remembered him. He was still breathing, but unresponsive.

"Okay, I'm just going to lift him out of the car. After I lift him up, help me spin and lay him on the cot." I reached my left hand under my dad's left armpit and pulled him toward me before lifting him up onto his feet. Several nurses grabbed his legs and helped me twist him around and lay him on the bed. Kendra unlocked the bed and pushed it toward the ER entrance. I don't think she heard who this was.

"Alex, I'll park the car and be right in," said my mother. "Oh, and you may want to get new scrubs. Sorry." She pointed at my pants, now covered with a smear of stool. Lovely. I looked back up and realized a plastic tarp covered her passenger seat. It was also soiled.

"Want me to throw the tarp out?"

"Yes, please. I'll be right in."

I pulled the tarp from her car and folded it several times before stuffing it into a garbage can by the entrance. My pants would have to wait until I was in the staff locker room. My record for the fastest shower and change is three minutes. Today I wanted it to take three hours. Anything to delay facing my parents.

Chapter 48

I stood in the hallway, staring into the room I liked least, looking at the patient I least wanted to see. If someone had asked me yesterday what patient I would least like to see, I would have said female conjoined twins. One of them pregnant with twins, the other seizing from eclampsia. Four patients at the same time.

Yet here I am, face to face with a man I thought I'd never see again. Though I'd been wanting to call and reconnect lately, I hadn't actually made the phone call. We had not yet reconciled. My hatred of him had lessened through my sessions with Trevor, but I wasn't ready to face him yet. Awake and talking, sure. But like this? Where I'm forced to feel bad for him? Not yet. I didn't want to take care of him today, but my oath demanded it. My conscience demanded it. My soul hated it.

My mother sat quietly in a chair next to the bed. She'd aged thirty years in the last seventeen, and my father even more.

"Hey, Mom."

Kendra looked up from her efforts to start an IV. The shocked look on her face was apparent even through the surgical mask on her face. To her credit, the look rose and fell from her face as fast as a wave crashing onto a rocky shore. There were remnants, such as a faintly raised eyebrow, but her jaw had closed and the lids were back to their normal position.

"Hello Alex. I'm sorry I haven't called in a while. Your father's been so sick. He's all I've had time to deal with."

Okay Mom, sure. I know Dad's probably been ill for some time, but I'm a freaking ER doctor. You don't think you could have combined his care with a phone call to me at some point in the last few months? His chest still showed rectangular patterns of old adhesive from recent hospital visits. Someone has obviously evaluated recently him in a hospital, so why again today? Why here? Why no call to let me know he was coming?

"What's going on with Dad? He looks awful. Is he still drinking?"

My mom shook her head slowly. "No, he has not had any alcohol in a few weeks. He's been too sick." She looked sad that he was too ill to drink. "His doctor said there's nothing else to be done. He's not eligible for a transplant and they said his kidneys are shutting down."

Hepatorenal syndrome. The death spiral of end-stage liver failure. When the liver hardens from cirrhosis, the pressure in the venous system builds to the point it also destroys the kidneys and there is no turning back. Death follows quickly.

Dad's body looked terrible. His abdomen stuck out like a pregnant woman a few weeks past her due date. Large blue veins wiggled their way down from his chest, ending somewhere inside his sweatpants. His swollen legs stretched the elastic of his pants, actually more than possible because Mom had cut a slice in each leg opening.

His skin was a sickly yellow and loose in places it should be tight. His once muscular arms were now fragile, emaciated remnants of their former glory. The humerus was clearly visible under his biceps, but the back of his arm looked like melted cheese. Just a blob of loose skin distended a bit by edema. Diffuse bruising covered the backs of his hands and arms.

His eyes were closed, which was fine by me. I didn't want him to look at me. His brain was probably poisoned by toxic ammonia, the byproduct of protein metabolism that his failing liver was incapable of clearing from his body. I could give him medication by an enema that might allow him to wake up, but then I'd have to talk to him.

What I mean is that if he were awake and able to interact, he'd be more miserable. Not that I don't want to talk to my father. He is going to die soon. The least I can do is to allow that to happen without more pain. Either from having to see his son who killed his first-born or from the discomfort of his medical condition.

Kendra finished with the IV and placed labels on the tubes of blood she had drawn. "I'm going to send this to the lab. Let me know if you need any medications, Dr. Lee."

I nodded at her voice but didn't take my eyes off my dad. It was like the scene in *The Last Crusade* where the Nazi aged quickly before everyone's eyes. My last memory was of my younger father and now he's old and dying.

"Mom, what do you want me to do for him? It sounds like he's beyond any hope of improvement at this point. What he needs is hospice."

"I know that. They've been wonderful with helping at home. He has a hospital bed in the family room, which is where I take care of him. The last few days, all he's said is that he wanted to see you. He..." her eyes bounced to the floor before continuing. "He said there's something he needed to tell you."

"Well, it seems like he waited too long, because I'm not sure he's going to wake up again. Do you want me to admit him to the hospital or try to get him home to die there?"

I wasn't trying to upset her; I was just trying to give her a clear understanding of where he was at medically. That didn't stop her from crying, though.

I pulled another chair close and sat next to her. I put my hand on her arm and slumped backward in the chair. "I'm sorry about everything. For what happened to Luke, for what happened after that, and for the last seventeen years. When Luke died, it basically ended your life and Dad's. It cost me my brother and my parents."

"No, you never lost me. I'm still your mother. I called; I wrote letters. But your father needed me."

Mom, I needed you too. I needed you differently than this drunk did. But she had enough on her plate. She didn't need to hear those words. "I understand."

"He wasn't always drunk, you know. He tried so hard to quit. He went to groups at church, went to see counselors, he even tried injections of something. But nothing worked. Even when we threw out all the alcohol in the house, he still found a way to drink. He must have stashed alcohol around the house. Once your brother died, the sober days were few and far between."

Yeah, I know. That's why he lost his job and the property probably looks like some abandoned haunted house.

"When you left for college, it ramped up and didn't stop." She pointed at him lying in bed. "Now look at him. At least Luke's death was fast and we could grieve the accident. This has been slow torture for me."

My mother used to be a head turner. She was the kind of mom your friends would make jokes about wanting to date, among other things. She could have had any man she wanted, and she chose him. I gave her credit for her loyalty. Most men would have run their wives off, but my mom honored her oath. For better or worse, in sickness and health, till death do they part. Looks like she's about to be free from her oath.

But he wasn't always an alcoholic. He actually used to be a pretty good father.

Chapter 49

Twenty-five Years Ago

"Come on, Alex. Can you please carry something?" asked Luke.

"I have the targets and cones," I said. "Dad doesn't want me carrying the gun or the ammo."

"But those are paper and plastic. Just carry a box of ammunition. My hands are getting tired."

"Okay, but don't tell Dad. He said he'll be out soon." I took a box of .22lr ammunition from Luke and held it while we walked. The rounds rattled a bit in their cardboard box, like they were excited to come out and play. They knew the routine. Every Sunday after church we'd go shoot targets while Mom made brunch. Just Luke, my dad, and me.

At first it was just Dad and Luke. I had to stay inside and help my mom make biscuits and gravy, or pancakes and bacon, or whatever she made that day. I wanted to be shooting a gun, not opening cans of biscuits. It was a completely different sort of bang. Then one day Dad invited me to come with them. It was completely out of the blue. I was still a year younger than Luke was when he started shooting. He only let me shoot once that day, but I was hooked.

Today, I was going to beat Luke. We nailed the targets onto old railroad ties Dad had stacked into a pile as a backstop. Two for me and two for Luke. Then we marched off twenty paces, and I set a cone down. I handed the last cone to Luke, and he walked five more paces before putting his cone down.

A wooden slap from behind us signaled Dad was on his way. He tossed something into his mouth and was still chewing when he was next to us. "You boys forgot your ear protection. Here, take these," he said, holding out two sets of earmuffs. When he spoke, I smelled bacon. Great, that's going to make it harder to concentrate. Mom's making bacon. I don't need that distraction today.

"Who's going first?"

"Dad, I'll go," said Luke. He unscrewed the end of the tube magazine and fed ten rounds into the rifle, then resealed it and brought it up to his shoulder. He took a moment to aim and then fired one shot after another into his practice target. All the rounds struck the paper and most were inside the five-point ring. Dang it. He's shooting well today.

"Not bad Luke, that's a pretty good warm up target. Alex, your turn."

I took the rifle from my brother, who was proudly smiling, his grin more of a prideful sneer. As if beating your younger brother in something you'd been doing for longer was an accomplishment. Luke was a better natural shooter than I was. But I worked harder at it. I was out here every time Dad was willing to take me out. And today Luke's going to see what hard work can do. I loaded the rifle and lined up the target in my sights.

"Hey, aren't you going up to your cone? You always shoot from the kiddie line," said Luke.

"Not today," I said as I pulled the trigger on my first shot. An eight. I followed that shot with nine more. When I had finished, there were only eight holes on my target, but all of them were inside the six-point ring or better.

"Pretty good Alex. You jerked the trigger on two of those shots. Remember to allow the trigger to reset before pulling again. Then don't jerk it when you fire."

My dad took the rifle from me and handed it back to Luke. "Well, let the game begin. Good luck to you both."

Luke reloaded and then lined up at the second target. He took his time between shots. This time as his pride was at stake. His dominance threatened. When he fired the last round, he engaged the safety and handed the rifle to my dad. We ran to the target and counted the points.

"Seventy-two!" Luke said, pumping his right fist. He was right to be proud. It was the best he had ever gotten. Crap.

I walked back to the cone, dejected. How am I supposed to beat him when he's on top of his game? My dad was rooting for me. Everyone likes an underdog. "Alex, take your time. You can do this. You just need to be confident and use what you've learned."

I lined up my target and began firing. I was counting the rounds in my head and stopped after nine shots. I handed the gun to my dad and walked toward the target, already counting my score.

"What did you get?" asked Luke.

"Hang on, I'm still counting." I waved my hand at him, trying to focus on the target. "Sixty-four," I said.

"Hah! I win again!" Luke pumped his fist again before sticking both arms up in the air. "Maybe someday, little brother, but not this day. Time for some victory bacon!"

"Hang on, I still have one more shot," I said. I was back by my father, who handed me the rifle.

"What? That's not fair!"

"What do you mean? You got ten shots, I get ten shots. What's unfair about that?"

"You tricked me into thinking I won already."

"No, I didn't. You just assumed I was done. Now be quiet. I have one more shot to take."

"Well, you need an eight to tie, and a nine for the win. Good luck."

I lined up my last shot, but I was too excited. My breathing was fast and the barrel of the rifle was bouncing up and down. There's no way I can hit a shot like this. I handed the gun back to my dad and sat down, facing ninety degrees away from the target.

"What, you're quitting?"

"Nope, going to take my last shot sitting down." I crossed my legs and held them off the ground, and then my dad handed me the rifle. I rested my arms on my thighs and now had a steady perch from which to fire. A gentle squeeze of the trigger sent my last bullet toward the target.

"No fair!" screamed Luke. "He can't shoot from the ground!"

"Says who? That was never in the rules." I jumped to my feet and ran to the target. When I was halfway there, I could see the new hole in the target, exactly where it needed to be. "Bullseye!"

"He cheated," complained Luke with a whine in his voice.

"No, he practiced and learned a better way to do it. Shooting from a seated position is more accurate than standing." My dad loaded the gun with ten more rounds and then quickly emptied the gun at both of our targets. My bullseye hole was now much bigger, and there was now a large hole in the center of Luke's target.

"Practice makes better. You don't have to start out naturally good at something to become excellent at it. Never stop trying to improve, boys. Now, let's get some breakfast."

Chapter 50

Dad's labs couldn't just report out through the computer system for me to review all at once. They were so abnormal that the lab tech had to call Kendra to report the critical values. His renal function, the creatinine, was over ten times normal, his hemoglobin half of what it should be. Both were significantly abnormal, but it was the potassium that was going to kill him. That was over eight. His heart showed many extra ventricular beats, some individual, some ran together in a series of abnormal beats called ventricular tachycardia. I watched the monitor, wondering when the series would continue instead of stopping after a few seconds.

"Mom, Dad's labs are terrible. I don't think he's going to make it another day. Do you want him to die here in the hospital or back at home?"

She sighed and looked down at her hands. "I just wanted him to be able to talk to you before that happened. If he's not aware of anything, does it really matter where he dies?"

"To him? Not really. But it does to you. When Luke died, everyone came over to the house and offered support immediately. If he dies here, there will be a delay before that happens. My shift ends in a few hours and I'm off for the next few days. I can come stay at the house if you'd like."

Mom nodded and accepted my offer. "That would be wonderful Alex. Thank you. We kept your room the way you left it."

And Luke's too, I bet. Stuck in the past, unable to move forward. No, that's not fair. I'm seeing a psychiatrist and therapist because I was stuck in my past, too. So was Kendra. Why is acceptance and moving on so hard?

"Let me call for an ambulance and we'll get him transported home. You should let the hospice team know so they can meet you there." I leaned down and hugged my mom. They say yawns are contagious even if you're not tired. It turns out tears are also, even if you're not all that sad. I silenced the cardiac monitor and then turned it off. No sense upsetting Mom with the frequent alarm tones. We all knew where this was going.

Kendra was waiting for me right outside the room. "I'm sorry, Alex. Can I do anything for you?"

"No, thanks for asking. I'm going to arrange an ambulance to get him back home." I started to walk away but paused and turned back toward her. "Actually, maybe you can do something. I'm going to spend the next few days at their house until he dies."

"That's nice of you. What do you need me to do?"

"Keep me company?" It was a statement, but my inflection showed a question. In case she missed that hint, my eyebrows were up so high they pulled my face into a slight smile.

"I'll have to get a shift covered, but it shouldn't be difficult. With Christmas coming up, there are plenty of people looking for extra hours."

"Perfect, thank you. Luke's room is right next to mine. You can sleep there." I winked as I passed by her shoulder on my way to the secretary's desk.

Carla informed me it will take about thirty minutes to get an ambulance here to get Dad back home. Apparently, the neighbors had helped Mom drag him into the car to come out here today. Had they come yesterday, he would have been able to talk to me. One freaking day. Why didn't I make the call sooner?

I made a mental note to thank the neighbors if I saw them at the funeral. It can't be easy to drag a mostly dead person into a car, especially one you'd known when he was healthy. It must have been like pallbearers at a funeral, except that he was still alive. Sort of.

I had time to see two more patients and begin their workups before I saw the transport crew show up for my dad. It was a disinterested crew, slowly pushing the stretcher as they meandered down the hallway. They did not know who they were about to transport or his relationship to the ER staff. They turned and entered the room before I could warn my mother.

Medics transport patients home from the hospital all the time. It's usually a straightforward procedure, but when I walked in, the medics were standing in the room looking confused.

"Doc, what gives? Did you know your patient was dead?"

What? He was fine thirty minutes ago. Well, not fine, but not dead. "No, I didn't. We turned the monitor off." I looked at my dad from the foot of the bed and could tell from there. He certainly was dead. His chest wasn't moving, his color was even worse, but that resting grimace of pain he wore had faded away. I didn't bother trying to stimulate him, listen for a pulse, or check respirations as I was supposed to. Obvious things are obvious.

I slowly eased myself down next to my mom, who was quietly sobbing.

She leaned against me and exhaled deeply. "He died about five minutes ago. I didn't want to bother anyone, so I just waited for someone to come in."

Yep, that's Mom. Not wanting to upset anyone. Just sit around and let life happen around her. Maybe with Dad dead she can start living again.

"I'm sorry, Mom. You've given your whole life to him. If you tell me which funeral home you want to use, I'll work on getting Dad out of here."

Kendra stepped into the room quickly, a shocked look on her face. "I just heard, I'm so sorry."

"Mom, I know it's a lot to take in right now, but this is Kendra. She's my girlfriend."

My mom looked up and flashed a brief smile, the movement of her facial muscles altering the flow of tears down her face. "Nice to meet you, dear." She turned to me and offered another brief smile. "Alex, she's beautiful."

"If it's okay with you, we'd like to come stay at the house for the next few days. You could use the company. We'll help you get through the funeral."

"That would be nice, thank you. But, the other guests…"

I knew where her conservative Midwestern mind was going. "It's fine Mom, she can sleep in Luke's room."

Chapter 51

The next afternoon, I picked up Kendra at her apartment and we headed toward my mother's home. To my childhood home. I'm embarrassed I only lived an hour away and hadn't been back in years. Kendra packed a full suitcase and a large purse.

"Expecting to stay longer than we planned?"

"What are you talking about? This is my weekend trip bag. Would you like to see what I'd bring for an entire week?"

Yes, I would. Let's skip this and go to the Caribbean. Maybe St. Barts. Or, on an ER doc salary, maybe St. Maarten would be better. Somewhere warm and sunny with private beaches. "Yes, very much. Maybe next trip?"

That earned me the smile I was after. Just because we're headed to my dad's funeral doesn't mean we have to be sad the whole time.

"Alex, it's been a while since you've been back home. Are you nervous? Are you afraid it will bring back terrible memories?"

I'd been wondering about this since my dad died. The memories never went away, so it can't bring them back. Trevor has helped me reprocess my feelings in a way that is healthier, and I think I'm ready to see the house and the barn again. "I think it will be fine. I'm in a different place now, thanks to Trevor. He actually suggested that I go back sometime soon as a test and a means to become more at peace with what happened. I had been putting it off because it meant dealing with my dad, but clearly that's not an issue anymore."

Once we got off the interstate, I took the scenic route to the property, which led us past Stacy Griffin's house. Then, a few more driveways up, I saw our familiar mailbox. A plastic largemouth bass mounted on a pole. Its dorsal fin was red and acted as the flag for outgoing mail. My dad loved that mailbox. Luke and I used to race to see who could bring the mail in first. But that was a long time ago.

Now the painted plastic had faded, and the grass was overgrown at the base of the pole. It was the perfect representation of what to expect when entering the property.

My parents owned just under ten acres that was carved off a neighboring farm a hundred years ago. The white two-story house sat back off the road and down a gravel driveway. They built it in an era where farmhouses were two stories with an attic and a basement, and it only took one bathtub to service five bedrooms. One of the first things my parents did when they bought it was to reduce it to a four-bedroom house and add a second bathroom off the master. My mom loved taking a bath and my dad didn't want her to have to do it in a tub covered with children's toys. The bath was her one escape, and Dad gave her a proper oasis.

The front of the house had a covered porch with a white swing, suspended from the ceiling with two chains. The wall behind it was still dinged from when Luke and I would aggressively swing back and forth. At first, my dad would fix the damage, but he eventually gave up because of the inevitability of another one showing up a week after he had repaired the last one.

I parked in the driveway next to my mom's car and unloaded our things. She must have heard the tires on the gravel because soon she was offering warm hugs and cold iced tea. We gladly accepted both.

I carried our bags into the house and upstairs to the bedrooms. Luke's room was the first one on the left and mine was next to it, further down the hallway.

"He certainly was a football fan, wasn't he?" said Kendra as she looked around the room. A huge Peyton Manning poster covered half the wall next to his bed, but a Purdue football banner held the place of honor over his bed.

"Was your brother going to play football at Purdue?"

I sat her bag on the double bed and shook my head. "No, they offered him scholarships to some lower Division 1 schools, but he had his heart set on attending Purdue. He set our school record, but we're a smaller school and that's not the same as setting records at a top tier program. It drove my dad nuts. We're IU fans. Part of me thinks Luke liked Purdue just to irritate my dad."

"Would you ever do something like that?"

"Me? Nah. But I liked basketball more. IU is easier to cheer for on the basketball court than they are on the football field." I cocked my head to the side and winked at her. "Do you want to see my room?"

"Why Alex Lee. What a thing to ask a lady. Your mother is downstairs," she whispered.

"We'll leave the door open. House rules." I grabbed my suitcase and laptop bag from the hallway, then brought them to my room. "Here it is, the place where magic happened."

"Shut up! You have a Britney Spears cardboard cutout?" Kendra's laugh was spontaneous and carefree, just like the rest of her. "And she just happens to be drinking from a straw in that outfit?"

Dang it, Mom. You couldn't have gotten rid of that? "Yeah, I got that in high school. Can't believe my mom kept it."

Kendra looked around the room and nodded slowly. "I think they kept everything. I'm surprised you didn't bring Britney to your condo with you."

This is the first time I've ever seen my desk organized, clearly the effort of my mother and not how I left it. A white envelope with my name written with shaky penmanship rested against a book. I recognized it as my dad's writing, or at least what it would look like if he were frail and unhealthy. Hopefully Kendra didn't see it.

"I'm going to freshen up a bit and then join your mom back downstairs. Come down when you're set." She kissed me on the cheek and then stepped out of my room. She had to have seen it and wants me to read it alone first. Nope, not going to do that. At least not right now.

I laid out my clothes and then jogged down the stairs to join the women.

"Mom, does the tractor still run? I'd like to get the lawn cleaned up before the funeral."

"And I can help you out around the house if you'd like," offered Kendra.

"Thank would be great, thank you both. It runs, as far as I know, but it's been a few months since anyone has used it. You know, I'm not sure what to do with this place. It's too much for one person, but I can't imagine not living here. It's where I've been since we got married."

And where Luke died. I get it. But it's time to move on. We don't need to stay anchored to our past. Trevor has helped show me that. Maybe I can do the same for my mom.

Chapter 52

"If you ladies don't mind, I'm going to hop on the tractor." I excused myself from the table and walked into the garage. It was pretty much as I remembered. Organized, but neglected. My dad loved his tools in the proper place. The tractor was really more of a mower. But living on a farm, we loved calling it a tractor. A zero-turn mower, to be more accurate. The kind you drive like a tank with an independent drive on each tire. The kind kids would fight each other to use instead of complaining about the chore.

After putting gas in and checking the oil, it fired up without a problem. Soon I was knocking down grass at nearly ten miles-an-hour, hoping nothing was hiding in the overgrowth. I'd lived in a dorm, apartment, or condo for almost half of my life now and haven't mowed a lawn in years. The smell of exhaust mixed with freshly cut grass brought back memories all around the property.

Trees had grown up and nearly covered the chicken coop from sight. Our experiment with chickens lasted an entire month. Dad helped us build the coop and covered the run to keep the chickens safe. Then we left the door open one night, and a coyote killed every chicken we had. Never even got an egg out of the ordeal. Dad never let us get more chickens after that and the coop became a fort to play in. He said it was cheaper to feed the coyotes directly than feed chickens and let the coyotes eat them.

He was probably right. We would have left the run open again. But we weren't the only ones who left things out. He once left his chainsaw outside all night. And of course it rained that night. He blamed us for it though, because Luke had hit me with a stick and gave me a big splinter. We had to run inside and have Mom use her tweezers to get it out, which ended the session with the saw prematurely.

As an ER doctor, I'm constantly juggling a hundred different things between direct patient care, phone calls to consultants, ordering medications, interpreting labs, and talking to the EMS crews. Can I blame one patient if I forget to do something for another? My dad wasn't an ER doctor, and he still forgot to put away his chainsaw.

I mowed around the small garden plot behind the house, which, to my surprise, contained several tomato plants and a few other vegetables. Mom was still gardening? Good for her. We used to have a massive garden that would yield bushel after bushel of food from June through October.

Luke and I would put them in our wagon and try to sell them at the street corner. It was hard to sell produce in the county where everyone was a farmer or had a garden, but we gave it our best. Until we left the wagon out and someone hit it with their car.

It wasn't really our fault. A neighbor invited us over to swim in their lake and it was so hot. We figured we'd only be gone an hour, but when we came back later that afternoon, the wagon was destroyed. I always wondered what would have happened if Luke and I had been sitting on it like we usually did. Dad never said it was a good thing we abandoned it, but he was glad we didn't get hit by the car. So it's not like he didn't care, he just couldn't tolerate laziness and not following direction.

After thirty minutes, I had the lawn around the house trimmed nicely and scanned around for more things to cut. Using that tractor is like riding on top of a BattleBot. Giant spinning blades of death and a powerful motor to take out anything in my path.

Kendra must have heard the tractor return because she was standing in the garage when I climbed down from its seat.

"This really is a beautiful property. I bet it was a lot of fun growing up here."

"It had its moments. Luke and I would often head to the back of the property and spend hours in the neighbor's woods. We used to build little forts and imagine all kinds of things back there."

"Will you build a fort with me? That could be fun."

I wrapped my arms around her and locked my hands together. "Here you go. All safe. What should we do now?"

"Eat. I'm starving."

"That doesn't sound like as much fun as what I was thinking, but that's fine. I'll go help your mother."

"Hang on," I said, maintaining my hold on her. "What do you think of my mom?"

Kendra paused and then sighed. "I think she's very nice and very broken. Like this house and property. At one point it was beautiful and full of energy, but over the years it's lost its luster."

"I agree. And it's so sad. I need–"

"Hey, don't interrupt me. I wasn't finished yet."

"Sorry," I said and kissed her. "Please, continue."

"Her beauty is still there. She just needs some help to find it. She needs to live for herself now."

"And I need to be a part of her life. Help her connect with friends and at church."

Kendra leaned her forehead against mine and pressed our lips together. "Now you're glad I packed a week's worth of clothes, aren't you?"

Yes, I am. But maybe you should have brought a lifetime's worth.

The door to the garage opened up and my mother's head poked through. "Oh, I'm sorry, you two. I didn't mean to interrupt."

I let my arms fall and Kendra turned around to face her. "It's okay," I said. "We were just about to come inside and help with dinner."

"Oh, I'd like that. I was thinking linguine tonight with my homemade pasta sauce."

"You're still making that?" I asked.

My mother smiled proudly as she pulled a quart-size mason jar off a shelving unit. "Before your dad got too sick, we put up twenty quarts of it. Should be enough to get me through the winter." She looked at the jar and shook her head. "It's so silly, but this was one of the last things we did together. Made pasta sauce."

"It's not silly, I think it's sweet," said Kendra.

"Thank you, dear. Take your time. I'll be inside making dinner."

Chapter 53

After dinner, the three of us gathered on the front porch with a glass of wine. Kendra sat with her legs tucked under her next to me on the swing as I pushed it slowly back and forth with my right leg. My mom was lying on a chaise lounger a few feet away.

"I have a question," she said.

"What is it, Mom?"

"Is it alright to feel a sense of peace right now? I know your dad only died yesterday, but as I lay here, I'm not sad. I'm almost relieved."

I get what she's saying. My dad was her full-time job for probably at least a year. For us it was a shock when he died, but she saw it coming slowly. Rolling closer toward the edge of the cliff every day. We were the ones walking below and surprised when he landed in a splat. She had to watch him inch toward the inevitable end the entire time, knowing there was nothing she could do to stop it.

"Yes, it's fine, Mom. You went above and beyond what was required of you over the years. You have nothing to feel ashamed about. Now it's time for you to relax and take a fresh look at the world."

Kendra nodded in agreement. "Nicole, have you given any thought as to what you'd like to do moving forward?"

"Are you kidding? I've been thinking about what I want to do for years. Everyone else is traveling the country and posting it all on the Facebook. I can't remember the last time I've left the state. Once everything is settled here, I'm going on a road trip, starting in Florida. I'm going to start in Destin and drive the entire coast all the way up to Jacksonville. I'll send you a postcard from Miami."

"Maybe Alex and I will fly down and join you for a few days. I love Lauderdale."

"That would be wonderful."

"I don't want to get too personal, but did Dad have life insurance or anything setup to take care of you? After raising us, you went straight into taking care of him and never really had a chance to establish a career."

"Oh yes, that was something he was very good about. I shouldn't have to work ever again. Plus, we own this property outright."

Good job, Dad. At least you took care of Mom the right way. It was the least you could do for her since you couldn't quit drinking.

"I'll leave you two alone. I need to get some rest if I'm going to make it through the viewing and the funeral tomorrow."

I stood up and hugged my mom tightly. "At least you won't have to do it alone. Kendra and I don't have anywhere to be for the next few days, and she brought enough clothes for a month."

That one earned me a slap on the butt. Positive reinforcement for negative behavior? Quit with the mixed signals, babe.

Kendra sat back on the swing and pulled me next to her. "I want a swing like this someday. My grandparents had one at their farmhouse."

"There's something relaxing about sitting on a porch swing in the evening, isn't there?"

"Yep, but I'm about to fall asleep. Between the food, the wine, and working yesterday, I'm ready for bed."

"Let's head upstairs, then. I'll tuck you in."

I led her upstairs and soon she was in Luke's bed, snuggled up under a set of sheets printed with NFL team logos. They were missing several of the newer teams and still contained a few older logos and names. I said goodnight and pulled her door closed gently. Normally, I would have dragged that out and found reasons to stay longer, but I had something I needed to do. Well, not do, but read.

My dad's letter.

Chapter 54

The envelope was still sitting on my desk, laying against a book. How long had it been there? Why didn't he mail it to me? Why didn't he just call? Why didn't I call? Or just show up?

I picked up the envelope and lifted the flap. It wasn't sealed and opened easily, exposing a single sheet of white paper, folded into thirds. Dad must have written this recently, when the toxins had begun building up. The penmanship was messy, as if the hand that held the writing instrument was barely attached to the wrist and flopped around frequently.

```
Alex, I'm writing you this letter
because I wasn't able to say these
words in person. Alcohol has taken
its toll on our family and that is my
fault, not yours. Your brother should
not have died, but I should not have
```

put all the blame on you. Luke was heading down the wrong path in life. I started catching him drinking more and more. Whiskey, beer, whatever he could find.

Luke's death was an accident, but I lost you because of my intentional actions. I had always dreamed of us reconnecting, but as the years went by, the alcohol consumed me to the point I was embarrassed about myself. You deserve a father who is stronger. Braver. I wish it would have been me that died that day, not Luke.

He'd be so proud of what you have become. An ER doctor, helping people in their darkest hour. I pray you will be the father that you deserved, not the one you received. When you read this, please come for a visit. I miss you dearly.

Love, Dad

As I read the letter, emotions rose that I hadn't felt in some time. I read it in the voice of my father from when we were young. When we'd sit on the porch and watch storms roll in, hoping to see lightning zap a tree or a tornado form in the distance. When I looked up to him as my hero and the man I wanted to become.

My face twitched around my eyes, and I waited for the tears to come. To cry over the failed relationship and missed opportunity for reconciliation. For the years of grief I carried and the emotional baggage that came with it. For the network of relationships affected by my internal conflict.

But my eyes stayed dry. I wanted to cry. It's expected when you find a letter from your deceased father. But I couldn't.

I put the letter back on the table and leaned back in my chair. Dad, why couldn't you have said all that while I was alive? You weren't trapped on an island; you didn't need to do this message in a bottle stuff.

When we were young, Luke and I had figured out a way to talk while we were stuck in our rooms at night. Mom and Dad wouldn't let us get up after bedtime except to use the bathroom, and we couldn't go at the same time. But sometimes brothers needed to talk things out.

That's when we found the air vent. The house did not have central heat or air conditioning, but it had a series of metal grates along the walls to allow air circulation between the rooms. I'm an adult now and could just walk into his room to talk to Kendra, and Mom couldn't do a thing about it. But I wanted the nostalgic feel of the secret communication. There was something calming about it.

I moved a few plastic storage totes away from the wall in my closet and found the grate, still in the same position. After laying down on my stomach, I pressed my face against it and began whispering. I could have spoken louder, but what's the fun in that?

After a minute, her face appeared on the other side of the grate. "What are you doing, Alex?"

"Luke and I used to spend hours talking back and forth through this thing."

"I thought a ghost was talking to me. It's not every day I hear my name whispered from an empty closet. Your sort of freaked me out."

"And you still went to check it out? Are you a ghost hunter?"

"If I wasn't interested in the paranormal, I'd never have asked you out. You're anything but normal."

She had a point. And an outstanding sense of humor. "It's more fun if you lay on a pillow. Did you bring one?"

"Hang on." She returned in a few seconds and laid down on her back. "Did you read the letter?"

So she saw it. "Yes, I did. It was from my dad."

"I figured. Do you mind if I ask what it was about?"

"He said a lot of things, but he mentioned Luke was drinking a lot. Said he had found him drunk several times and was trying to get him to stop. I never knew that."

"Did you know he drank at all?"

"We snuck the occasional beer, but I didn't think it was anything serious. Guess there were some things going on in the family that I wasn't aware of."

"I'm sorry, Alex. Alcoholism is strong in generations and can start earlier than you'd think. Most of the people I work with think it's normal to drink at least half a bottle of wine a day. It's all a big joke until it isn't."

"I know. I just didn't think Luke would have done something like that."

"Did he say anything else?"

"He said he wished he could quit drinking, and that he was sorry for yelling at me in the barn. Said he should have apologized years ago, but as the anger waned, the guilt worsened and made it too hard. So he wrote the letter hoping I'd find it and then we could talk after I'd read it."

"The timing of that didn't work out so well," she said.

"No, it didn't. I don't understand. If he felt bad for saying what he said all those years ago, why not make amends? I lived an hour away. I carried around so much emotional baggage that could have been erased with a few quick conversations."

I could hear her sigh through the vent before she spoke. "So why didn't you go home and talk to him?"

"That's the million-dollar question. Why didn't I? I guess at first it's because I was mad at him for what he said to me that day. I didn't know how the conversation would go and the last thing I wanted was to be blamed all over again. Then I thought it was because he must hate me for what I did to Luke."

"And what do you think now?"

"Maybe because we both hated ourselves? I know my dad would have laid down and taken Luke's place on that barn floor. He was so broken that day. But I don't think I would have. I was a coward."

"You weren't a coward Alex; you were a teenage boy. It's natural to focus on yourself at that stage of your life. You weren't negligent, it was just a tragic accident."

"Do me a favor, will you?"

"What's that?"

"Every once in a while, ask me if there's anything I need to talk about. Not in a brief, superficial way as we pass each other in the hallway. But a sit down, phones off, look each other in the eye sort of way. I want to stop the lack of communication in its tracks."

"I'll do that. You know, I really enjoyed sitting out on the porch with you and your mother after dinner. It was so nice to enjoy a slow moment with nothing to focus on except relationships and memories."

"And wine," I added. Can't forget the wine. Just not too much, obviously.

"Yes, and wine. I'm going to head back to bed if that's okay. See you in the morning?"

"Good night, love you."

"Love you too, Alex." I heard her slide along the hardwood floor as she backed away from the grate and headed back to bed. Luke's bed springs creaked a bit when she lowered herself down. The same squeaks I'd heard years ago. I'll never stop missing my brother.

Chapter 55

My mother planned a traditional Christian funeral. One where the pastor regaled the crowd of mourners with funny stories from the highlights of the decedents life and wove in references to eternal judgment and opportunities for salvation.

Mrs. Blanchard played a soulful rendition of "Amazing Grace" on the piano on stage. The same one Luke and I took lessons on twice a week through grade school. She loved music and did her best to get us to feel the same way. I wonder if our names are still scratched into the soundboard or if someone sanded them off.

I sat dutifully next to my mother and played the role of grieving son as best as I could. It wasn't that hard, I truly was grieving. Not for the death of my father, but for the ruined lives that extended from the train wreck that was his alcoholism. My mother's life. Mine. Though it may not be fair to blame all my issues on my dad. Killing your brother through your own horny stupidity can cause some serious issues for anyone. Indirectly, that is affecting my girlfriend, my patients, and potentially my future children, if I'm blessed enough to have them.

Kendra's occasional squeeze of my hand kept bringing me back to the present. Without her time warp hand squeeze, I would have missed the call for pall bearers at the front of the sanctuary. I joined Officer Lindy and several other people I hadn't seen in over a decade. We acknowledged each other with a slight head nod and went about our task of escorting my father's casket down the center aisle and out into a waiting hearse.

The actual burial ceremony was brief and poorly attended. It's striking to see a visual representation of how alcohol abuse alienates people from their friends and family. The number of witnesses to your final descent is a clear indicator of how much damage was done while you were above ground.

When Luke died, my parents bought three burial plots right together. One for Luke and one for each of them. I took the hint. Why would you want to be together forever with someone you didn't want to be with on earth? At least that's what I thought. Now, seeing it again, I realized people move during their lives. They bought the plots next to Luke because they didn't want him to be alone. I might move to Florida or Oregon and have my own family burial plot someday. It wasn't a sign of disrespect; it was probably both an exercise in thrift and hope that I would start my own family someday.

Afterward, the church hosted a bereavement meal at our home in honor of my father. The ladies of the church had brought crock pots full of home cooked classics and we all stood around talking, catching up on years of lost interactions.

I never realized how much I missed my former life until I got a glimpse of where it went without me.

"Alex, you've sure made something of yourself," said Officer Lindy as he stretched his hand out toward me. "And who is this you brought with you?"

"Hello, sir. And thank you. This is my girlfriend, Kendra. She's an ER nurse at St. Luke."

He shook her hand next and then settled into conversation mode. "It's a terrible thing that happened to your father."

"Well, he did it to himself. The body can't take that sort of abuse and not fail at some point," I said.

"No, not the alcohol. I meant the reason he drank so much more after your brother died. He kept complaining about a rake that was on the ground."

Great, more guilt trips. Exactly what I needed. Why did I even come back for this funeral?

Kendra handled this one for me. She must have felt me tense up after that comment. "What do you mean? What happened?"

"I'm talking about the rake your brother fell on. I guess Luke had been using it to sort through the pile of garbage your father burned."

"Right, we used that to pick out metal and other things that didn't burn so they can cool before we threw them away. It was Luke's job to do that after the fire was out. I knocked it off when I climbed up the ladder."

Officer Lindy took a drink from the cup he was holding and shook his head. "I'm not trying to upset you, Alex, but that's not what happened. The rake your brother fell on was about fifteen feet inside in the barn. You couldn't have knocked it off the wall and had it land there. It would have had to go end over end three times. That would not happen by knocking it off a hook a few feet off the ground."

What is he saying? That it wasn't my fault? It's not possible. It was all my fault. That guilt and knowledge have shaped my life for the past seventeen years. It's got to be true. It's a part of my story. I stared at the ground, picturing the barn that day. "I specifically remember knocking it off the wall when I went up the ladder."

Working with Trevor, I had almost convinced myself that it wasn't negligent of me to knock off the rake that killed Luke, but I couldn't fully buy into that. It felt like I was trying to shirk my responsibility. Now he's telling me it's true?

"Maybe you knocked something off, but it wasn't the rake your brother fell on. I remember picking up a bale of hay that day. It had blood on one side of it."

"Yeah, that's the one I threw at Luke."

"Well, I found it laying on top of a shovel, next to all the other tools that were hung up on the wall. Maybe you just knocked that shovel off?"

Suddenly, my legs weren't as interested in supporting my body weight as they had been until that point. I sat down in the closest chair I could find, still holding onto Kendra's hand.

"That hay bale landed on his chest. When I got down to him, I couldn't tell what he landed on. I thought he just landed on his back and knocked the wind out of him. He was struggling to breathe, so I lifted that hay bale off him and threw it over my shoulder. That's when I saw the rake sticking through his chest. That hay bale must have knocked the other shovel off."

Officer Lindy shook his head again. "Nope. Not possible. There was blood on the handle of the shovel, but not on anything else hanging up. That shovel had to be lying on the ground when the bale landed on it. Otherwise, everything else on the wall would have been covered in blood as well. What you're saying just can't be possible. I put all that in the report. Did you ever read it?"

I shook my head. No, they did not offer me the chance to read the report on what I did to my brother. But I saw what happened. I didn't need a report written by someone who wasn't there.

"Then how did the rake get there?" Kendra asked what I was struggling to verbalize.

"I can't answer that one. Just heartbreaking that it was."

And that I caused him to fall off the loft.

Chapter 56

Officer Lundy made his way through the crowd, talking to others at the luncheon. Maybe he had more life-shattering news to drop on someone else's head.

"Alex, you've been blaming yourself for that rake ever since. What if this wasn't your fault? What if it really was just a sad accident?"

"No, it was more than the rake. I scared him. The floor of the loft wasn't screwed down, and he fell over the edge."

"You're an ER doctor. What would have happened to him had he just landed on his back?"

"From ten feet up and landing on dirt? Maybe some broken ribs, a concussion. Broken wrist."

"Right, but not death." She sat down across from me and grabbed my other hand. "Honey, you didn't kill your brother."

I heard the words but could not accept them. Luke's been gone as long as he'd been alive at this point. My relationship with him now consisted of the knowledge

I had killed him, along with other memories from our youth. I couldn't give that up. It was too drastic of a change. I owe it to Luke to keep it as it was. He's my brother, and this is our relationship. Trevor has helped me come to terms with it, but I can't change the facts. Trevor was very clear about that. History is just that. What we can do is change how we react to the memory of it.

Kendra's face showed the empathy that I love her for. It's what makes her an amazing nurse to care for critical patients, but it's also the thing that will cause her to burn out and leave the bedside. Like many nurses before her, she knows the final endpoint, but continues to do it despite the negative impact on her.

A black-haired woman emerged from behind the shadow of Kendra's head. She was walking toward me with a man in tow.

"Hi, Alex," she said. Luke's old girlfriend. Becky Townsend.

"Kendra, this is Becky Townsend. She was friends with Luke."

Becky smiled at us both. "Actually, it's Cobb now. This is my husband, Chad. It's good to see you, Alex. How have you been?"

It was a fair question. I hadn't talked to her much since Luke died. Neither of us wanted to discuss it since it was too fresh. I know she stopped by to talk to my mom about it a lot in the year after Luke's death, but then the visits slowed down and eventually stopped. Memories fade and life continues.

"No complaints." That I'd tell you about. Why do we even ask questions like this? "It's hard to come back here, you know? Brings up a lot of old memories, and not all of them good."

"I know. That day has haunted me for years. I couldn't even look at a barn for the longest time. I shouldn't have even been there, but I wanted to see Luke."

What is she talking about? She wasn't there. She was at the funeral, but she wasn't there the day he died. "I'm sorry. I don't believe you're remembering it correctly. It's been a long time. You weren't there that night, but you were at the funeral."

"No, I was there. I heard everything. I still have dreams about it once in a while."

"What? How? I never saw you."

"That's because I was inside the room Luke built in the haystack. I had passed him a note at school and told him to meet me up there that night." She looked at her husband and winced before continuing. "Sorry Chad, but I need to get this off my chest."

He nodded and squeezed her hand. "It's fine. It was a long time ago. Go ahead."

"Thanks," Becky said, wiping a tear from her eye. "We had been seeing each other for a few weeks. Sneaking away any chance we got. The corn fields were convenient, but a hay loft was way better. He would sneak beers out and we'd spend hours talking and," she paused and looked at Chad, "looking at the stars." Right. Sure.

"I thought I heard Luke climb into the loft, but I was in a playful mood, so I kept quiet, hoping to surprise him. Then I heard his voice outside the barn and realized it must have been you who had climbed up, so then I really tried to keep quiet. That would have been awkward, right? Anyway, then you jumped out, Luke fell down and everything happened so fast. I wasn't supposed to even be there, so I stayed put and tried not to make any noise. I just froze. After a few hours I was really thirsty so I drank the beers and then I guess I fell asleep. When I woke up, everyone was gone. I almost fell myself, but fortunately, I regained my balance and then snuck back home."

I was stunned. All this time I thought Stacy passed me that note and then stood me up. I blamed her for my presence in the loft that night, but really, it was Becky's fault. She stuck the note in my pocket. She must have thought I was Luke! I was standing next to his friends when the note was stuffed in my pocket!

"Becky, Luke wasn't planning to meet you in the barn that night. I was."

That elicited a single soft laugh from her and a confused expression. "What are you talking about? Why would you go to meet me?"

"Because you put the note in my pocket and slapped me on the rear!" I must have said that part louder than I realized because the room went silent and everyone turned to look at us.

Kendra squeezed my hand and leaned toward me. "It's okay, it was a long time ago," she said.

Yes, it was. Seventeen years. Ever since that night, I'd believed that my booty call killed my brother. I blamed the wrong person for having put me in the loft that day and internalized all the guilt and shame. It destroyed my family and gave me borderline psychosis from PTSD. And now here she is with her husband. Probably a few kids at home with a babysitter today so mommy and daddy can go out to lunch at a funeral. She was clearly less bothered by what happened than I was.

Becky must not have picked up on my growing anger because she continued speaking. "I know the rake was there, but I think he fell because of that loose board."

You've got to be kidding me. "What board? What are you talking about?"

"When I crawled out of the hay, I tripped and almost fell off the loft too. As I walked up there, a board flipped up like a teeter totter when I stepped on the end. I remember a screw on the far end sticking up and heading straight at my face. I had assumed that's why he fell over the edge. Isn't that what happened?"

"I remember his foot catching a screw right before he fell. I went up there the next day, but the screw was all the way in and the board was tight."

"Someone probably fixed it, so no one else was going to fall."

"Yeah, that makes sense," I said to those around me, but my brain was back in the barn. Why would there be a loose board in the loft? We were up there all the time and I don't remember loose boards other than that one. That day. I need to get out to that barn.

"Becky, it was good to see you. Thanks for coming out today."

"You too, Alex." She offered a smile in the shape of a frown before grabbing Chad's hand and walking away.

Back then, I had wanted Stacy Griffin, but ignored her after the event because I thought she had stood me up and put me in the position to scare Luke. I never even got the chance to date her. Kendra leaned forward and hugged me across the chair during my self-pity memory. It's funny how you can not get what you wanted and end up happier for it.

Her breath against my neck usually drove me wild, but today it just made me feel hot. Her hair acted like an insulated blanket, suffocating me. I leaned back quickly and took a few breaths, but was still feeling penned in. "Let's go outside. I need to get away for a bit."

Chapter 57

She caught up to me on the front porch, where I was leaning onto the railing and breathing deeply. "Hey, what's going on?"

"Sorry. I think I panicked back there." I rubbed my face in my hands and exhaled through my spread fingers. "Look, I had come to terms with what happened, but now I'm thinking about it again and doubting the version of events that I have carried with me. That event defined who I am and now it may be changing. It's a lot to take in."

Kendra stood next to me and looked out over the yard. The barn was still there, along with a well-worn narrow path leading to it from the house. I could still see the pile of railroad ties stacked against a fence row. Many bent rusty nails dotted the sides of them, the paper targets long since decomposed.

"Can you show me the barn? I'd like to see where it happened," she said.

What? Why would you want to see where my brother died? Where my family broke apart. Delroy's voice interrupted my thoughts and agreed with Kendra. *You may need to confront the event again.* Fine.

"Sure, let's go." I flexed my left arm and lifted my elbow, allowing Kendra to slide her arm through mine as if on our way to a fancy dinner. Like our wedding reception. It's okay to think positively. My counselor gave me permission.

We started toward the barn, but a shout of my name interrupted us just a few steps into the journey. "Alex, wait." It was my mother.

She hurried out of the house and joined Kendra and me along the path. "I want to go with you. There are too many people inside. I haven't even seen half of them for years. Some of them are here just for gossip, it seems."

My mother hooked her arm through the opening I made with my other arm. Halfway to the barn, we passed a round gravel patch where no weeds were growing. The burn pile.

My mother smiled and pulled us to a stop. "You and your brother used to love burning things. I swear you and Luke would find all sorts of junk and bring it home, knowing your dad would toss it in the burn pile."

I laughed at her accusation. "There may be some truth to that. The burning was fun, but not the cleanup. Luke always hated that."

"Well, he was the older one, so we had him sort through the ashes for things that didn't burn. He would always forget to put the rake away and your dad would have to do it. Roger would get so mad because the dew would cause everything to rust."

She's right. Dad would get angry when we would borrow his tools and then leave them outside. We ruined an entire set of wrenches one time we were working on the basketball goal. He made us spend two days scrubbing them to remove all the rust. We got it off, but they rusted again, anyway. This led to a screaming fit and ended with him throwing the wrenches across the yard. We would find them from time to time over the next few months. Dad threw a lot of things when he was mad.

"Luke left that rake out all the time, didn't he?" I asked.

Mom laughed again. "Yes, that boy was great at the start of a project but got too distracted to finish them. It would sure set your father off."

Kendra and I shared a quick glance, but neither of us spoke the thought. She pulled me forward by my left arm, dragging my mother along as well.

The barn door was shut, and I had to lean hard to get the old door to slide along the corroded track. The squirrels had filled the track with walnut husks, which made the job even harder. Kendra helped push, and we eventually got it all the way open.

It was as I remembered, except now there was an old recliner and a small table sitting where Luke had landed. The barn was dark but illuminated by dozens of streams of light shining through openings between the boards on the walls.

"Your father used to spend hours out here when he was strong enough to walk this far. He was so tormented by what happened that day. Unfortunately, he could never let it go and it consumed him. One drink at a time."

The wall to my left contained many tools hanging quietly on their hooks. Exactly where we kept the rakes and shovels. Years of dust and bug debris created a patina that would make any haunted house envious.

I looked at the distance between the wall and the chair. Officer Lindy was right. There's no way that rake fell off the wall and landed where it did. Maybe if someone tossed it into the barn from outside. I kept that opinion to myself, though I suspect Kendra thought the same thing.

The ladder still looked sturdy. Built from hardwood before the age of dimensional lumber. The two by fours were actually two inches by four inches.

"I have to go up there."

"Just be careful, Alex." Thanks Mom, I know.

Kendra released her arm as I reached for the rungs of the ladder. I scaled it quickly and stood on the solid loft floor. There was still a large pile of hay, but it had been decomposing for several years. The sides had sunk in like there was a hole in the bottom, slowly pulling the bales through.

I leaned over the edge and looked down at the two women in my life. My eyes saw the chair next to my mother, but my heart saw Luke laying there instead. Gasping for air, unable to get up.

Turning around, I continued along the floor, testing each board to see if any were loose. They all appeared attached. Until I took one more step and a board flipped up toward me. The same thing Becky described happening that night.

"Hey, be careful," added Kendra. More good advice.

The board was missing the rusty screw heads the other boards had, but the holes were still there. It was not secured to the joist below and simply rested on it. This board was over the small stable where we used to keep a goat years ago. I knelt down and pushed one end of the board, causing it to pivot on the joist and lift its far end into the air.

I moved to the end of the board and pulled it toward myself, sliding it between my legs and exposing a cavity between the two by twelve floor joist and the roof of the stable below. Another pull and the board moved further, exposing the space on the other side of the joist. As I did, the thick bottom of a glass bottle came into view.

Sliding the board further, I exposed the entire space between the joists. Someone had hidden a few large glass bottles inside, most of which were empty. A few had a golden liquid in it that looked like dilute maple syrup, but I'm sure tasted like bourbon. The label confirmed it.

Suddenly, I felt the same way I did inside a few minutes ago. The barn was now too small and full of old, stale air. I had to get outside before I couldn't breathe again.

"Alex, are you okay?" The words came from the ladder, and I turned to see Kendra's head at the top of it. She finished the climb and hurried over to me, her nursing instincts clearly kicking in. She probably saw a pale guy who looked like he was about to pass out.

She knelt behind me and helped support my back. In doing so, she looked down into the space under the floorboard.

"Are you two okay? What's going on?" asked my mother. She was on the ground and couldn't see what we were looking at.

Kendra squeezed the left side of my neck and she leaned forward, resting her face on the right side of my neck. Close enough to whisper without being heard. "I'm so sorry, Alex. But this wasn't your fault. You need to let it go."

I had been waiting seventeen years for someone to say that to me. The words struck my soul like a lightning bolt, shattering the wall of guilt that I had built over the second half of my life. It released a torrent of emotion, which must have further worried my mother.

"Alex? What's wrong. I'm coming up."

That caused me to sit up quickly. "No, Mom. Don't come up here. It's nothing. Just something I wasn't expecting to see. I'm fine."

"Well, what is it?" she asked.

I looked down at my mother, frail and standing behind the chair. From this vantage point, I could see the erosion in the barn floor in front of the chair where my dad's feet likely rested all those years, and a path leading toward it from the front of the barn. But I could also see another path behind the chair, narrower than the other eroded area. Exactly in line with where my mother was standing now.

She had stood by my father through the worst of times and loved him well to the very end. Past when she received anything from the marriage. Past when most people would have ended the marriage over rampant alcohol abuse. Past when he was no longer able to control his bowel and bladder. Her legacy is one of loving sacrifice to a man she promised to love forever, till death do they part.

I looked down at the liquor bottles. One of my dad's stashes for when he wanted to hide his drinking from us. The stash he had to unscrew a board to access. The stash he likely forgot to replace a screw in. The same screw that Luke tripped over and fell off the loft. Onto the rake that Dad probably threw into the barn because he was pissed Luke forgot to put it away.

But I couldn't say that to my mom. "Remember that barn cat we used to have?"

She nodded up at me. "Yes dear, why?"

"Turns out it didn't run away, but we won't need to worry about feeding it anymore. I'll come back later and get rid of it and then replace the floorboard."

Kendra helped me stand up and escorted me back to the ladder. My dad had to have realized where the rake came from. Either he threw it there in a fit of rage, or Luke left it out. He knew it wasn't all my fault. That's probably why he drank so much. To suppress the guilt. But why not just come clean? Why not talk to Mom and me? Why let the knowledge destroy you and the family? But I knew the answer. You can't reason with mental health; you can only treat it.

When the three of us were outside in front of the barn, I pushed the door closed again. I hooked my arms, and both women snaked their arms through again as we headed back toward the house. Kendra popped a piece of candy into her mouth and chewed the soft sugary goodness.

"Mom, I've been thinking a lot since Dad died. I think it's time for me to sell the condo and buy a house. Something with a nice yard, and far enough away from the neighbors that we can target shoot." I let that sink in a moment before continuing. "Should I look for a place with an in-laws' quarters?"

She pulled her arm out from mine and wrapped it around me instead. "I would love that. I think it's time to sell this old place, anyway."

"I agree. It's time for some major changes."

"Hey," said Kendra, stopping short. Her right arm pulled me backward, spinning me toward her. Her left hand grabbed my right cheek and held me still. "You're not planning to get rid of me, are you?" A few pieces of sugar decorated her lips from the candy she was still chewing. I leaned my head against her hand, closed my eyes, and inhaled. Vanilla and sugar. I wanted cake again. But a huge one this time. One big enough for hundreds of our friends, family, and coworkers. I smiled and shook my head no.

"Not today. Not ever."

Epilogue

Five Years Later

"Okay, Luke. Keep your eye on the ball. Keep that bat off your shoulder and take a nice level swing." I watched as my son mostly followed my instructions and smashed the 'ball' sitting on the tee as hard as he could. It exploded into a mist of red juice and coated both of us.

"Oh no, do you know what this is?" I asked my son, who was standing still, surprised at the watery eruption after he made contact.

"What is it?"

"Tickle juice!" I ran at him while I wiggled my fingers, causing him to scream, drop the bat, and start running the bases. He was rounding third when the back door opened and his mom stepped onto the porch.

"What is he covered in?" she asked.

"Tickle juice!" he screamed as he ran toward home in a full sprint, sliding in for no reason other than the pure joy of childhood. "Safe!"

I caught up to him and helped him off the ground. "Great hit, buddy."

"You need to save a few tomatoes for your mom's sauce, you know."

I smiled at Kendra and then pointed at Luke. "Tell that to Babe Ruth here. We found a few that had bugs in them and didn't want to just toss them back in the garden."

"What do you think? Is it Mom's turn?" I held the bat out toward Kendra, who was shaking her head no but grinning broadly.

"Yes! I'll get a ball," said Luke. He put a fat, juicy tomato on the tee and stood back.

"I think she's afraid to take a swing with that enormous belly in the way. Can pregnant women even play baseball?" I was goading her, and she knew it. But what's the fun of not stepping up when someone calls you out?

She stepped off the porch and marched toward Luke with her hand out. "Give me that bat. This momma's going to show you how to hit a tomato."

And show us she did. Kendra took a huge back swing, shifted her weight forward, and exploded the tomato over all three of us.

"Yes! Home run!" yelled Luke, but no one ran anywhere. We were too busy laughing. Lucy joined in with excited barking to complete the chorus.

"What am I missing? Are you three having fun without me?" My mom must have heard the commotion and came to investigate.

"Just getting rid of some of the bad tomatoes. Alex found a fun way to smash the ones with bugs in them."

"Kendra dear, there were no bugs in those. I picked them all myself and they were perfect. Alex used to do this with his dad and brother all the time when they were little. I'm going to get Granny Mary. She'll want to see this." My mom went back inside, probably to wheel Kendra's mom outside, too.

"Luke, we're going to need some more balls. Looks like this game is going into extra innings," I said.

"Yes!" he screamed, before running out toward the garden.

"So it's come full circle, has it?" asked Kendra, tapping the bat on her hand while smiling at me.

"Yes, it has." She dropped the bat when I stepped close in order to pick a small piece of tomato off my cheek. Kendra wrapped her arm around my neck and pulled me in for a hug. She didn't smell like vanilla this time, just tomato. But she felt like happiness.

Author's Note

Post-traumatic stress disorder is a serious condition that is under-diagnosed, and, as a result, under-treated. This novel explored a character's battle with PTSD stemming from the sudden loss of his brother and the ripple-effect of the damage to his entire family. This example was obviously extreme, and the therapy sessions simplified because of my lack of training in the field. If you struggle with depression or other mental health symptoms, seek evaluation by a licensed mental health practitioner. If you do not have an existing relationship with one, speak with your primary care physician to obtain a referral, or use online resources to make an appointment yourself. You deserve to be healthy.

For more information on EMDR and what it can offer, visit EMDR International Association online at https://www.emdria.org/

Acknowledgements

It Happened In the Loft is my first novel in the psychological drama genre. Any time we step into a new role, it's helpful to have others give feedback to ensure we're on the right track. I'd like to thank my beta readers who volunteered to read the first draft and provide feedback on a novel that had not gone through proofreading and was surely a grammatical mess.

I am trained as an emergency medicine physician and have treated patients in acute mental health crisis for twenty years but have limited knowledge of how to treat mental illness on an ongoing basis. When I developed the concept for this novel, I realized I needed help understanding EMDR therapy in order to represent it accurately in the story. I reached out to Megan Hudson, a licensed clinical social worker who employs EMDR therapy in her practice here in Indianapolis. She was kind enough to walk me through the process and answer questions I had along the way. I appreciate her time and effort to help this novel more accurately spread awareness of EMDR therapy. Any errors in the portrayal of EMDR are mine alone.

Finally, I want to thank my wife, Cheryl, for again reading the alpha draft of my novel, the one with chapter headings that ruined any potential for surprise. She continues to be my biggest cheerleader in this incredible adventure of self-publishing.

If you enjoyed this book, please leave a positive review and then check out *Redemption*, Book One in the Dr. Bryce Chapman Medical Thriller Series. This is my debut novel and the first book in the series. I am planning to release book four in the fall of 2023.

$13.99 Paperback
$3.99 E-book

About The Author

Dr. Brian Hartman is a practicing Emergency Medicine Physician in Indianapolis, Indiana. He is married to his wife Cheryl, a dentist with whom he has two boys, Evan and Andrew. They enjoy traveling to tropical locations, including several of the settings of Redemption. Brian began the formal pursuit of writing as a creative escape from the stress of the COVID-19 pandemic.

Redemption is the first novel in his medical thriller series starring Dr. Bryce Chapman. Brian has written dozens of short stories and has several independent novels in production. He transfers his experience as a practicing physician to the characters and events of the books, letting the reader see inside the mind and emotions of the team caring for patients. The lives of doctors and nurses do not stop when they leave the hospital and his books explore the events and back stories that make our lives interesting.

Brian enjoys interacting with his readers via email and social media. Find him online:

Website: https://www.brianhartman.me/
Email: brianhartmanme@gmail.com
Facebook: https://facebook.com/brianhartmanme.

Also By Brian Hartman

Bryce Chapman Medical Thriller Series:
Redemption (Book One)
Deception (Book Two)
Vengeance (Book Three)

Short Story Anthology:
The Muddled Mind

Psychological Romance Drama:
It Happened In The Loft

Psychological Thriller
Lake Sinclair (Spring 2023)

Also by Brian Hartman